RIO GRANDE BLOOD

CONCHO BOOK SIX

A.W. HART

The characters and events portrayed in this book are fictitious. Any similarity to real persons, living or dead, is coincidental and not intended by the author.

Special thanks to Charles Gramlich for his contribution to this novel.

Published by Wolfpack Publishing
5130 S. Fort Apache Road, 215-380
Las Vegas, NV 89148

Paperback ISBN 978-1-63977-606-1
eBook ISBN 978-1-63977-218-6
LCCN 2022940598

RIO GRANDE BLOOD

CHAPTER ONE

Beneath a frosty January dawn, Texas Ranger Concho Ten-Wolves rode a borrowed horse to the banks of the Rio Grande. It was a leisurely Saturday under a brightening turquoise sky. Until all peace shattered.

In a good mood and humming softly to himself, Ten-Wolves crested a small rise and saw the river below. The smell of wet muck stabbed his nostrils. A slow, dark current tugged the muddy water downstream through stretches of bare dirt interspersed with greener patches of riverside bush—sage, blackbrush, holly, and others.

Here, the Kickapoo Reservation where Concho lived bordered directly on the Rio Grande. He'd come here often as a kid to swim. Few of the reservation children did so today. They swam at the big pools of wealthier friends or in small backyard pools filled by water hoses. Maybe that was better, though Concho had important memories of this place. They'd shaped him, for the good and the not-so-good.

The river was familiar to the Ranger, with its water and brush and dirt. The four-wheelers and green flat-bottomed boat pulled up on the United States side of the bank were not. Concho reined his big bay gelding to a halt a quarter of the way down the rise. Nine men milled around the boat some forty yards away, all armed. He recognized not a one, which was suspicious given his knowledge of just about everyone who lived on or near the reservation.

The men were unloading things from the flatbottom, nylon satchels and chests. One item appeared to be a body bag. Concho didn't have time to get a good look at anything before someone among the crew spotted him and straightened. The first man gestured to the others. They straightened too. The moment held. Perhaps one man noticed the glint of the Texas Ranger badge on Ten-Wolves' shirt; he swung a rifle off his back and opened fire.

Concho was already moving. He'd seen the metallic spill of light off the rifle's swinging barrel and didn't relish a surprise gunfight against nearly a dozen shootists. Kicking the gelding savagely in the flanks, he yanked the bay's head around by the reins. The horse was a gentle sort, unused to such treatment. It squealed and laid its ears flat, but it moved under digging heels.

For protection against flying lead, Concho swung his body down alongside the horse's big bulk like a Cheyenne rider of the western plains while he urged the animal back up the rise. Bullets slashed up dirt all around him, followed by the sharp crack-crack-crack of gunfire. Something must have stung the gelding across the withers to galvanize it. It squealed even louder and surged over the top of the small hill with a little extra giddy in its gallop.

More than one weapon spoke now but the bullets whipped overhead as Concho drummed his heels into the horse's ribs. Pursuit was bound to come and the bay, which the Ranger had borrowed from a friend who owned a small ranch at the edge of the Kickapoo Rez, was built more for strength than for the sprint.

The gunfire fell silent as Concho disappeared over the rise, but engines began to boom and rev. *The four-wheelers*. And on any relatively flat and clear terrain, those machines would quickly run down a horse.

Concho never left home without a Colt Double Eagle .45 semiautomatic slung on each hip. He drew his right-hand Colt and twisted around in the saddle to look over his shoulder. A stripped-down red four-wheeler topped the rise, moving fast enough to catch air. Two men rode it, the driver and a passenger carrying an Uzi machine pistol or some knockoff clone of the Israeli weapon.

Concho fired his Colt from under his left arm. Aboard the jouncing horse and with his target moving, the Ranger never expected a hit. He got one anyway. Almost sheer luck. The .45 slug caught the helmetless driver of the ATV right at the bridge of his nose and punched blood and gore out the back of his skull.

As the ATV driver slumped limply forward and the passenger flinched away from the spraying tissue that slapped him in the face, the nose of the vehicle came down sharply. It hit the ground head-on and the four-wheeler flipped forward, spinning back into the air before crashing down on top of the men astride it. The driver was beyond noticing but Concho heard the passenger scream as the weight of the machine came down on him like a fall of cement.

Two other four-wheelers burst over the rise. Like the first, they were sport models, shark nosed and sleek. Concho fired his Colt again but had no luck this time. Gunfire ripped from the ATVs toward him. Bullets whined like hornets past his head. The bay horse squealed again but did not slow its run.

The Ranger jerked the horse's reins to the left as a desperate ploy shouted in his mind. A narrow, red-dirt arroyo snaked through the landscape to that side. It was almost invisible to those who didn't know it was there. But it was deep. Concho sent the gelding plunging toward it.

The ATVs turned with him, closing the gap as dust churned up under their wheels. Guns chattered like magpies. A streaking bullet tugged at Ten-Wolves' hair. They were nearly to the ravine. Concho booted the gelding in the ribs and pulled up on the reins as he leaned forward to urge the beast into a jump.

Just at that instant the horse caught a burst of lead. It shrieked and stumbled. Its rear legs folded. Concho threw the reins away from himself and kicked his boots loose from the stirrups. The horse sounded almost human as its front end went over the edge of the arroyo and it voiced pain and fear.

Concho bailed out of the saddle as the poor horse tumbled into the ravine, its neck snapping on impact. His feet missed the edge of the arroyo; his back scraped it. He landed in a crouch in the smooth, sandy bottom. His right-hand pistol still hung in his hand.

The driver of the leading four-wheeler saw the ravine too late. He tried to spin the vehicle to a stop, but it toppled over the edge in a spray of orange dirt. Concho leaped backward as the machine smashed into the bottom of the arroyo on top of its riders.

The driver shrieked like the horse as bones in his right leg broke with an audible snap. The passenger was flung free, slamming into the opposite wall of the ravine. His gun went flying. He dropped to his knees with the wind hammered out of him.

Concho glanced up. The driver of the second ATV managed a sliding stop before going over the edge. The vehicle rocked back and forth as dirt from under its wheels cascaded in a whisper into the arroyo.

This four-wheeler had a passenger too. With a gun. But the ATV's sliding stop beside the ravine had left the man with his back to the Ranger. He wore a helmet; the visor caught and flung morning sunlight. He tried desperately to twist around so he could find Concho and kill him. Ten-Wolves shot him in the side of the neck before he could turn.

Taking three steps, Concho leaped upward. The arroyo was maybe seven feet deep. He hooked his arms over the bank and pulled himself up. The dead passenger still sat slumped on the ATV, his back against a sissy bar. The driver shoved the body to one side as he leveled a pistol in the lawman's direction.

Ten-Wolves leaped forward, clubbing downward with the butt of his Colt. The heavy, almost square handle of the gun chopped into the driver's face, smashing the nose and tearing open the cheek.

The man shouted in pain and Concho kicked him out of his seat and into the ravine. The Ranger leaped onto the ATV himself. The engine was still running. Concho holstered his Colt and punched the throttle lever with his thumb. He twisted the handlebars as the four-wheeler lurched forward. Its back wheels caught, and it slewed around.

The dead passenger finally went flying off as Concho accelerated. But the Texas Ranger wasn't running now. He was mad. They'd attacked him on his own ground; they'd killed his horse. Steering and working the throttle with his right hand, he pulled his left-hand Colt and made ready as he aimed the ATV back in the direction it had come.

Toward the Rio Grande and blood.

CHAPTER TWO

CONCHO PUSHED THE FOUR-WHEELER HARD BACK OVER THE rise and down toward the banks of the river. The green boat no longer nosed into the shore; its outboard motor roared as it churned toward the far bank, where a military-looking Jeep awaited.

Two men rode the boat; only one man remained on the US side, and he wasn't expecting to see Concho astride the returning four-wheeler. From amid a pile of unloaded supplies, the man lifted a hand in a wave. Until he realized who it was.

As the fellow's welcoming smile fled and he swung up a rifle, Concho opened fire with his Colt from the back of the moving ATV. Four shots. Five! Three slugs missed; two didn't. The man dropped his gun and grabbed at his chest as the four-wheeler rolled up to him. A look of surprise fled the fellow's face to be replaced by the glaze of death as he collapsed.

Concho slid off the ATV and ran to the water's edge. He shouted at the men in the boat. "Texas Ranger! Halt!"

But the two fugitives were already leaping onto the far shore. One threw himself toward the Jeep. The second took an instant to kick the loose boat into the river current before following.

Concho lifted his pistol but held his fire. The men were in Mexico now and he had an inkling of the trouble that would ensue if he shot one of them across the river. Five seconds later, the point was moot as the Jeep's engine thrummed to life and the vehicle went skidding away down a narrow dirt road heading south.

For the first time in minutes it seemed Concho took a deep breath. He turned toward the man he'd shot, taking only the time needed to slide a fresh magazine into each of his .45s. He holstered both Colts as he knelt beside the dead man and emptied out the fellow's pockets.

No identification. No surprise.

Various items and containers lay piled along the shore, but they'd have to wait for examination. Concho straddled the four-wheeler again and sent it tearing back up the hill toward the arroyo and the site of his recent battlefield.

He found three more dead bodies, two under the ATV that had flipped over and another lying beside the ravine. An injured man lay trapped under the ATV in the arroyo, but two others were nowhere to be seen, the one he'd hit with a gun butt and another who'd been flung into the ravine's wall when his vehicle wrecked. Both had left footprints behind in the soft, sandy soil of the arroyo floor. They were running.

Concho followed the tracks with his gaze. The men had headed down the arroyo to a low spot in the bank, then run east into a thick stretch of brush and briars impassable for a vehicle. He wasn't going to catch them. Roughly a mile past that dense growth rose the streets and houses of a local subdivision.

Turning back to the arroyo, the Ranger dropped into it and knelt beside the bay gelding who'd carried him here this morning. The animal was dead with a broken neck. It wasn't suffering, but the unnecessary pain it had felt before it died made him grind his teeth. He rose and stood over the man who remained trapped under the flipped four-wheeler. His deep, brown eyes laser cold.

"Please!" the fellow begged. He lifted a hand. Tears of pain streaked his cheeks. Snot dribbled from his nose.

"If I shot you now, no one would ever know it didn't happen in the heat of combat," Concho muttered savagely.

"Please. Don't. Please, I…give up."

"Your name!"

"Holt. Doug Holt."

"Where'd your buddies go, Doug?" Concho pointed toward the tracks leading away down the arroyo.

"I…don't know. They ran. Didn't even try to pull the four-wheeler off me."

"Good friends, then?"

Holt shook his head. "I just met them. We were just… working a job."

"What job?"

"Please, can you get this thing off me? My leg's broken. It hurts."

"What *job*?"

"Just a delivery. I don't even know what. Supplies, I guess."

"Delivery to whom?"

"I don't *know*. Someone on the reservation. Or close by. I wasn't told the name. Only the guy who hired us knew the name."

"And who was that?"

"Presley Dickerson."

"Where would I find Dickerson?"

"I think you killed him."

Concho shook his head in irritation. He yanked his cell phone out of his pocket and swiped the number for Roberto Echabarri, the head of the local Kickapoo tribal police. After hearing that help was on the way, he hung up again.

Holstering his pistol, the Ranger squatted next to the injured man and took hold of the ATV. He lifted it slowly, rising as he did so, and flipped it onto its wheels. Doug Holt cried out as the weight came free of his leg. He started to draw the limb toward his body but shrieked in pain and stopped.

The fibula of the lower leg was clearly broken and had punctured the skin. The knee and femur were twisted.

Holt grabbed the upper part of his leg with both hands. "God, it hurts! Please, you have to give me something! You got anything?"

"Afraid not. At least you're better off than my horse." Concho pointed toward the dead gelding. "If not as innocent," he added.

Holt rocked his upper body back and forth. Agony filled his voice as he spoke. "You called someone. How soon before they get here?"

"Half an hour maybe."

"God, God, God," the man moaned. "I can't stand it."

"God didn't have anything to do with this morning's events. That's all on you and your buddies."

"Up yours!" Holt snarled.

Concho offered him a grim smile in return. "You have the right to remain silent," he began.

A whirring noise claimed Ten-Wolves' attention. He glanced up. A drone with a camera installed zipped over them and slowed to a hover. Concho's hand flashed for a Colt; he palmed the pistol and fired. The bullet tore into the drone and sent it spinning away. Smoke trailed from the device as it wobbled in the air. With a loud buzz, it flipped over and dove straight into the ground in an eruption of sparks and parts.

Concho holstered his pistol. "Where were we?" he asked Doug Holt.

* * *

Kickapoo Sheriff Roberto Echabarri and three of his deputies arrived at the Rio Grande scene in a pair of white SUVs. They found a handcuffed outlaw with a broken leg yelling for help. Neither SUV stopped to investigate as they continued over a rise and came down to the riverside where a big half-Black, half-Kickapoo Texas Ranger stood talking on the phone. The SUVs parked. Echabarri and his deputies climbed out and joined Concho amid a pile of unknown baggage.

Ten-Wolves swiped off his phone and tucked it into his jeans. "FBI," he said by way of explanation. "Figured they might wanna know about my morning's work."

Echabarri nodded. He glanced around. A body lay on its back nearby with open eyes staring emptily into the sky.

"I noted three other dead men on the other side of the ridge," Echabarri said to Concho. "Like to shoot a few guys before breakfast, I see."

The Ranger flashed a wry grin. "Need something to wake me up and I don't like coffee."

Echabarri nodded distractedly. "What happened?"

Concho explained.

"And what is all this stuff?" Echabarri asked, gesturing around at the piled baggage.

"Probably the strangest collection of materials you've ever seen confiscated from a group of criminals," the Ranger replied.

Echabarri arched an eyebrow. "That would take some doing."

"I think you'll reevaluate after the tour."

CHAPTER THREE

"ALL RIGHT," ROBERTO ECHABARRI SAID. "I'LL BITE. WHAT'S so strange about all this stuff?"

"I'll show you," Concho said as he gazed at the sheriff and the three deputies who stood near their chief. These were Arturo Ramon, Timbo Corbett, who was only a quarter Kickapoo and who could easily pass as white, and Nila Willow, the first woman to join the Kickapoo Tribal Police. Nila never used an unrequired word.

Leading the small crew over to a line of three army-green duffel bags stacked together, the Ranger leaned over an unzipped one and used the tip of a handy stick to spread it open. Inside lay stack after stack of brand-new greenbacks tucked into plastic sandwich bags.

Echabarri gave a small gasp. "Wow! All three bags full of that?"

"Yep. All in twenties. At least on top. I didn't dig down into the bags."

"How much you reckon?"

Ten-Wolves shrugged. "Can't even guess. A bundle. If it's all twenties like on top."

Roberto nodded. "A lot of money. But not that unusual, is it? I mean...some kind of drug deal maybe?"

"Agreed" Concho straightened. "Though it all being in twenties is weird. But what about this?"

He walked over to a large ice chest sitting across from the duffel bags. Again, the others followed. Slipping his hand inside the cuff of his long-sleeved blue work shirt to avoid leaving fingerprints, Concho sprang the catch and opened the chest. Frost smoke streamed out. Roberto watched it clear and gasped again, louder this time, as he saw the contents.

"That's…that's…" he stuttered. "What the—"

Abruptly, Arturo gagged and turned away. Timbo Corbett spat to one side.

"It's a human heart," Concho said. "Kept on ice. There's two of them in there. And a liver. And a couple of organs I don't recognize."

"Two hearts?" Echabarri stared. "You mean two murders?"

Concho shrugged. "Could be. Maybe is. But I think they're organs for transplant."

"Ah. Right. Makes sense." Echabarri frowned. "I guess. But drug dealers who also transport black market organs? Crazy!"

"Told you."

"You did."

"Saved the best for last," Concho said.

"I'm afraid to ask," Roberto replied.

* * *

DOCTOR GUTIERREZ AQUILA WATCHED SMOKE CURL FROM THE twin barrels of his Holland & Holland side-by-side twelve-gauge shotgun. The expensive weapon had a spring system that clicked the barrels open automatically after firing. Aquila pulled the empty shot casings out himself and tossed them aside, then reloaded two fresh shells.

"Pull," he said.

The young redheaded woman who managed the thrower, or "trap," for the doctor had already placed two new clay target disks into the mechanism. She tripped the lanyard to release them into the blue sky.

Aquila held his gun down by his side until the targets neared their highest trajectory, then whipped the weapon up to his shoulder and pulled the front trigger. Before that shot had time to strike, he shifted his aim and pulled the back trigger.

Both clay pigeons disintegrated into fragments and began to rain down onto the field of scrub brush and cacti stretching from the rear wall of the doctor's hacienda to the horizon. The young woman clapped wildly.

The doctor, a Mexican citizen from the state of Coahuila, just across the Rio Grande from Eagle Pass, Texas, and the Kickapoo Reservation where Concho Ten-Wolves lived, paused to take a sip of fragrant sherry from a glass sitting on a cloth-covered table at his right. He glanced at the woman and nodded for her to load two more targets.

Before Aquila could give the order to "pull," however, a thin, balding man in a dark blue Mexican policeman's uniform came hurrying from the house. Aquila frowned.

"I did not plan on being interrupted," the doctor said curtly as the man reached him.

"I'm very sorry to do so, sir. I wouldn't have if it weren't important."

Aquila said nothing. The policeman's name was Eduardo Diaz, a lieutenant by his insignia. He held an iPhone in his hand and fidgeted.

"Well!" Aquila snapped. "Tell me."

The policeman jumped as if he'd been tasered. "Of course, sir. It's a drone video from the site of the operation." He stepped toward the doctor and held up the phone. A swipe across the screen brought a video to life. The image was quite clear considering it had been fed to the phone from a flying drone many miles away.

Aquila watched the Rio Grande pass beneath the drone's

camera. He saw what looked like a small riverside camp where various supplies had been piled. A man of Hispanic ancestry lay on his back among the materials with two bullet holes in his chest. He was clearly dead.

The drone continued over a short rise and came to a hover over an arroyo and two living men. One leaned with his back against the arroyo's bank; he appeared to be hurt. The second fellow looked to be a Black man with straight, long but somewhat coarse, black hair. He was a very large individual and held a large pistol.

Aquila watched the big man point the pistol seemingly directly at him. A muzzle flash lit up the screen, which immediately went black, leaving only an instant of shrieking audio feedback.

Aquila frowned and the policeman jerked the phone away with a "Sorry, sir!"

"So," Aquila said, "you're telling me this American Negro killed one of my delivery men, injured another, and shot a drone out of the sky when it tried to observe him."

"Yes, sir. And he wears the badge of a Texas Ranger."

"What about the rest of the delivery crew?"

The policeman shrugged. "We don't know, sir. But given the…uhm, Ranger's location, we think they may also be dead. Probably killed in some planned ambush by the Americanos."

"And Jañega?"

"We don't know for sure, sir. He hasn't checked in. But the drone was his, so we believe he was still alive when it was being operated in the video."

"And the delivery?"

The policeman swallowed hard. "There are...containers visible at the site, sir. But we're not clear on how everything was packed. We fear it's been compromised, though."

Aquila snorted a quick angry breath and tapped his fingers on the stock of his shotgun. "Well find out!" he snapped. "Everything. And identify this Tejano Ranger for me. I want to know who it is I'm about to have killed."

* * *

CONCHO LED THE KICKAPOO POLICE OFFICERS OVER TO WHAT looked like a body bag. It lay in the back of a small trailer obviously meant to be pulled by a four-wheeler.

"Not a corpse in there, I don't think," Echabarri said. "It's too flat."

Concho said nothing. Using his sleeve as a glove again, he unzipped the bag and folded down the top.

"Damn!" Nila Willow said. They all looked at her with shock, then stared again at the shape revealed within the bag.

A small, densely woven sack made from plant fibers rested inside the bag. It had been further surrounded with modern bubble wrap, but through the plastic everyone could see a mask positioned over what appeared to be a small skull. The mask was of turquoise with polished obsidian for eyes.

"Is that…a body?" Echabarri asked.

"A mummy," Concho replied. "Aztec, I think." He tapped the pocket of his jeans where his phone rested. "At least when I looked up American mummies on the net that was the closest image I could find to this."

"And only a child," Nila Willow said, her voice hoarse with emotion.

CHAPTER FOUR

Doctor Gutierrez Aquila was still shooting clay pigeons when Lieutenant Eduardo Diaz returned from making inquiries concerning this morning's fiasco on the Rio Grande.

"What have you discovered?" Aquila asked without looking at the policeman.

"Jañega has disappeared. He may be dead at the scene."

"He is not," Aquila said. "You do not know people, Diaz. That is why you will always work for others rather than yourself. Jañega has fled rather than face my wrath for his failure. Keep looking. I'm sure he left some trail. Let me know as soon as you have it."

"Yes, sir!"

"And what about the American Negro?"

Diaz cleared his throat while he opened and reread the text he'd received from a contact in Eagle Pass, Texas. "He is not a Negro, sir. At least not fully so. He is named Concho Ten-Wolves. A Texas Ranger and a Kickapoo Indian."

"Texas Ranger!" Aquila snapped. "*And* an Indian? I did not think the Tejano devils allowed Indians or Blacks in their ranks."

"Things have apparently changed, sir," Diaz said. "This

particular Texas Ranger is actually rather famous across the border. He recently stopped a raid by American fascists who tried to take over a mall in Eagle Pass. And he has solved several high-profile local crimes."

Aquila made a face. "All right, you're dismissed."

Diaz fled.

Aquila tucked his shotgun under his right arm, then picked up his glass of sherry and drained it. He handed the empty glass to the redhead who stood by his side.

"Throw," he said.

The woman looked discombobulated but wound up an underarm throw and hurled the glass as high into the air as she could. Aquila brought the shotgun smoothly to his shoulder and pulled both triggers at once. The glass shattered into glitter in the late morning sun.

Aquila lowered the shotgun. "It's going to need more than that moron Diaz to deal with this," he said to the woman. "Bring me my phone."

She rushed to obey.

* * *

ONCE YOU CROSSED THE CAMINO REAL INTERNATIONAL Bridge outside of Eagle Pass, Texas, you entered the city of Piedras Negras, in the state of Coahuila, Mexico. Piedras Negras was much larger than its US sister city of Eagle Pass, with a population in excess of 160,000. It offered many amenities to its inhabitants and visitors alike, including Holiday Inns and Domino's Pizza.

On the outskirts of the city, many other, less-savory attractions were offered at a cantina called *Vida Salvaje*—*Wild Life* in English. *Vida Salvaje* was a large, barn-like structure painted mostly rust red. Its two stories of entertainment sat just off the side of the highway with ample parking in front and more in the rear.

As noon came and went, the bar's parking spaces began to

attract old pickups and cars half made of Bondo. Each forlorn vehicle would wait for its owner's stumbling return. Such waits would likely be long.

A vintage orange Pontiac Firebird in mint condition wheeled into the lot and slid to a stop in a shower of gravel near the bar's front entrance. A young woman got out. She was blonde and tall, though only the height was natural. Low-rider jeans with their cuffs tucked into burnt-orange cowboy boots encased her legs. A tight, ivory T-shirt bared her tanned midriff and accentuated other elements of her anatomy. The shirt depicted a fantasy character on the front known as "Death Dealer."

Death Dealer woman opened the door to *Vida Salvaje* and stepped inside. Though the day was bright outside, the interior of the bar remained smoky dark and filled with the odors of tobacco, cannabis, spilled beer and whiskey, and the musk of the mostly unwashed clientele.

The woman crossed the littered wooden floor to the bar and slid onto an empty stool. The half dozen men in the room provided her with an immediate and attentive audience. She ignored them.

The bartender, also a woman, walked down the bar dragging a dirty rag along the wood behind her. She was even taller than the blonde but with darker, shorter hair, and a heavier build—mostly gym-toned muscle.

"Liana," the bartender said. "Qué quieres?"

"Dos Equis," the woman named Liana replied. She leaned a little forward and placed her pale hand on the darker brown one of the bartender. "Por favor. And grab one for yourself, mi hermana. I'm buying."

The darker skinned woman pulled her hand away. "I am working. *Mi hermana*!"

"You are always working, Zoe. You should have more fun."

"You have enough for both of us."

Liana faked a pout. "I know, and it is so sad. You are old before your time."

The woman named Zoe reached under the bar and pulled out a tall, dark bottle of Dos Equis beer. She opened it and sat it down sweating in front of Liana. The blonde picked it up and took a long swig, then placed it slowly down on the dark wood while she closed her eyes and smiled orgasmically.

"Oh, that's good! Can't get it like that across the border."

"Many things one cannot get across the border," Zoe replied. "And some you can get there but not here. What is it you want, Liana, that you can only get here? Besides the best Dos Equis, of course?"

"That would be you, Zoeita."

Zoe did not seem impressed. "If you have a point, get at it."

Liana faked another pout. "All business with you, Zoeita. Always so. Well, I got a call a little bit ago for some business. Thought of you immediately and came straight here."

"I'm out of it."

Liana looked around pointedly. "Going to make a career out of bartending?"

"Maybe."

"I doubt that Zoeita. And this job may have personal meaning for you."

"What kind of meaning?"

Liana rose from her stool and leaned across the bar to whisper in Zoe's ear. After a moment, she sat back down.

Zoe sighed. "How much?"

"A certain doctor of our acquaintance is doing the hiring, so you tell me."

Zoe lifted an eyebrow, then nodded. She straightened and rolled her shoulders to loosen a kink in her back. Reaching behind her waist, she undid the strings of her apron, pulled it off and tossed it on the bar.

"Wait here," she said. "I'll only be a moment. Don't kill anyone."

Liana smiled broadly. "I'll try."

Zoe walked past the end of the bar and down a short

corridor to a door marked "OFFICE." She knocked but entered without waiting to be invited. The middle-aged fellow behind a cluttered desk inside was Asian. She thought he might be Chinese but had never bothered to ask.

He frowned at her, then spoke in perfect, non-accented English since he didn't understand much Spanish. "What do you want, Zoe? I'm quite busy."

"Li," she said. "I appreciate you giving me this job and I'm glad to have had it, but something has come up. Family-wise. And I'm afraid I have to leave. Today. Right now. I wanna collect the pay I've got coming."

Li frowned again. "That's not policy. You get paid every two weeks. We're not there yet."

Zoe nodded. "I know. But I *have* to leave, and I need money for the trip. Just pay me out of the petty cash in your desk and replace it when my normal check would go through."

"Be reasonable," Li said. "This isn't how business is done and, besides, you are leaving us in quite a bind."

Zoe stopped smiling. She took two long steps toward Li's desk and leaned over it with her shoulders hunched. The manager flinched.

"I *am* being reasonable." Zoe spoke slowly. "You've got more people willing to bartend here than you can count, and I'm not leaving without the money I've *earned*."

Li licked his lips. He glanced around the small, claustrophobic room as if he might find someone to call for aid. There was no one. His gaze dropped. He sighed. Pulling out a side drawer on the desk, he took out a small gray metal tin about the size of a safety deposit box. Opening this, he began counting out money from the stacks inside.

Zoe's smile returned. She straightened and seemed to shrink in size, making her suddenly much less threatening. Li placed a small pile of cash on the desk and slid it across to her. She took it, counted it, folded it, and stuck it in the pocket of her green corduroys.

"Thank you, Li. Glad we could reach an agreement on the

issue."

"Go," Li said.

Zoe snapped the man a quick two-fingered salute as she left the office. As she came back into the bar area, she found a young Hispanic fellow in his thirties sitting on the stool next to Liana. He appeared nervous, and as Zoe approached closer, she glimpsed the butterfly knife Liana held pressed to his right carotid artery. A few tiny droplets of blood had already fallen to splash on the wooden bar.

Zoe stopped and frowned at Liana. She put her hands on her hips. The blonde shrugged. She stood up, folded the knife blade into the weapon's handle and slid it into the front pocket of her jeans. Her glance returned to the man on the stool. He hadn't moved.

"You can go," she said.

The man swallowed but quickly got up and darted away. A spreading stain on the front of his jeans indicated where he'd wet himself.

Zoe shook her head. "Let's head out," she said to Liana. "I don't suppose I wanna know what that was all about?"

The two women started toward the front door of *Vida Salvaje*.

"As soon as you left, that pig came over and tried to hit on me," Liana said. "When I turned him down, politely, he got ugly and called me a name."

"What name?"

"Manflora!"

Zoe laughed. "And for that you needed to bleed him?"

"Only a few drops."

"Enough to make a mess on the bar. And probably on the floor."

Liana shrugged. "What do you care? You don't have to clean it up."

Zoe laughed again. "You're right. I don't. Screw it."

In another few minutes, both women had piled into Liana's Firebird and were tooling west down the highway.

CHAPTER FIVE

The crime scene along the Rio Grande roiled with activity most of the morning. The FBI dropped in by helicopter. They'd been invited onto the Rez by Echabarri. This was a bigger scene than the young Kickapoo sheriff ever hoped to take charge of.

Special Agent Della Rice, with whom Concho Ten-Wolves had a complicated relationship marked generally by both caution and mutual respect, arrived to take over for the FBI. Rice was African American, tall, athletic, competent, and occasionally a bit brash. Two other agents accompanied her—Bihn Bui, of Vietnamese descent, who almost always wore a suit and tie, and Will Bolin, an all-American football-player-type with crew cut hair and a ruddy face. Concho had worked with both and liked them.

Agent Rice grilled Concho for half an hour. He told her what he knew and what Doug Holt, the outlaw with the broken leg, had told him—that a man named Presley Dickerson had hired him and had probably been killed by Concho, and that the money and other materials were to have been delivered to someone on the Rez or close by.

"We can get Holt to identify this Dickerson," Rice said.

"I'll show him pictures of the bodies. But what do you make of this 'delivery to someone on the reservation' issue?"

"It makes no sense," Concho replied. "I know everyone on the Rez. To move the kind of items these men brought in would require someone with a lot of money, influence, and connections. I can't think of anyone here who'd have that combination. We've got criminals. Same as everywhere. But none who swim in those kinds of ponds."

"What about among the Kickapoo Council members?" Echabarri asked.

Concho shook his head. "They're powerful. Yeah. But only on the Rez. This kind of thing…" He gestured around at the money, mummy, and the ice chest of organs. "This requires a whole other level of influence."

Rice nodded. "OK. What about nearby? Maybe someone whose land butts up against the reservation and would be easily reached from here?"

"I've been racking my brain. They were using four-wheelers rather than trucks or SUVs to move the stuff. Suggests rough terrain to me. Without a lot of roads. You go east off the Rez and you find a lot of houses and highways. ATVs would be conspicuous. But to the west, it's pretty empty. A few ranches. Mostly small. But there are a couple of bigger spreads. As soon as I get to my place I'll file a report and copy it to you about my thoughts."

"All right," Rice said.

She got on the phone to her superiors. Echabarri went to check on his deputies, leaving Concho alone with his thoughts. Soon, more agents arrived, along with various other specialists. Evidence—including the four bodies of the men the Ranger had killed—was recorded, fingerprinted, and bagged, then loaded for shipment to still more specialists, including the Maverick County coroner, a man named Earl Blake, who was a mutual acquaintance of Rice and the Ranger.

Concho had little to do during this time other than answer questions. Eventually, officers began to clear out and Rice returned to the Ranger where he stood along the banks of the river watching the muddy water twist its way downstream.

"You ever think about taking some downtime, Ten-Wolves?" Rice asked.

Concho shrugged. "I try but things happen."

"A lot of things happening around you involve bloodshed."

"Don't I know it!"

"You call your boss? Got a new one, don't you?"

Concho nodded. "Dalton Shaw. A whole lot better than the old one."

His previous commander in Texas Rangers Company D had been Max Keller, who'd become the brutalized victim of the serial killer Concho had tracked down in his most recent case. That killer, who went by the name Jericho, was now in prison awaiting a trial that would probably give him life. Or death.

"Well," Rice said. "Let's hope this Shaw has the patience of a saint if he's going to be working with you."

Concho quirked a grin. "I'm trying to be good. Honest!"

Rice nodded. "Well, I expect you'll be liaising with us again on this one. Keep me in whatever loop you're hanging yourself with and I'll let you know what we find out from the materials we sent off."

"Thanks," Concho returned dryly.

"The money looks to be counterfeit, by the way."

"Ahh. I wondered. Everything in twenties. Any preliminary thoughts on the organs or the child mummy?"

"Nothing I'd care to venture at this point. Earl will be having a look. He's a very fine coroner. I'm sure he'll figure some stuff out."

Concho chuckled. "Earl? You and old Doc Blake getting right friendly, huh?"

Rice flashed a smile, easing her normal stern demeanor and making her seem younger. "You know how it is. Maybe we just both like the cut of the other's *jib*."

It was a joke Concho had started but which had taken on a

life of its own. An approaching Roberto Echabarri overheard the comment and groaned.

"I don't want to hear about *anybody's* jib right now," the young sheriff muttered.

Ten-Wolves and Rice both laughed. Concho plunked his baseball mitt of a hand down on Roberto's shoulder. "If you give me a ride, I promise not to mention jib the whole time."

"Sure, I can run you home."

"One stop first. I need to drop by Martino Fonseca's place."

"What for?"

The Ranger winced. "I have to tell him I...got his horse killed."

Echabarri tsked in sympathy.

Della Rice snorted. "It's a skill, Ten-Wolves. You've got a talent for causing mayhem." She didn't notice that the Texas Ranger failed to smile at her gibe. Maybe she was hitting a bit too close to home for comfort.

* * *

A WHITE SUV BEARING THE EMBLEM OF THE KICKAPOO Tribal Police turned off the main highway. It rattled across a cattle grate and sped up a gravel road toward a small ranch house sitting on the edge of the Kickapoo Reservation.

Roberto Echabarri, the driver, glanced over at his passenger.

"You OK?" the sheriff asked.

Concho Ten-Wolves snapped out of the reverie he'd been caught in. "I guess. Just wondering how to tell Martino that his daughter's favorite horse is dead because of me."

"Wasn't your fault."

"I reckon."

A moment later, they pulled into the front yard of the ranch and parked. Both men climbed out. A beautifully maintained and painted windmill creaked slowly next to a white, smallish, two-story home. A cow bawled from the red barn on the other side of the house. Close to the barn stood a garden patch, already tilled and waiting for seeds to be planted. It had warmed up enough today to plant, but most local gardeners would wait, knowing there were still some chilly days to come.

The house's front door opened, and a small dynamo of a girl raced out. She looked six or seven, wearing tennis shoes and a denim overall dress. Through dark braids, her smile threatened to split her face. She threw herself at Concho and he laughed and caught her, then swung her high and around. He slowly lowered her back to earth, but she kept a clutch on his hand, or on two fingers of it anyway. A sudden shyness bloomed in her dark, olive eyes.

Concho bent over and tapped her chin lightly with one finger. "Pequeño soñador," he said. "You grow taller each time I see you."

"Mama says I'm eatin' right," the girl replied, giggling.

Concho sniffed her breath. "It smells like you've been eating cheese."

The girl clapped her hands. "I have. Mama made it. From our cows. I love how you can smell things."

The Ranger chuckled. He looked up as the girl's father came through the open ranch house door onto the porch. Martino Fonseca also smiled and raised his hand in greeting. But a quick frown followed as he recognized that Concho was returning without the horse he'd been loaned.

Wearing the frown like a mask, Martino stepped off the porch and walked over to Concho and Roberto. Fonseca was a short man, no more than five feet seven. He was in his early forties, still slender and with his dark hair full and as black as youth. His younger brother, Manuel, who'd been Concho's age, had been killed with the army in Afghanistan.

Martino replaced his frown with a smile for his daughter, who still held Concho's fingers. He dropped his hand to her shoulder, then leaned over to speak. "Sofia, mi hija, would you go to the barn and check on Bessy? She is bawling. Maybe she needs to be fed some hay, no?"

"Oh, Papi, I want to talk with the Ranger."

"You will talk to the Ten-Wolves more later. Right now, Bessy needs your attention. Si?"

Sofia sighed but nodded. She let go of Concho's fingers and started toward the barn, kicking her tennis shoes against the dirt.

Martino straightened. His gaze met Concho's. "I see, perhaps, there is a problem."

Concho sighed. "Yes. Sugar Man, the horse. He was…killed."

Martino's pupils dilated. "How did this happen?"

"I was riding down by the Rio Grande. Stumbled upon some kind of crime. Sugar Man was shot."

Martino took a deep, gasping breath. He blinked rapidly. "Were you…Are *you*…well?"

Concho felt agony well up inside, for this man, for the little girl who'd just walked away, for the gentle family horse named Sugar Man, and maybe a little for himself. He wished he had some explanation to make everyone feel better. He didn't.

"They were shooting at me," he finally said. "But Sugar Man took the bullets."

Martino considered, then nodded. He looked down, wiping his mouth with his hand. "I am happy you are all right. Sofia will also be glad. But the horse...it was her favorite. It will be hard to tell her."

Concho winced. "I know. If you want, I'll tell her. It was my fault."

Martino shook his head. "Only the fault of those criminals. And I will tell her. Such news as this must come from her father."

"I understand. I am so sorry. I can pay—"

Martino held up his hand to forestall further words.

"Do not speak of such. It is not a matter of money."

"Yes. Perdóname."

"I will go to the barn and tell her now," Martino said. "It should not wait."

"Do you want me to stay?"

"Perhaps not. Her mother and I will see to it. I will call you if Sofia wishes to hear more. Where is the horse?"

"In an arroyo near the river. I pegged a tarp down over him to keep scavengers away. I'll bury him if you want."

"It is good about the tarp. But wait until I speak with you."

Concho nodded.

Martino flashed a quick but sad smile. He patted Concho on the arm, then headed for the barn. The Ranger glanced at Echabarri and the two men climbed into their SUV. Roberto turned around and headed for the highway. He drove slowly, casting frequent glances at his passenger, who sat chewing his lips.

Finally, Concho slammed one fist into an open palm. "I'm a hex," he snarled. "A Jonah. Just as bad for the innocent as the guilty."

"That's not true," Roberto said. "Those men came onto *our* land. You were minding your own business. Having a day. *They* are the ones who hurt the innocent. You cannot be blamed for this."

"Tell that to the child whose heart I broke," the big Ranger growled.

Echabarri couldn't think of anything to say.

CHAPTER SIX

THE ORANGE FIREBIRD ROLLED LIKE SWIFT LIGHTNING WEST down the highway, cleaving a passage through the Mexican sunlight. The passenger, dark-haired Zoe, glanced over at the driver, blonde Liana.

"You wanna slow down before we're in a police chase and on the news?" Zoe suggested.

"Firebird wants to fly," Liana replied. She pressed a little harder on the gas and the 400-cubic-inch V8 responded with a higher-pitched growl. The speedometer eased toward a hundred. Liana laughed raucously.

"Either slow down or stop and let me off!" Zoe snapped.

Liana glanced over at her friend, saw the grim line of the lips, and sighed as she took her foot off the gas.

"I swear you used to be more fun," Liana said.

"No," Zoe replied. "I used to be a drunk and didn't give a shit."

"Exactly. More fun. Like I said."

"You wanna tell me where we're headed?" Zoe asked, changing the subject.

"Chihuahua. In particular, the town of Ejido Rancho Ojo Laguna."

"At the bar, you said we were looking for Jañega. That right?"

"Si. Your old boyfriend."

Zoe made a face. "He was never my boyfriend. We grew up together."

"Oh," Liana said. "So, what the Tejanos call 'friends with benefits'."

Zoe glared. "Not funny. I can't stand the bastard. Why are we looking for him?"

"He was in charge of a very important shipment for the doctor. Apparently, he did not take all the precautions required. A Texas Ranger disrupted the delivery and captured everything. Jañega ran."

Zoe snorted. "So, the doctor thinks Jañega was bought?"

"He does."

Zoe shook her head again. "He's not that stupid. I imagine he ran because he could read the doc's mind and knew he'd get blamed."

Liana shrugged. "I only know we're supposed to find him and ask him some questions. And get paid."

"So that's the only reason you brought me in on the deal?"

"Not true. Your knowledge of Jañega is only gravy."

Zoe nodded. "All right. We need to go to another town, though. Even smaller than Ejido Rancho Ojo Laguna."

"Smaller? I don't think there's a hundred people live there."

"And less than ten live in Estacion Ojo Laguna."

"Why there? Jañega grew up in Ejido. His family still lives thereabouts. Figured we could find a lead."

"Trust me," Zoe said.

Liana shrugged. "OK. Reprogram the GPS for me will you."

"No need. I know the way."

"Gotcha."

"We need to stop somewhere and pick up some coats," Zoe said.

"Coats?"

"High elevation there. It'll be colder than *your* heart. At least at night."

Liana laughed. "I'll believe it when I see it."

* * *

AFTER LEAVING MARTINO FONSECA'S PLACE, ROBERTO AND Concho drove in silence for a while. They passed a McDonald's and Roberto pulled his SUV through the drive-in. He ordered a burger for himself and an extra bag of burgers and chicken nuggets for his deputies on the reservation. Concho ordered two quarter-pounders with cheese, with fries and a Coke. The silence continued as the two men ate their fries hot and drank their sodas. Before long, they pulled up in front of Ten-Wolves' trailer on the Rez.

"Thanks for the ride," Concho said, as he opened the door and stepped out holding his brown Mickey D's bag.

"No problem. You gonna be OK?"

"I'll be fine."

"I'd stay a while, but I need to get these rations to the troops." He patted his own big bag of extra burgers and nuggets. "And I better get my report on the incident down while it's fresh."

"Same here," Concho said. He forced a smile. "And I *will* be fine."

Echabarri nodded. It seemed he wanted to say more but couldn't think of anything. He shifted the SUV into reverse and Concho closed the door and watched his friend drive away.

Ten-Wolves glanced around his familiar yard. A cool breeze tugged at his hair and clothing. To his right grew a massive mesquite tree, with a stone fire ring beneath it and several nylon lawn chairs perched about. He would have liked to have seen his friend Meskwaa sitting in one of those chairs, but all were empty.

Turning toward the trailer, he unlocked the door and stepped inside. His trailer was a double-wide, built on an open floor plan that gave him plenty of room to move his big frame around. He'd recently added several rows of bookshelves, but they were still sparsely populated with titles. An arson fire had taken his previous trailer and all the books he'd accumulated over time; he was only beginning to replace that collection.

Normally, he enjoyed the quiet of his place, which was well outside the main reservation village. Today he felt lonely. He missed Maria Morales. His girlfriend had been spending a lot of time here over the past week but was at work today and planning to be with her family tonight.

Concho slapped his two quarter-pounders on a paper plate and poured himself a glass of tea. Heading into his home office, he flipped on the computer and spent the next half hour eating while typing his report on the morning's events. After sending the report off to Dalton Shaw, his new commander in Company D of the Texas Rangers organization, he forwarded it to Echabarri, and to Della Rice at the FBI.

His phone rang just after hitting send on the reports. He grabbed his cell, expecting it to be Martino Fonseca about his daughter, Sofia. But the caller ID indicated someone calling from Dominguez State Jail in San Antonio. He frowned but swiped to answer.

"Yes," he said.

"Hello, Ranger," a voice spoke.

Concho startled. Of all the calls he might have expected, this was not one of them. "Jericho," he said.

"Glad you remember my voice."

"After all that happened, I'm not likely to forget for a long time. Even if I might want to."

"Hmm. I...wanted to tell you. I don't hold it against you for killing my sister. She was about to kill you. Which was not what I wanted. Anyway, you did what you had to do."

Concho considered what to say. A couple of weeks earlier, in the process of investigating a child kidnapping, he'd uncovered Jericho, a serial killer who also stole children in some bizarre attempt to create the perfect family he'd wanted as a child but never had.

Jericho had developed a delusion that if he helped Concho by getting rid of the Ranger's previous boss, Max Keller, and helped him break up a child-trafficking ring, that Concho would join his "family" and they'd do great things together. Unknown to the lawman at first, Jericho's sister, a woman named Persephone Wiebke, had actually been working with the Ranger as a deputy sheriff on the case. But only to keep an eye on him for her brother.

After a final confrontation at an old movie set called Alamo Village, Concho had captured Jericho but been forced to kill Wiebke before she shot him and Roberto Echabarri dead. He hadn't realized Jericho was being held for evaluation and trial at the state jail in San Antonio. He wasn't looking forward to testifying in the case, or on any case involving the suffering of children.

"I didn't want to kill her," Concho finally replied to Jericho. "As a deputy, I rather liked her. But, of course, all that was a lie."

"Not entirely," Jericho said. He didn't expand further. Instead, he asked another question. "How is Mandy?"

Mandy was a fourteen-year-old young lady who Jericho had kidnapped when she was about ten. He'd essentially raised her as his daughter for four years. He'd not sexually abused her, though the "raising" could not in any way be considered typical. Concho had been instrumental in getting Mandy away from Jericho and back to her family.

"I'm not going to talk to you about Mandy except to say she's adapting well to a more normal life."

"I'm glad. I worry about her. Please watch over her."

"I'm staying in touch. Is that why you called me? To ask about Mandy and tell me you weren't holding a grudge for your sister?"

"For one more reason."

"What?"

"You are not very well liked in this place."

"I may have put a few of your fellow inmates away."

"Yes. I wanted to tell you that one of them, a man named Wayne Quaite, has definitely *not* forgiven you for getting him locked up in here."

Ten-Wolves chuckled. Quaite had been the bodyguard for a gun smuggler who Concho had busted. He'd wounded Quaite in a gunfight and put him away. The man hadn't *seemed* the forgiving-type.

"How is old Wayne?" Concho asked.

"He's lost a lot of weight. Wasting away. I think he may have some disease. But before he goes, he wants you to pay."

"How so?"

"He's sending someone after you. I don't know the name. Only that he got out of here recently and is something of a freak. And he's big enough, strong enough, and mean enough to beat you to death."

"I've heard that one before," Concho said.

"Well, just a friendly notice. He might be on his way to you."

"Thanks, I guess. You sound different. Your voice. You sick, too?"

"In a way. They've got me on…meds."

"Are they helping?"

"They're killing me. The real me. But it doesn't matter. None of it does. I've got to go. Take care…Ranger."

The phone clicked off. Concho frowned, then slowly pocketed his cell. A weird day had gotten weirder. And it had time to get stranger still.

CHAPTER SEVEN

As expected, Concho got an email from Commander Dalton Shaw assigning him to investigate the smuggling incident further. Shaw indicated that he'd contacted the Mexican police in Coahuila to ask for their cooperation but wasn't expecting much.

Ten-Wolves' first official act of his investigation was to take a slow, late-afternoon drive along the roads outside the reservation bordering on the Rio Grande. He was looking for any sign of the two men who'd fled the scene. He didn't really expect to find anything; the area was too big. He was right about the nothing.

As dusk began to fall, the Ranger returned home with a double order of takeout chicken wings and French fries from the Wagon Wheel Restaurant. He'd become used to eating with Maria but she was staying the night with her mother, so he ate alone and felt lonely. A phone call from her didn't help much.

Deciding to read until bedtime, he selected an older collaborative effort from two writers whose work he'd enjoyed separately—Stephen King and Peter Straub. He was used to the horror works he'd read by King and Straub and *The Talisman* was more of a fantasy. It took him a while to get into the tale of young Jack Sawyer and his adventures, and just when he was becoming hooked, his phone rang.

The caller ID read Earl Blake, the Maverick County coroner who Concho had worked with on several cases recently. The Ranger frowned. It was after 9:00 PM, late for Blake to be calling. It must mean the man had some information on the case at hand.

"Hola," Concho said as he swiped to answer the call. "You're working late."

"Ten-Wolves," Blake replied. "I figured you and Della would appreciate whatever information I could glean from the organs and the mummy I received today."

Concho grinned to himself. "Yes. I know *Della* will be happy."

A tinge of irritation crept into Blake's voice as he responded. "Yes, *Della*. Or, if you'd rather, Special Agent Rice of the F.B.I."

"A very special agent, I'm guessing."

"Are you through?"

The lawman chuckled. "Mostly. What kind of information you have to share?"

"The organs were two hearts, a liver, two kidneys, and a pancreas."

"I've heard of a pancreas but I'm not quite sure what it does."

"Makes insulin for one thing. Overall, it's critical for converting food into energy and allowing body cells to use that energy. Considering how much you eat, you oughta know what a pancreas does and make an effort to keep yours in good shape."

"I'll take it under advisement. Were the organs healthy?"

"In excellent condition. Perfect for transplanting. We're looking at multiple thousands of dollars for these."

"I don't suppose you can tell anything about where or who they came from, or how they were taken?"

"You mean, if they were taken from murder victims?"

"Something like that."

"I won't be able to tell that specifically. However, they are pretty clearly from younger donors, and organs from young donors are relatively rare except when family is involved."

"Or from accidents."

"Yes, but that's still relatively rare."

"Meaning they could have been killed for their organs."

Blake grunted. "It's a possibility but I wouldn't want to speculate. They were certainly harvested and preserved by an expert. But as for where or who, I might know more when I finish running DNA tests on the tissue."

"How long?"

"Three days maybe. If I do all the work myself."

"I'm sure Della would appreciate it."

"Anyone ever tell you you're an SOB?" Blake asked dryly.

"A better question would be, who *hasn't* told me that? What about the mummy?"

"It's consistent with Aztec work but I'm no expert. I'm calling an academic anthropologist friend of mine tomorrow. Maybe I can get him to take a look. I'll let you know. What I can say is, it's female, probably around nine years old. Definitely preserved. It's not a natural mummy…"

Blake trailed off and Concho frowned. "And?" the Ranger asked.

"This one could have been murdered. Or, I guess, ritually sacrificed. There's a hole in the chest and the heart is definitely missing."

Concho winced. He knew the Aztecs supposedly sacrificed victims to their gods by cutting the chest open with an obsidian blade and pulling out the pulsing heart. It was hard enough to imagine such a thing, and harder to think of it happening to a nine-year-old.

"Any idea on a time frame?" he finally asked.

"No, but there's a process called Carbon-14 dating that

might come in handy. My friend will probably be able to help me with it."

"What's Carbon-14?"

"Well, you probably know that humans are largely made up of water and carbon."

Concho did know, but he tried to make a joke to ease the burden of his thoughts about a child who'd likely lived and died before he was born, a child he could not possibly have saved.

"I think I'm mostly made up of chicken wings at the moment."

"Well, normal people," Blake replied. "Carbon-14 is a special type of unstable carbon. All living things contain it and constantly recycle it. But when an organism dies, the stuff stops being renewed and starts to break down. We know the rate at which it breaks down so you can count the amount of Carbon-14 in something that was once living and get a pretty good idea of when it died."

"Sounds very helpful."

"It's been used to date the age of mummies before. It can be used to estimate when wood was cut, when leather was made, and so on. They even use it to measure the age of coprolites."

"And that would be?"

"Fossilized feces."

Concho half choked. "What? Now you're just making stuff up."

Blake snorted. "Look it up. And imagine how much of that stuff they'll have to carbon date when you're gone."

"You're too kind."

"I know."

"Let me guess, you've already called Della with this information. I'm an afterthought."

"Definitely an afterthought. And yes, I called her."

"Did you talk about coprolites? I hear women love that sort of thing."

"Eat a coprolite, Ten-Wolves!" Blake said. He hung up, laughing.

* * *

LIANA AND ZOE DROVE UNTIL LATE SATURDAY EVENING AND stopped briefly to sleep and pick up a couple of jackets for cold weather ahead, as well as supplies for kidnapping and interrogation. Just after noon on Sunday, they rode the Firebird down main street in the small village of Estacion Ojo Laguna. The town consisted mostly of a set of railroad tracks and a few scattered houses. Population—virtually nonexistent.

The bright Firebird stood out like a thoroughbred in a field of pack mules. Or it would have if anyone had been outside to see it. The place sat tomb-like, empty. A dust devil whirled down the middle of the highway.

"They filming a zombie apocalypse movie here or something?" Liana quipped.

"Folks here don't care much for strangers," Zoe replied. "But you can believe they're watching and noticing. Just keep driving. We're going farther up the mountain."

Liana shrugged but kept the car rolling. Straight ahead, a series of short, jagged peaks arose against the setting sun. The road climbed toward them. The landscape outside the car was arid and desolate, but when Liana cracked the window a little a chill wind came rushing in.

"Must be in the forties out there," she said, rolling the window back up.

"And it'll get colder after dark."

"So, who in the world lives out this way? And why?"

"Agate mines," Zoe replied.

"That some kind of rock?"

"A very pretty rock. At least when it's cut open and polished. People make beads and necklaces out of it."

"So poor people have to dig it up? Ain't that always the way?"

Zoe grinned. "Guess you never heard of the Agate Mafia."

Liana looked startled. "What? That's not a real thing! Is it?"

Zoe laughed but shook her head. "No. The stuff is not worth a lot but people do make a subsistence living out of yanking it from the ground. It's how Jañega's family earned their livelihood. My family too."

"No wonder you both turned to crime."

"Could be."

"Pull off over here," Zoe said, gesturing toward a wide spot in the road that created an overlook.

Liana obeyed. In the distance below them, they could see a very large lake sparkling in the early afternoon light.

"Laguna Encinillas," Zoe said.

"I'm good," Liana replied. "I don't need all the geographical features. Not like I'm moving out here."

"Yeah, I imagine it's a little quieter than you're used to. But, anyway, here's where we part ways for a bit."

Liana looked confused. "What are you talking about?"

"Jañega doesn't know this car. If he sees anyone other than me get out of it, he'll start shooting."

"So what am I supposed to do? Stand here in the cold with my thumb up my ass?"

"As pretty a sight as that might be, you've actually got the harder part of the deal."

"Say it."

"About a quarter mile up the road. Off to the right, there's a turnoff. There's a little cabin there. Not much more than a shed. If Jañega is around, that's where he'll be. I'll pull off the road and show myself. I don't think he'll shoot me immediately. Meanwhile," Zoe pointed off to her right, "you see that rocky trail over there?"

Liana squinted, opined that she did.

"You take that trail. Stay low. It circles around behind the cabin. I guess you can figure out what to do after. Just be careful. He might not be alone in there."

Liana considered. She scratched her head, then nodded. Leaving the car running, she climbed out, folded the seat forward and grabbed a fringed buckskin jacket out of the back.

Beneath the jacket lay a Glock 29 Gen4 in 10mm, a compact handgun ideal for concealed carry. Liana clipped the holstered semi-automatic on her belt and pulled the jacket on over it. She stepped out of the way so Zoe could climb into the Firebird's driver's seat.

"There's a Glock 40 in the glove box," Liana said before Zoe could close the door. "Just for you. But do *not* let anything happen to this car." She gave Zoe a stare. "If it comes out of this with bullet holes, I'm going to be very unhappy."

"If *I* come out of it with bullet holes, *I'm* going to be even more unhappy."

"So we're agreed. No bullet holes."

"Agreed. I'll give you twenty-five minutes to get in position. Then I'm driving in."

Liana nodded and started across the highway toward the dirt trail Zoe had pointed out. In another moment, the blonde woman disappeared among the rocks. Zoe sat in the car, letting it run to keep it warm but turning off the radio and leaving the window cracked so she could hear if anything went wrong, or if guns started to boom.

CHAPTER EIGHT

After the call Saturday night from Earl Blake, Concho tried to return to *The Talisman*, but his mind kept working over the coroner's new information, seeking to incorporate it with the facts he already had. He'd gotten up and paced, thinking of what they knew and didn't know about this mystery.

One—a set of organs from young donors. Brought into the USA even though many illegal transplant surgeries took place in Mexico where the organs originated. Two—a mummified child. With the heart missing. Could there be any connection between *that* missing heart and the hearts in the ice chest? He couldn't see how. Three—a whole lot of money. Probably counterfeit. For what purpose? To fund something? The transplants? Surely not with fake money.

Eventually, he went to bed, hoping for a dream to make sense of things. It had happened in the past, but when he awoke Sunday morning, he had no better ideas than the night before.

He ate a quick breakfast and spent the morning researching organ transplants, counterfeiting, and mummies online, using the databases available to him through the Texas

Rangers. Nothing clicked. Just after noon the phone call came that he'd been dreading.

"Hello Martino," he said into the cell.

"I am calling to ask your help," Martino Fonseca replied. "With the horse."

"Of course."

"I will come by your place. I have borrowed a truck with a winch so we can load her. If you can show me where."

"I'll be here."

"Thank you."

"How is Sofia?"

"Understandably, she is upset. But she is a strong child. She'll be all right."

"OK," Ten-Wolves said. "I'll see you shortly."

Half an hour later, Martino arrived driving a GMC flatbed. Concho climbed into his own truck and led the way to the Rio Grande where they spent a half hour hooking hip clamps on the dead gelding and hauling it out of the arroyo. At least the tarp Concho had covered the horse with had kept away coyotes and buzzards. The carcass was still in good shape, for what that was worth.

After strapping the horse onto the flatbed, they headed to the Fonseca ranch. Martino, or perhaps Sofia, had chosen a good place for Sugar Man's burial—a small rise behind their barn. Martino had already used a backhoe to dig the hole. As the Ranger and the rancher pulled up beside the gravesite, Sofia and her mother, Theresa, came walking from the house.

Concho helped unstrap Sugar Man from the flatbed. Martino worked the winch to lift the dead animal. The law officer glanced over at Sofia. The little girl wore a blue polka dot dress with white stockings and white shoes. Her Sunday church clothes. It was colder today than yesterday, and windier under gray skies. The sharp breeze pushed Sofia's hair against her cheeks and tugged at her dress.

Concho bit at his lower lip. He felt sure Sofia would be angry with him, but when she saw him looking at her, she ran over and grabbed his hand, giving it a fierce squeeze. He squeezed back, and they watched as Martino slowly lowered the gelding into the ground.

Sofia stood unblinking, not crying. Her gaze remained fixated on the horse. Concho felt a sting of salt in his own eyes. He blinked rapidly and cleared his throat. Sofia glanced up at him, saw the wetness on his face. She began to pat his hand with hers, to offer *him* comfort. The Ranger's shoulders shook. Tears began to roll down his cheeks to his chin. He didn't bother to wipe them away.

Martino climbed into the grave for a moment and unhooked the hip clamps. He pulled up the winch and climbed onto the tractor to which the backhoe was attached. Only when he began to bucket dirt into the hole to cover Sugar Man did Sofia start to cry. Concho picked her up and held her while she wept into his shoulder.

TWENTY-FIVE MINUTES AFTER LIANA LEFT THE CAR TO CIRCLE behind Jañega's probable hideaway, Zoe pulled the Firebird back on the road. She eased around a curve and thirty yards beyond turned into a narrow, rough driveway of dirt and stone. A low cabin—no more than a shed really—stood about fifty yards in among an outcropping of rock slabs. Shadows cloaked the place, and it would have appeared abandoned if not for a thin trickle of smoke spilling from a rusted tin pipe on the roof.

Zoe pulled to a stop about fifteen feet from the cabin's front door and slowly climbed out of the car. Though the chill grew in the air as the day began to count down, she threw her jacket in the backseat to give herself more freedom of movement.

"Jañega!" Zoe called. "It's an old friend. I want to talk to you."

Although she couldn't see anything through a single front window nearly black with grime, someone inside heard her. Or already knew she was here. The front door of the cabin creaked open. A rifle barrel poked through but at least it wasn't pointed directly at her.

"Rafael!" Zoe called. "You remember me. Surely. I heard you were back. I wanted to talk."

"How did you know where I was?" a voice called from behind the rifle.

"Estacion Ojo Laguna is a small village. Besides, I've always been the type to know things others don't." Zoe's voice softened. "And I…remember this particular place."

"You alone?"

Zoe gestured toward the car. "You see anyone else with me?"

The rifle barrel lowered. The door opened and a man stepped onto the rickety front porch. He was perhaps thirty-five, a little under six feet, with thick, dark hair slicked back and hanging to his shoulders. Zoe could almost smell the pomade he used on his hair from here.

Rafael Jañega looked a little like Antonio Banderas in the movie *Desperado*. And that look had opened many doors and hearts for him. Unfortunately, Rafael had none of the *Desperado's* morals or bravery. He was a con artist and thief, a trifler and grifter. He'd skated by on his looks and charm for years but had largely exhausted that particular genetic trust fund. Now, he had the air of true desperation about him, the look of a man on the run. It was what he was; maybe what he'd always been; and what he'd never change.

"I thought you had…left here," Jañega said.

"I come and go," Zoe replied.

Jañega nodded. His shoulders slumped. The barrel of his gun drooped toward the ground. Zoe knew it was likely an act, though it still had a certain power to disarm. She couldn't let it. She could not allow this man to mean anything to her. Not anymore.

"I'm glad you're here," the man said. "I'm very much alone. I…need somebody."

From the cabin behind Jañega, a shout of shattering glass

rang out. Gunfire followed. Two shots. The man on the porch startled convulsively. He spun around. Zoe charged him, moving almost silently.

Jañega swung his rifle up toward the open door but heard Zoe's rushing footsteps. He tried to turn again but Zoe hit him in stride like a linebacker hitting a ball carrier. Zoe was a gym rat, muscled from neck to toes. She smashed Jañega against the cabin wall. The rifle went flying as the man grunted.

Zoe clipped Jañega on the left side of the neck with an open-handed karate strike. The man's muscles spasmed on that side. He went to one knee. Zoe smacked him on the head, then grabbed his left arm and twisted it up behind him.

Jañega cried out, but before he could react, Zoe grabbed his other arm too and twisted a large zip tie around his wrists. She shoved him down on his belly and drew the Glock 40 Liana had given her from behind her back. It wasn't needed.

Liana stepped into the frame of the doorway. "All clear inside." She glanced down and saw Jañega on his belly whimpering. "I see it's all in order here, too. What a wuss."

"What were the shots for?" Zoe demanded.

Liana gestured toward Jañega. "The Butt-Munch had a friend inside. Armed to the teeth."

"He still alive?"

"Mostly."

"Puta!" Jañega snarled.

Zoe frowned. Liana laughed and booted the man lightly in the side with the sharp toe of a cowboy boot. "We're not here to talk about your momma, Dickwad!"

Jañega growled and tried to get his knees under him; Liana put her boot on his back and pressed him flat.

"Relax," the blonde said. "We don't want to have to hurt you before we even get you to good old Doc Aquila."

"Aquila?" Zoe said, startled. "I thought *we* were going to question him!"

"Oh?" Liana replied. "Did I say that?"

* * *

By the time Concho got home from the Fonseca place, it was late afternoon. He was tired, more exhausted than he remembered feeling in a long time. He called Maria Morales and she immediately sensed his mood.

"I'm coming over," she said.

"You don't have to."

"I know. But I'm coming. I've got something going on here until 6:30 and then I'll stop by."

"Thanks. It'll be good to see you."

"Want me to bring you something to eat? The food court in the mall will still be open."

"Uh, well, sounds good. They have that Chinese place, don't they? I could have a boneless fried chicken and rice."

"I'll get it for you."

"You're a lifesaver."

"Gotta keep the Texas Rangers happy so they don't investigate my criminal activities at the mall," Maria joked.

Concho chuckled, his mood lifting a little. "Don't worry, I'll quash any reports of your nefarious deeds. For a stash of boneless fried chicken, that is."

Maria blew him a kiss and hung up.

Next, the Ranger called FBI agent Della Rice to see if she had any more information on the materials they'd recovered on the banks of the Rio Grande. She had a little.

"Four hundred thousand dollars in counterfeit twenties," Rice said. "Excellent work, in general, though not perfect enough to fool the experts."

"What about the organs and the mummy?"

"Didn't Earl Blake call you?"

"He did, but he didn't have a lot of intel yet."

"Then you'll have to be patient," Rice said.

"Not my strong suit."

Rice chuckled. "You're telling me."

"So, did Earl give you the story of the coprolites?"

Rice laughed louder and longer. "He did."

"A real romantic, our coroner. Wouldn't you say?"

"Screw you, Ten-Wolves!" She hung up.

No sooner had the laughing Ranger put the phone down than it rang again. He plucked it up and checked the caller ID. Sheriff Echabarri. A premonition clutched at his heart, speeding it and killing whatever humor still lingered in the evening.

"What is it?" he snapped quickly into the phone.

Echabarri's voice was wired tight, higher pitched than normal. "Ten-Wolves, can you get to the casino? We've got a bomb threat. I'm calling everyone in I can think of."

"On my way."

CHAPTER NINE

CONCHO BUCKLED ON HIS GUNS AND RACED FOR THE DOOR. His white Ford F-150 extended cab sat in the driveway. He leaped in, cranked the engine, and tore out, leaving dirt flying.

Concho's trailer stood about twenty minutes outside Kickapoo Village, where the majority of the reservation's population lived in a variety of houses ranging from old cinderblock homes to new, modern brick structures. Just beyond the village rose the glitter of the Lucky Eagle Casino and Hotel.

The casino paid every tribal member a monthly dividend, which had significantly raised the standard of living for many. That explained most of the brick homes and the new model cars and pickups parked in front of them.

It was easy for a law officer to feel conflicted about the casino. The decrease in poverty on the reservation had definitely been a good thing. But sometimes more money brought more problems, particularly crime. Despite his issues, though, Concho played the cards as they were dealt. The casino was here, and any threat to it was a threat to the whole Texas Kickapoo nation.

Well before he reached the casino itself, Concho saw the darkening sky lit up ahead with blue-and-red emergency lights.

He also began passing cars heading swiftly away from the casino as the building was shut down and visitors began to abandon the area.

Pulling up behind a row of SUVs with Kickapoo police emblems on the side, he skidded his Ford to a stop. Leaping out, he saw Roberto Echabarri in the center of swirling activity —his own officers, local Eagle Pass police, firemen, and other emergency workers. A local news crew had arrived and were being held back from the Kickapoo sheriff while they shouted questions at any uniform venturing within striking distance of them.

The casino itself, with the floors of the hotel above it, blazed with light. Fire alarms whooped like banshees. Most of the afternoon and evening gamblers had fled in their cars; most of the patrons of the hotel had been pushed all the way to the edge of the big parking lot where they huddled together in the deepening chill. A few civilians still milled around too close to the scene, either out of confusion or out of excitement that demanded a closer look.

Concho bulled through the crowd, his size and badge helping clear the way. He reached Echabarri just as men and women first responders began rushing away on assignments. For the first time he saw that Melissa Nolan stood next to Roberto. She was still dressed in her day's business attire, a green blouse under a blue jacket and short, blue skirt.

Nolan managed the casino for the tribe. She was even on the tribal council, though officially only as a financial adviser. Her ancestry included one-eighth Kickapoo blood, though you couldn't tell it by looking at her. She was blonde-haired and hazel-eyed, with very light skin.

Another young woman stood near Nolan, a contrast, as dark skinned and dark haired as the casino manager was light. She wore jeans and a starched white shirt. Her gaze rested on the Lucky Eagle, without even a speculative glance for Concho.

The Ranger nodded to Nolan, who stared wide-eyed at him. He'd not really seen her discombobulated before. It was almost refreshing. Stepping past Nolan, he spoke to Roberto. "What have we got? A call-in threat, or has some possible device been spotted?"

Dark half circles of swollen skin under Roberto's eyes indicated his stress level. His whole demeanor suggested he was "too old for this," although he was only twenty-six.

"Both," Echabarri answered. "First, a call. Then at least three reports of devices. Only one seems credible." He nodded toward Melissa Nolan.

"The trash can outside my door," Nolan said. I saw a pair of wires sticking out of it. Red and green. I didn't stop for a closer look. I took the originating call too. I was in the office alone."

"What did the caller say?" the Ranger asked.

"He—" Nolan began, then broke off. "Well, I'm not sure it *was* a he. The voice was distorted. Anyway, he said he'd planted bombs all over the casino and they'd blow in less than an hour."

"That it?"

"He didn't ask for anything or make any statements other than that he'd called me as a courtesy."

"Courtesy?"

"That's what he said."

"How long since the call?"

Nolan glanced at the expensive watch on her left wrist. "Maybe thirty minutes."

"So, the bombs could go off at any time," Echabarri said.

"If there *are* bombs," Concho replied. "Any bomb squad members on the scene yet?"

"No. Ms. Nolan triggered the fire alarms. We think most everyone is out of the hotel but…"

"Any law officers inside?"

"Terrill Hoight. He went in about five minutes ago."

Concho nodded. "OK, I know a few things about bombs from my days in Afghanistan. I'm going in. I'll find Hoight and anyone else who might be in there and get them out."

Roberto sighed. "I'm not your commander so you'll do what you want to do anyway. Just be careful."

Concho took off at a run for the front door of the casino. The electronic doors slid open as he approached. He stepped through into the first-floor gambling area. Immediately, the oddness of the ambient sound struck him.

The fire alarm shrieked but there was none of the jingling, jangling, clinking, clacking of slot machines working and coins falling into tin trays. Nor were there any voices raised in joy or anger. The room was empty, though glaringly, garishly lit, like a tomb decorated in Las Vegas chic.

Concho called out for Terrill Hoight, who was a deputy in the Maverick County Police Department. A good man. But he didn't answer the hail. Ten-Wolves trotted toward the stairs and took them to the second floor. He passed meeting rooms until he came to the manager's office. Melissa Nolan's office.

The trash can the woman had mentioned stood next to her door with red-and-green wires sticking out from under the metal lid. Their tips had been scraped bare of insulation but were not twisted together, and no sound came from within suggesting a countdown.

"Faked," he muttered to himself.

But he couldn't be sure. And despite his mention of "experience in Afghanistan" to Echabarri, he'd never disarmed an actual bomb. He left the can alone for the bomb squad to investigate when they arrived.

"Hoight!" he called again, and again got no answer. That wasn't terribly surprising; the hotel was a big place.

To the right of Nolan's office ran a corridor leading to bathrooms. A hunch sent Concho jogging that direction. He passed men's and women's rooms, checked them quickly and found them empty.

Stepping back into the hallway, he looked toward a water fountain, which appeared to mark the end of the corridor. Recently, he'd found it didn't. Another corridor, cleverly constructed to be invisible until you reached it, branched off the first. That one led to a door marked *Maintenance* and a stairwell beyond that took you to the casino's roof.

Still working off his hunch, Concho turned down the maintenance corridor. The door at the end of that short hall read *Authorized Personnel Only. Alarm Will Sound.* But the door was ajar, held open by a crushed soda can crammed beneath it. And no alarm was going off except the fire alarm.

An odor lingered in the corridor. Grease. Not industrial grease but more like cooking oil reused too often. An electric tingle arched down Concho's neck. A warning from his subconscious. He drew his right-hand Colt.

Slowly pushing the door open wider against a faint squeak of hinges, he eased his head through into the maintenance area stairwell. Cables and pipes filled much of the dank space beyond, lit by a bare bulb. A spiderweb fluttered in the dim light. This place *did* smell of industrial grease, and of rust.

Concho stepped out onto a concrete landing anchoring a set of metal stairs winding up and down. The only sound was his own breathing and a slow, faint drip of water from somewhere. The sound of the fire alarm was muffled here, distant.

The Ranger glanced at the stairs leading downward. They descended into shadow. It was lighter going up. From past experience, he knew that way led to the casino roof. He'd been involved in a shoot-out there once before and the place didn't hold any cherished memories.

He took the first step upward, then stiffened. On the landing above him, he could just make out the scuffed bottom of a cowboy boot pointed his direction. Whoever wore it lay on their back on the landing—perhaps injured, or dead.

CHAPTER TEN

Liana wanted to cram Rafael Jañega into the trunk of the Firebird immediately and haul him off to Doctor Gutierrez Aquila. She wanted to get paid and wash her hands of anything more. Zoe overruled her.

The two women pulled Jañega to his feet and dragged him protesting into the small cabin where he'd been hiding. The inside was a mess, full of the stench of unwashed bodies, burned tortillas and beans, and raw spilled Tequila. Smoke-blackened dirt covered everything.

A wounded man in his early twenties lay moaning next to an ash-filled fireplace where only a few sticks smoldered. As Zoe shoved Jañega into one of two barely functioning chairs, Liana went over to the wounded fellow and kicked him in the ribs.

"Get up!" she ordered. "You aren't hurt that bad."

The man cursed but pushed slowly to his feet, using the stones of the fireplace to lever himself up. Blood stained the right shoulder of the dirty white T-shirt he wore. He covered the wound with his other hand as he limped to the small room's second chair and sank into it.

Zoe tossed Liana two large zip ties. She linked them together, then fastened the man to the chair by his neck. She pulled her Glock 29 from her belt holster and pushed it into the guy's face.

"You try anything and I'll finish the job I started," she told him.

He nodded, with scared eyes.

"What's your name?" Zoe asked the wounded man.

"Jorge Gonzales," he murmured.

"All right, Jorge. You be very still and cooperate and you might just live through this."

"Una diablo," Jorge muttered, his gaze focused on Liana.

The blonde grinned. "You betcha!"

"Enough," Zoe said. She turned and studied Jañega. He spat at her feet, though she noted he was careful not to get any spittle on her. She shook her head and sighed.

"Tell me what happened?" she asked.

"Happened where?" Jañega asked.

Zoe shook her head. She thumped Jañega on the skull with a flick of her middle finger. "Don't be stupid or I'll let Liana do the questioning."

Jañega paled. He licked his lips. "We were delivering… items to the USA. At the Kickapoo Reservation in Tejas. One of their Rangers. He came from nowhere. Started shooting. Killing everyone. We fled. Jorge and me. Before we, too, were shot down."

"This Ranger. Was he alone?"

"No. They had men in the trees. All of them shooting. We escaped barely with our lives."

"What were you delivering?"

Jañega's pupils dilated further. He glanced over at Jorge, mumbling something Zoe could barely hear.

"Speak up! What were you delivering?"

"I don't think I should tell."

"Let me ask him," Liana said, as she started toward Jañega.

"No, no!" he shouted. "It is only that the…the man knows and he would not like me to tell anyone."

Liana cursed. She holstered her pistol and drew the butterfly knife from the pocket of her jeans, flipping it open with a snicking sound. "That's it!" she snarled.

Zoe held up her hand to forestall Liana. The blonde stopped walking but the look on her face spoke volumes about how much she'd like to take the knife to Jañega's hide. The bound outlaw whimpered.

"We know the delivery was for Gutierrez Aquila," Zoe said soothingly. "We're here working for him. He wouldn't have sent us if he didn't expect us to find out everything. So tell us… or I let Liana do what she loves."

"Money!" Jañega said. "But it was counterfeit. And there were some…organs. In an ice chest. For transplant."

"That all?"

Jañega hesitated for a fraction of a second before saying, "Yes, all."

"Who were you making the delivery to?"

"I do not know the name."

"The hell you don't," Liana snapped. She started forward again, flicking the butterfly knife open and closed with a *click, click, click*.

"I swear!" Jañega shrieked, trying to pull back against his bonds and away from Liana and her blade. "I swear it! We were given a GPS location. Aquila told us there'd be a...a kind of cave to put everything in and leave it."

"Leave money and unprotected black market organs alone?" Zoe said. "You expect us to believe that?"

"I swear it! I thought it strange, too. But Aquila insisted someone would pick the material up, and *they* wanted it done that way."

"What were the GPS coordinates?" Zoe demanded.

"I do not remember them but they're in my phone. He looked down at the pocket of his jeans.

Zoe frowned but stuck two fingers into Jañega's pocket and

tugged out his phone. The cover plate was scratched and the screen filthy but it came on when Zoe pressed the button on the side.

"A text," the man said.

There wasn't even a password. Zoe swiped through the text messages and found the one Jañega had mentioned. A single text with GPS coordinates. From an unidentified source listed as "restricted."

"And this location is on the Kickapoo Reservation?" Zoe asked.

Jañega nodded.

"It was the Tejano Ranger," Jorge suddenly said from the chair where he'd been bound.

Zoe turned sharply toward him. "What do you mean?"

"It was the Ranger," Jorge repeated. "The one who started the shooting. I am sure he was the one we were to deliver the goods to. Perhaps he decided his cut was not large enough. He decided to take it all. To betray Aquila. He is a devil, that one."

"Sounds like you know him," Zoe said.

Jorge nodded. "I know him. He lives up on that reservation. I have a cousin who lives too on the reservation. Leticia Garcia. She and her family have been terrorized by this Ranger. She had to send her young ones to Mexico to protect them from his evil. And they are but niños and niñas."

Zoe frowned. "What's this Ranger's name?"

"He is called the Ten-Wolves," Jorge said. "Concho Ten-Wolves."

* * *

Holding his right-hand Colt at the ready, Concho Ten-Wolves eased up the steps toward whoever lay on the cement landing above. Two steps revealed the figure's identity—Terrill Hoight, the Maverick County deputy. The man lay supine, completely still. Dark red blood dribbled from a cut on the left side of his forehead.

The rest of the stairwell looked empty. Concho shoved his Colt into its holster and quickly dropped into a crouch next to Hoight. He pressed two fingers against the right carotid and puffed a breath in relief as he got a pulse—a strong one.

"Terrill!" he called, giving the deputy's shoulder a shake. "Terrill!"

The man stirred and moaned. He opened his eyes, then closed the left one again. He tried to sit up and Concho kept him pressed flat with his hands on the deputy's shoulders.

"Don't move yet! What happened?"

Hoight groaned. He lifted his left hand to his head, winced as his fingers touched his wound and came away bloody.

"Heard someone. In the stairwell. Something hit next to me when I came through. I saw a...a shadow. Big one. He threw something at me. Or…I don't know. Started up the steps and he hit me again. In the head. I guess he did. I blacked out."

"All right. Can you get up?"

Hoight started to nod but quickly stopped. He reached out a hand and Concho grasped it and rose. The deputy grabbed hold of the stair railing with his other hand and climbed to his feet with the Ranger helping.

"My pistol!" Hoight mumbled. He turned to look for it.

Concho saw the weapon, a blue-steel .38 revolver, lying in the corner of the landing. He scooped it up and handed it to Hoight, who stuck it in its holster.

"You get on outside," Concho ordered. "Get a paramedic to check your skull. You might have a concussion."

"What are you gonna do?"

"Whoever hit you must have gone up the stairs. Maybe to the roof. I'm going to check it out."

"Be careful."

"Forewarned is forearmed," Ten-Wolves replied.

Hoight groaned and closed his left eye again against the ache in his head. "I don't think I'd be much good to you anyway. Holding onto the railing, he shambled down the stairs toward the maintenance door.

Concho watched the deputy until he reached the door and pulled his way through, then turned and gazed up the stairwell. It looked empty. But was it? He drew his pistol again. Time to find out.

CHAPTER ELEVEN

"He is called Concho Ten-Wolves," Jorge Gonzales had said. He added again, "I am sure he must have been the one Aquila was dealing with. His greed is legendary on the reservation. He must have decided to take it all himself. He is to blame for our failure in the delivery. Not us!"

Zoe rubbed her lips with a finger. She glanced at Liana and jerked her chin toward the door. The blonde followed her out of the cabin, and they stood close together in the cold dark where they would not be overheard by their captives.

Night had fallen; a glittering stream of stars flowed through the sky overhead. A knife-edged breeze came stabbing in the dark. Zoe shivered. "What do you make of Jorge's story?"

Liana shrugged. "The Texas Devils are all corrupt. It's not hard to believe one of them could be in cahoots with Aquila."

"And be stupid enough to betray him?"

"You know how arrogant Americanos are."

Zoe nodded. "We need to call the doctor. See what he has to say."

"Sounds good," Liana replied. "Go ahead. You have his number?"

Zoe started. "Me? You're the one he hired to find Jañega. It's your call to make."

Liana smirked. "How can you still be so naive, Zoeita? I figured you surely knew I was fibbing when I told you that. Aquila wanted *you* for this job. He called *me* because he had my number and knew I could find you."

Zoe took a quick breath and snorted it out through her nostrils. "One of these days, Liana!"

Liana laughed. "But not this day." She pushed back through the door into the cabin.

Zoe tapped her fingers on her hip, then pulled out her cell phone. She did have Gutierrez Aquila's number, although not linked to him by name. She'd worked for him before, and he paid well, although she didn't particularly enjoy the kind of jobs he offered. In fact, she no longer enjoyed any of this kind of work. But here she was.

She called up the appropriate contact number and hit send. The phone rang twice before it was answered. The voice at the other end spoke in cultured and educated English.

"Yes."

"Dr. Aquila. This is Zoe deSaint. We've spoken before."

"Yes, Ms. deSaint. I was expecting a call from you. I am sorry I misplaced your own number. Can I assume you have some information about a certain Rafael Jañega?"

"You can, sir. We have him. I've questioned him. He and a companion named Jorge Gonzales."

"I do not know Jorge."

"I imagine he was hired by Jañega for the task you assigned him. I'll find out for sure."

"Good."

"Both men claim they were surprised by the arrival of a Texas Ranger at the site of the landing. Both claim the Ranger was not alone and that they…Jañega and Gonzales and their men, were outnumbered and barely escaped with their lives."

"Some part of that is a lie, of course," Aquila said. "Perhaps all of it."

"Perhaps, sir. Gonzales told us one other thing. He recognized the Ranger as a man named Concho Ten-Wolves. Gonzales says he's crooked and probably confiscated the delivery for his own uses. He even thinks Ten-Wolves might be the contact to which the…materials were to be delivered."

"Hmmm," Aquila murmured. "We have also determined that Ten-Wolves was the name of the Texas Ranger who disrupted the delivery. We don't have any evidence he had others with him but cannot at present prove it one way or another. However, as for a 'contact', he is definitely not the person for whom the delivery was intended."

"Right," Zoe said. "I believe Liana and I should investigate this Ranger and see what we can find out. How did he know about the delivery? We both have joint citizenship, so it won't be hard to get into the States."

"I was hoping you would say that, Ms. deSaint. As long as *you* are in charge of all of it, I concur."

"I'll be in charge. And I appreciate your faith in me."

"Faith is well rewarded."

"Thank you, sir."

"You will bring Jañega and this Gonzales to me first."

Zoe felt a chill flash the length of her spine. Every aspect of this conversation from here on had to be handled with the most delicate of touches. You did not want Gutierrez Aquila mad at you. Not only was he the kind to order torture, but he was also said to enjoy administering it himself. And physically, he was big enough to do it. The man might have been in his early forties but when she'd met him she'd found him to be powerfully built and in peak physical condition. Gym rats recognize their own kind.

"If possible, sir, I'd like to keep both men handy to talk to as we begin our investigation. I've asked them everything I can think of but unforeseen questions always arise on any job. And from what I hear of this Ranger, I might need information quickly. I have a place close to the Rio Grande where they can be kept safely. And people I trust to watch over them and keep them available to me."

Even as she spoke to Aquila, Zoe wondered why she made any effort on Jañega's behalf. She owed the man nothing. Why was she trying to keep him from falling into the doctor's hands and surely being tortured? True, they'd grown up together. Jañega had been a couple of years older. He'd once seemed full of worldly coolness to her. She'd had a crush on him. He'd been her first kiss. When she was twelve.

But it hadn't been long before she'd discovered what he was—a coward and a con, a weak boy who'd grown up to be a weak man. And yet, she'd just put her neck on the line for him. It was stupid. She wasn't cut out for this anymore.

Last job, she thought. *I'm truly done!*

Across the phone line, Aquila drew a long, slow breath and released it. "Very well. For the moment. But keep me informed of any of these 'unforeseen' questions you end up having. And after all is done, I'll be expecting the two men brought to me."

"Of course, sir." Zoe swallowed the sigh of relief she wanted to vent. She'd only postponed the inevitable of the doctor getting his hands on Jañega. But who knew what might happen or occur to her in the interval?

"One other thing," Aquila said.

"Yes, sir."

"It appears I have some kind of leak in my organization. Someone who is in league with the Texas Rangers. Or one of them at least. If it turns out *not* to be Jañega, I still need to know who. Ten-Wolves will have that information. I expect you to get it. However, regardless of what you find out from and about this Ranger, in the end he has to die. And badly. I cannot have my...projects so disrupted without consequences."

"We'll make sure of it, sir."

"*You* make sure of it, Zoe deSaint. You!"

Aquila hung up before Zoe could respond. The dark-haired woman sighed in relief and returned to the cabin. Liana glanced at her questioningly.

"We're going to Texas," Zoe said by way of answer.

Liana frowned, then offered, "Well, you know what they say."

"No. *What* do they say?"

"Nothing is sure except death and Texas."

Liana laughed quite a while at that one. Zoe only rolled her eyes.

* * *

CONCHO STARTED UP THE STAIRS, MOVING FROM THE SECOND floor toward the third. He had a feeling he'd have to go all the way to the roof to find whoever had knocked out Terrill Hoight.

Months back, he'd been forced into a shoot-out on the roof. A man named Wayne Quaite and a Kickapoo tribal gang member named Tall Horse had ambushed him. He'd killed Tall Horse and wounded Quaite, who'd spent the days after that in prison for attempted murder.

A thought occurred. Could Hoight's "big shadow" figure be the man Jericho had warned him about from prison? The "freak" hired by old enemy Quaite to beat the Ranger to death? That would mean he was being led deliberately toward the roof for a new showdown. It sounded like Quaite, who'd want to make sure he knew who was behind his pain.

If so, that changed the whole complexion of tonight's events. The bomb threat wasn't about a real bomb. It was about getting Concho to the casino and getting him alone. It seemed egotistical to make this all about himself, but there'd been enough attempts on his life recently to create some paranoia.

Ten-Wolves shook his head. He'd find out soon enough. He started faster up the stairs. Third floor, fourth floor, fifth. He reached the door to the roof. After his gunfight with Quaite and Tall Horse, the roof access had been multiple locked.

Those locks hung loose now. The bolt cutter used to savage them leaned against the wall nearby.

Cautiously, Concho pushed open the door and peered through into the outside world. Full night had fallen while he'd been inside. The moon had not yet risen; a few scattered yellowish lights on the roof merely accentuated the shadows around them. Only the earliest stars spotted the velvet-black sky beyond.

The lawman crouched to make himself a smaller target and eased onto the roof. Gravel crunched under his boots, and he froze. He could see no one but there were plenty of big air conditioning units to hide behind and sets of big pipes running every which way. It was an ambusher's paradise.

Ten-Wolves duckwalked over to a dark mass of unknown machinery and straightened. "I figure you're up here," he spoke to the night. "Why not introduce yourself? Tell me what it is you want."

A deep laugh rumbled out of the darkness, a laugh like something out of a Kaiju behemoth's throat. He couldn't localize it. One of the roof lights to his right suddenly exploded, sending sizzling glass flying.

A light on his left went next, shattering as if struck by a bullet, though he heard no sound of a shot, only a kind of high-pitched whistle. A third light followed. The darkness grew in strength and began to close in on the Ranger as if it were alive.

CHAPTER TWELVE

Concho fired a shot in the air. The lights stopped breaking but there were only two left that he could see. Neither of them very close. The dark surrounded him, submerged him in a lake of black air. It was deep but certainly not empty. Ten-Wolves listened hard. He was not afraid of the dark, but something was going on here he didn't understand, and it left him wary. The darkness would blind his enemy as well as himself.

Unless…

"Unless he's got night vision goggles," Concho murmured softly.

He had such goggles himself, but they were in his truck. Light-years away at the moment. Whoever stalked him had probably watched him come onto the roof. He'd also called out to them, which would have helped them identify his location. Time to try something that might bring him information in return.

"How's old Wayne doing?" he called. "Wayne Quaite. I imagine he's the one hired you. What's he after anyway?"

"You!" a voice answered.

It came from somewhere to the Ranger's left, a low, raspy

voice that sounded as if its owner were gargling a scurry of cockroaches.

"He tried once before and got a bullet for his troubles."

"That was him. This is me."

Now the voice sounded like it came from the Ranger's right. *Impossible!* No one could have moved that quickly *and* silently past him.

Unless there are two of them?

Concho shifted position behind the pile of machinery that hid him, trying to get a better view of the rest of the roof. Something struck him brutally on the right hand, just behind the knuckle of his little finger. He cried out as the hand went numb and the .45 he held dropped away.

The blow had come from behind; he spun, drawing his left-hand pistol. With a rushing sound, a huge shape appeared out of the darkness, powering toward him like a runaway dump truck.

Concho swung up the gun. The moving shape struck him first, smashing him savagely against the machine behind him. His arm went up; the gun went flying. The shape was big, tall as a stilt but with shoulders wide as a bull. Ten-Wolves couldn't see a face; the man's night vision goggles turned him into a monstrous insect.

Hands like post-hole diggers clamped around Concho's throat. A knee slammed toward his privates, and he just managed to block with his hip. A huge body pressed him back; he smelled greasy hair and rancid breath.

The hands around the lawman's throat tightened like a steel collar. He grabbed at the wrists, tried to twist them aside. The Ranger knew how strong he was. Usually when he exerted his strength to make something move, it moved. Not this time. He clawed at the wrists, but the man's grip was relentless.

Dark spots began to swim through the law officer's vision. His breathing came in gasps. He slammed a fist into his opponent's midsection. It hit something hard beneath the long-sleeved sweatshirt the man wore—maybe a bulletproof vest. The man barely grunted.

In desperation, Concho punched lower, into the testicles. He hit with his right hand, the one struck moments before by a blow from nowhere. Agony arched up his wrist, but his attacker cried out in even greater pain and doubled over.

Concho tore free of the man's grip. He slid to the side and slammed a left hand into his foe's jaw. It was like hitting ceramic tile, but it knocked the goggles askew. The man shook his head and straightened. He ripped off the goggles and let them drop.

Beneath, he wore a balaclava that still concealed his head, although the massive square thrust of the face was visible beneath the cotton. With a roar, the fellow lunged, swift as a bullet. His open hands came down on Concho's shoulders and tried to latch on.

Concho twisted away. He slammed an open palm from his right hand into the man's chin, snapping the head back. Again, a shock of agony flashed through his injured hand, and the blow scarcely slowed his attacker. The man responded with a fresh roar and charged.

Ten-Wolves darted aside. The Ranger was six feet, four inches tall. He weighed between two-fifty and two-sixty. The other man was bigger, by far. At least five inches taller and well over three hundred pounds. He had three or four inches of reach on the lawman. Concho couldn't stand toe-to-toe with him.

At least his huge attacker wasn't a trained boxer. The man swung his giant fists like anvils. Any one of those that connected would have ended the fight, but Concho ducked and wove and stayed alive. After each roundhouse blow slung in his direction, he fired back a left jab. Most of these connected but had about as much impact as a spitball. The man kept coming, stalking the Ranger, hunting him.

"What's your name?" Concho shouted.

He hoped for even a momentary respite in the duel. He

wasn't used to backing up for anyone. But he'd felt the power of the big man's hands around his throat. He couldn't let those hands close on him again. This had to be the "freak" Jericho had warned him about, a man who'd only recently been released from prison.

The big man didn't *stop* to answer the question, but he did answer as he kept advancing. "Law Dog Killer!" he snarled.

A huge fist cannoned through the air, missing Concho's chin by less than an inch. The Ranger popped another jab into the man's lips, spraying blood that seemed of no concern to the fellow.

"And you work for Quaite?" Concho asked, still backing up.

A quick glance behind showed they were getting close to the edge of the roof. He couldn't let himself be cornered there. He snapped a kick toward the giant's thigh. A wrist as thick and hard as a 2x4 blocked it.

"No," the man answered. "But he sends his regards."

"So, you're willing to go back to jail for him?"

For the first time the man grinned, showing block-like teeth through the mouth line of the balaclava. "Not if there ain't no witnesses alive to testify."

Now, Concho snarled. He spun, lashing out with a roundhouse kick. His boot slammed into the man's side but barely moved him. Again, the giant hands grasped for him, trying to lock on and drag him near. Concho avoided the grab but now they were even closer to the edge of the building and a six-story drop.

The idea of such a fall had clearly occurred to Concho's huge foe as well. He almost seemed to be 'herding' the Ranger, forcing him toward a death plummet. Concho had to stop retreating. He snapped a kick toward the big man's groin. A knee blocked the strike.

But then Concho lunged forward on the attack. He slammed an open-handed left up under the man's chin, staggering him for an instant. His right hand latched onto his opponent's wrist, and despite the pain blazing through his fingers he gave a savage tug.

The man swung a windmill right. Concho let his legs fold; he started to fall backward. The punch whiffed over his head. His left fist knotted in the man's gray sweatshirt.

The big fellow stumbled a step forward, off balance for the first time. Concho's back hit the roof. He swung his legs up, snapping his boots into his enemy's midsection while holding his grip on the man's shirt and wrist. With all the power of his legs, the Ranger drove his feet upward, lifting his foe into the air and flipping him over his head.

The man cried out in shock. Concho released his grip on the giant, who did a complete flip and came down on his spine right across the punishing edge of the roof. Shock turned to pain in the man's voice, then into fear as he felt himself sliding over the side.

Concho bounced to his feet though every part of his body shouted with pain. Somehow, the giant flopped over onto his belly. His hands scrabbling frantically at the top of the roof, scraping up tar and gravel. Three-quarters of his body already hung free in the air, though.

One of the last of the rooftop lights flashed in the huge man's eyes. Terror grew stark as toadstools in that gaze. His powerful hands clawed at gravel and found it no more substantial than water. He slid backward; his right elbow caught on the edge; the muscles of his arms bulged like steel cables.

"Help!" he pleaded.

Concho stepped forward, not quite sure if he planned to help the man or finish him. Before he could do anything, the man's elbow slipped off the roof. The nails of his right hand dug in but tore away under his immense weight. He screamed as all his support disappeared and he plummeted downward. A heavy thud came from below, followed by silence.

"You son of a bitch!" a new voice shouted. "You killed him!"

Something small and hard, like a marble, struck Concho

between the shoulders. It stung but not much more. The Ranger spun around, dropping into a crouch, wondering what new enemy he faced but prepared to crush it.

* * *

THE SLEEK FIREBIRD POWERED EAST NOW, RETURNING TOWARD Piedras Negras, in Coahuila. Liana drove, keeping to the speed limit. Or at least close to it. Zoe deSaint was grateful. It gave her time to think.

She had a lot to cogitate about, the new job from Gutierrez Aquila involving a certain Texas Ranger named Concho Ten-Wolves, and what she was going to do afterward if she decided not to turn Rafael Jañega over to Aquila. That was not a pleasant place for her thoughts to dwell.

From the backseat of the Bird, where Jañega and Jorge Gonzales were handcuffed, a voice spoke. It was Gonzales. "If you seek for help with the Texas Ranger, I can call my cousin on the reservation. Leticia Garcia. She and her family will be happy to help send him to hell."

Zoe turned in her seat to look at Gonzales. "What makes you think we have any plans about Ten-Wolves?"

Gonzales shrugged. "It is not hard to imagine who you called when you left the cabin at Ojo Laguna. And if you spoke to the doctor, you would have mentioned what I told you about Ten-Wolves. From there, the course is inevitable."

Zoe studied the man. He dropped his gaze. She kept studying.

"Perhaps he's not as stupid as he appears," Liana said from behind the wheel. She wrinkled her nose. "Or as he smells."

Zoe glanced over at her companion. "Maybe we should have thrown them in the lake before we let them in the car."

"Maybe we should have just shot 'em and covered 'em in dirt."

"We'll have to keep our options open," Zoe said.

Both women laughed but the men didn't find it as funny.

CHAPTER THIRTEEN

As Concho turned, he saw the figure who'd shouted at him limned against the ambient light fifteen feet away. The shape stood barely more than five feet tall, with short, crew cut hair. As it lifted its hand, the weapon it gripped showed in silhouette. A slingshot.

The boy—for that's what the figure was—whirred the sling. Even as the youth let fly, Concho dodged. The pellet, or whatever it was, whistled past, missing him by a foot. The boy stabbed his hand into his pocket, probably for another slug, but realized Ten-Wolves was charging him. He turned to run but the Ranger already had momentum building. The youth barely made three steps before Concho caught him and wrapped a long arm around his chest.

The boy twisted and threw an elbow. The lawman blocked, then kicked the youth's legs from under him with a swipe of a boot and put him on his back. He straddled him, using enough weight to pin the lad down without crushing him.

"Get off me! Get off me!" the boy yelled. "You killed him! You killed him!"

"Killed who?" Concho demanded roughly.

"My dad. My dad!"

Despite the fact that this boy's father had been trying very hard to kill *him*, Concho felt a momentary gut punch at the words. This was just a kid; he looked no more than twelve or thirteen, and small for his age.

"I couldn't help it. I didn't want to."

"Son of a bitch!" the boy yelled again. He thrashed his head.

Concho grasped the boy's chin and forced him to stillness. "Who are you? What's your name?"

"Deke!" the boy snapped. He tried to spit up into the Lawman's face but the spittle only fell back into his own mouth. He choked and hacked but quickly caught his breath.

"Deke what?"

"Deke Cooper."

"And your father?"

That question aroused the youth's suspicions. His face narrowed. "I don't have to tell you nothin'."

"How old are you?"

"Eighteen!"

"That's a lie."

"Screw you!"

"You're probably thirteen. And your father brought you along on an attempt to *murder* someone?"

"He didn't have no choice," Deke said hotly. "When he got home, Mom told him to take me and leave. She wouldn't even let him in the apartment. He didn't have no choice."

Again, Concho felt the gut punch. This boy's mother had sent him off with a father who was fresh out of prison. She'd thrown him out like trash.

"Who's your mother?" he demanded.

The boy stopped struggling; his voice went sullen but at least he was talking. "Dana."

"Dana Cooper?"

Deke shook his head. "She don't go by that."

"What does she go by?"

"Dana Angel."

"Angel? Sounds like a stage name. Your mother an actress? Or an exotic dancer?"

A shrug. "I guess."

"Where?"

"Dallas." He made a face. "She works at a place called *Fatty's*. But it won't do no good to send me back there. She don't want nothing to do with me. And now you done gone and killed my dad."

The teenager's eyes welled with thick tears. He fought to crush them back but couldn't even get his hands up to wipe his face because Concho had them pinned. Sobs racked him. His whole body shook.

Concho rose to his feet. He reached down and grasped the boy's arms and pulled him to his feet. He almost draped an arm over the youth's shoulders as a comfort, but Deke pushed away from him and slapped at his own face to beat away the tears. He glanced toward the door into the hotel.

"Don't even think of running," Concho warned. "My legs are a lot longer than yours."

"Screw you!" Deke shouted again. But he stood still.

Concho ignored the curse. "I need you to answer two more questions. First, is your dad the one called in the bomb threat?"

"Ain't telling you nothin'."

"Any chance the bombs are real?"

"You go die!"

* * *

DOCTOR GUTIERREZ AQUILA CONTINUED TO THINK ABOUT THE phone conversation he'd had earlier with Zoe deSaint. He had worked with deSaint before. He trusted her and she'd always delivered. But now, something in her voice on the recent call suggested she was conflicted about his orders.

One reason he liked deSaint was because she had a moral center that her colleague, Liana, did not possess. That meant she would not try to fleece him and would show no more than the minimal deceptiveness that made up the weave of even the most honorable human beings.

However, he also knew the morals of his employees could create problems when they conflicted with his desires. He hoped this would not become an issue with Zoe deSaint. His previous interactions with her had been profitable, though he'd never asked her to carry out a killing before.

Putting thoughts of the woman aside for the moment, Aquila entered the home office in his hacienda, locked the door, and went around behind his desk. It was eight o'clock in the evening, time for a conversation he was not looking forward to having.

Ignoring the top-of-the-line office computer on his desk, he opened a drawer and took out a disposable tablet computer he'd ordered from Best Buy. It looked like standard issue, but this one was loaded with software he'd acquired through Lieutenant Eduardo Diaz of the Mexican police, which they—no doubt—had acquired elsewhere still.

Powering up the tablet, he set that software in motion. The computer searched for and found a Wi-Fi network other than the one he ran his home systems through. It then immediately routed his connection through a series of increasingly distant sites. Screens opened and closed, until only one was left.

Aquila entered a web address on that screen. The connection went through, and a fresh blank screen appeared with a flashing green prompt. Using the tablet's virtual keyboard, Aquila typed, *Good evening.*

A minimal lag followed before words appeared in response. *Is it?*

Aquila considered, then wrote, *I suppose it is not. From either of our points of view. However, a full investigation is under way.*

Which will not provide the materials to me I expected. Nor will it refund moneys already spent.

Irritation swept over Aquila. His fingers stiffened over the tablet, but he forced them to relax. *If there is a cost that requires refunding, I'll refund it. As for the other materials, I assure you they will be recovered.*

I care about only one.

It will be recovered.

What went wrong? was the only reply.

Primarily, one man. His name is Concho Ten-Wolves.

This time, there was a much longer lag before words appeared on the screen. *I should have guessed. If there is a problem for my people on the reservation, he is at the center.*

Options are being considered, Aquila typed.

The screen came back with, *Good. We will consider them as well.*

The cursor blinked but Aquila could see the connection had been severed. He shut off the tablet. Rising, he took the device over to the wall safe in his room. He opened the safe and stuck it inside, where a powerful magnet would scramble its memory. He locked the safe behind it.

One couldn't be too careful in a world full of lies.

CHAPTER FOURTEEN

UP ON THE ROOF OF THE EAGLE PASS CASINO AND HOTEL, Concho searched Deke Cooper's pockets. He found a handful of ball bearings to use as ammo in a slingshot, and a small device that took a moment to puzzle out. It was a voice changer, which explained why he'd heard Deke's father's voice coming from two different places.

He confiscated the ammo and the device while handcuffing the boy to his left wrist. A quick search across the roof revealed his two Colts, which he holstered again after brushing them free of dirt. He also found the slingshot the boy had dropped.

It was a professional job with a solid rubber grip and even a laser sight mounted on the handle. A dangerous weapon in the hands of a skilled enemy, which Deke's father had apparently been and his son not so much. Concho's right hand still hurt from the blow he'd taken from the sling. Examining it revealed a clearly broken little finger. A knot had risen behind the knuckle. He'd have it looked at as soon as he got off the roof.

The Ranger also picked up the night vision goggles Deke's father had dropped. They were professionally made, as well. Better than the ones he had in his own truck, in fact. Given their quality, he might be able to trace where the slingshot and goggles had been bought. He needed more information now, though, and only Deke Cooper—a big name for a small fellow—was around to supply that info.

Concho pulled Deke around to face him and read the boy his rights in a stern and menacing voice. By the time he was done, the youngster stood hunched and shaking and the Ranger felt like a heel.

"I don't…wanna go to jail," Deke protested. "I can't!"

Time for some *good cop*. Concho softened his voice. "I understand, but the law is the law. Making a bomb threat is a Class B felony. A pretty serious crime. Cooperation might have helped some but…" He shrugged.

Deke glanced up at the Ranger, then looked quickly away. "What if I…if I cooperated…a little?"

"What's a little, Deke?"

"I…maybe I heard something my Dad said on the phone."

"What?"

Deke's shoulders slumped even lower. "I heard him talkin' to somebody and he told them there was a bomb. More than one actually."

"But there wasn't, was there?"

Deke shook his head. "My dad, I don't think he knows nothin' about bombs. He had some wires he pulled out of an old fuse box. He hooked 'em to a motorcycle battery and stuck it in the trash can outside some woman's office, with the wires outside so it would look like a bomb."

"What woman?"

"I don't know her name. I guess she runs the place."

Concho nodded. "And was that the only 'fake' bomb he put up?"

"Yeah."

"Just one more thing. What's your dad's name?"

"Ron Cooper. Well, he told people to call him 'Ron.' His name was Myron."

"Wouldn't have imagined it."

Deke shook his head back and forth. "He hated it."

Concho sighed. "Thanks." He pulled out his cell phone and placed a call to Sheriff Echabarri, who answered promptly. A lot of ambient noise bled through the airwaves, but he made out his friend's words.

"Ten-Wolves? You OK? Where are you?"

"I'm fine. I caught our perpetrators on the roof. One of them called in the bomb threat but it was faked. Only one device and it's just wires attached to a motorcycle battery in the garbage can outside Melissa Nolan's office. The bomb squad in?"

"Yes. One of them just entered the building."

"Get in touch with him. Let him know."

"Will do," Echabarri said. He sounded relieved. "What about you?"

"I'm coming out with a prisoner."

"One? I thought you mentioned 'perpetrators.' With an 's'."

"There were two." Concho glanced at Deke and lowered his voice, though the boy would still be able to hear him. "There's only one now."

"I understand," Roberto said.

"By the way, is Sam Reyes around?"

Reyes was a Kickapoo tribal member and nurse practitioner. He ran the clinic for the casino and had stitched up the lawman's wounds in the past.

"Yeah, he's around. Having a look at Terrill Hoight. Why? Somebody else hurt?"

"Me. A broken finger. I'll need him to set it."

"Glad it's no worse. I'll have him here when you get outside. I'll tell him you need to have your arm sewn back on. That'll make him jump."

Concho wanted so badly to arch an eyebrow at the comment but didn't have the brow construction for it. "Seems a little extreme," he offered instead. "Maybe just a hand."

Roberto laughed. "Sorry. Just really relieved there's no bomb and we didn't lose any of ours."

"Yeah," Concho said. He swiped off the call. His glance took in the thin frame of Deke Cooper standing next to him with shoulders bowed. *None of ours*, his thoughts echoed.

* * *

THE DRONE CIRCLED ALMOST SILENTLY IN THE SKY OVER THE Kickapoo Lucky Eagle Casino and Hotel. Its camera eye took in the crowd, focusing primarily on the actions of police and firefighters, and fed the images to a laptop located in a truck with blacked-out windows parked near the rear of the casino lot.

Two men in the truck followed the drone's movements on the computer. They each leaned closer to the screen when Texas Ranger Concho Ten-Wolves came walking out of the emptied establishment with a kid in tow.

One of the men took a deep breath and let it out slowly. "All right," he said. "I'll call the boss."

"Better you than me," the other replied.

* * *

SINCE IT APPEARED THERE'D BE NO "BOOM," THE CROWD outside the casino had thinned. The local news crew still clamored for attention and Echabarri had finally gone over to brief them. After Concho had briefed *him*.

Ten-Wolves sat on the tailgate of his pickup while Samuel Reyes examined his hurt right hand. Concho winced as Reyes set the bone in the pinkie finger and taped that finger to the one next to it.

"They call this a 'buddy splint'," Reyes said.

"Good thing those two fingers like each other," Concho replied.

Reyes chuckled. "You really need an X-ray. Go hit up an emergency room as soon as you can."

"Will do. Thanks for the temporary fix."

"My job."

Both men paused to stare at a gurney being pushed past from the casino toward a waiting ambulance. The paramedics pushing it were in no hurry. The man who lay beneath the white sheet on the gurney was beyond any healing care. He'd just fallen six stories to his death.

"Big fellow," Reyes said, eyeing the large, somewhat misshapen mound beneath the sheet.

"Even bigger in life," Concho said. "Excuse me."

The Ranger signaled the paramedics to stop. He lifted the sheet covering the dead man's face. The medics had removed Myron Cooper's balaclava and placed it on his chest. The revealed face was huge and almost square, with thick brow ridges, almost flat cheekbones, and a large nose with its tip bent to one side. Short, curly red hair adorned the head.

Both Sam Reyes and Roberto Echabarri walked over for a look. "So that's Myron Cooper?" Roberto asked. "Doesn't look like a 'Myron'."

"I had the same thought," Ten-Wolves replied. "Apparently he went by 'Ron'."

"What's wrong with his face?" Roberto asked.

"Could be acromegaly," Reyes responded.

"I've heard of that," Concho said, "but I'm not exactly sure what it is."

"A hormonal disorder. The pituitary gland releases too much growth hormone. It causes the bones to thicken. That's where the squareness of his features come from. And the brow ridge and big nose. Maybe also why he's so tall and has such large hands." The medic pointed toward the outline of Cooper's platter-sized hands under the sheet.

Concho folded the sheet back over Myron Cooper's face and signaled the paramedics to continue. As they rolled away, the Ranger glanced over at Roberto. "Where's his son now?" he asked. He'd turned the boy over to Echabarri while Reyes was treating his broken finger.

"With Nila Willow. She'll keep an eye on him. But what are

we supposed to do with him? You plan to charge him with a crime?"

Concho shook his head. "No. I guess the only thing we can do is contact his mother. But from what he told me, she doesn't really want him around."

Roberto winced, then sighed. "You know her name?"

"I think it's Dana Cooper but apparently she goes by the name Dana Angel. Sounds like she works as an exotic dancer in Dallas. At a place called '*Fatty's*'."

"You're kidding me."

"Nope."

Echabarri nodded. "All right, I'll give them a call. Find out what she wants to do. But what if she doesn't want him?"

"I don't know. Social services, I guess. If it comes to that, I'll call Beth Pennebaker. She's a local social worker. She can probably tell us how to proceed."

Roberto glanced over at Reyes, who got the message and drifted away. Concho had given the Kickapoo sheriff a brief explanation of what transpired on the roof, but he wanted more.

"So, this man was after you?" Roberto asked.

"Yep."

"And the bomb threat was just to get you here and get the place cleared so he could murder you?"

"So it seems."

"How could he know you'd even be called in? Or that you'd go in alone?"

Concho shrugged. "A calculated guess, I suppose. Someone had been feeding him information about how we work around here, though."

"Wayne Quaite?"

Ten-Wolves shook his head. "I'm thinking someone closer."

"On the Rez?"

"Yeah."

"I don't like that."

"Me neither, though my money's on the Whitehearts or Letty Garcia."

"Likely," Roberto agreed. "Or both. One last question."

"Ask."

"Tell me tonight's events don't have anything to do with the smuggling operation you uncovered on the bank of the Rio Grande the other day. Tell me we don't have some kind of conspiracy working."

Concho grinned. "That's a statement, not a question. And there's two of 'em."

"Ten-Wolves!"

The Ranger stopped grinning. "I wish I could," he said soberly. "But the timing is an awfully big helping of coincidence to swallow."

Roberto sighed. "I was afraid you were going to say that."

CHAPTER FIFTEEN

After leaving Echabarri, Concho sought out Terrill Hoight. He found him talking to an Eagle Pass fireman, who moved away after Ten-Wolves arrived.

"You OK?" the Ranger asked Hoight.

"OK enough. Thanks for coming in after me."

"No problem."

"Sounds like *you* had a rough few moments on the roof."

"Over now," Ten-Wolves replied. He offered the deputy the night vision goggles and the sling. "The guy had these. Maybe you could try to trace down where they were sold? You'll have better connections than Roberto."

"Gotcha!"

The cell phone in Concho's pocket vibrated. He pulled it out and immediately excused himself as he saw who it was. Stepping a few feet away, he swiped to answer.

"Maria! I'm sorry, I should have called."

"What's going on? I'm at your place. Where are you?"

"At the casino. We had a bomb threat."

"Oh my God! Is everything OK? You OK?"

"I'm fine. We got everything resolved a little bit ago. We got the perps and there was no actual bomb."

"Thank God. Anybody hurt?"

Concho considered what to say and settled on, "Mostly minor injuries."

"I'm coming over."

"No need. I'm actually just getting ready to leave. I should be home in twenty minutes."

"All right. I'll be here. Love you!"

"Love you, too!"

Concho swiped off the call and hurried toward his truck. He desperately wanted to see Maria. Right now. To hug her. He needed it.

* * *

MARIA MORALES GASPED; HER BODY JERKED AS SHE SAT astride Concho's hips. She was looking down at her lover. His brown eyes brightened, then softened. He gave a little groan. She smiled.

After a moment, she slid to the side and lay down on the bed. He turned his head toward her, and she kissed his forehead, faintly damp with sweat but smooth now that his worry wrinkles from earlier were gone.

"Feel better?" she asked.

"Much."

She stroked his broad cheek with a finger. Stubble met her touch; he needed a shave. "I'm glad you weren't seriously hurt." She drew back slightly, then added, "I...hate your job."

He smiled gently. "You hiring security guards down at the mall?"

Maria managed the Eagle Pass Mall. She could, in fact, have hired Concho as a guard there, but she knew he wouldn't go for it. Her boyfriend was the hero-type. No matter how much he might deny it, he was built physically and emotionally for taking risks in the service of others. And as much as she wanted to come between him and danger, she couldn't. Their relationship would never survive. Not that any of it was easy to deal with.

Smiling fondly to cover up her fears, she made a joke. "I was thinking more of hiring you as a tree. Or maybe as a food critic."

He laughed. "That last is the job I was born for."

"Not really. A *critic* has to occasionally *criticize* food. Not just love it in all its forms."

Concho made a frowning face. "Sounds…weird."

Maria chuckled. "You know, I was thinking…"

"What?"

Maria sighed and shook her head. She pushed away from her lover and slid out of bed. "Bathroom," she said.

Concho closed his eyes. "Go for me. I'm too tired to get up."

Maria blew him a raspberry of a kiss, then slipped into the bathroom and shut the door. When she came out a few minutes later, Ten-Wolves was sound asleep, spread three-quarters of the way across the bed. He snored.

It was barely 10:00 at night. Maria wasn't tired. She closed the door to the bedroom and let the Ranger sleep.

* * *

CONCHO HEARD LAUGHTER. OR THOUGHT HE DID. HE OPENED his eyes. Or so he believed. The room should have been dark but was strangely lit in ethereal blue. He found himself standing, though he didn't remember rising.

The door was open, and he stepped through. Maria stood in the kitchen some thirty feet away, her back to him. Hair tumbled down her spine, drenched in black against the white nightgown she wore. She laughed again.

Concho grinned and started toward his love. She turned. He froze. Her face smiled; her hands lay linked over her belly. She was pregnant. Not just a little pregnant but months along.

Even as he watched, Maria's belly moved as the baby inside kicked. That couldn't be.

Maria was looking directly at him but didn't *see* him. He started forward again, confused, and she turned casually and stepped out of his view into the den. He sped his pace. Rushing through the kitchen, he saw no sign of Maria in the den except for an open back door. She could hardly have moved so fast, but he followed, out the door onto his deck. The sky above was dark, empty of stars and light, but the moon shone in his backyard.

No, the moon had *come to rest* in his backyard, shrunk to the size of a circus tent. It had settled there like a fairy ship anchored in a strange port. It glowed a scorched orange. He could see the details of its face, the craters and lunar seas, the rays of ejecta shining like silver spiderweb threads across the surface.

And, he could see dimly through its surface, through its translucent skin. A distorted shape moved inside. A woman, he thought. Maria! She held something. And he knew it for a baby when it vented a high-pitched cry.

A baby! *His* baby!

Concho felt a huge grin break across his face. He began to run toward the moon, which suddenly was nothing more than a brightly lit tent in a midnight yard. Something blocked his way, though. A shape on the ground. It looked like a tow sack with a head on top. He almost stepped on it before it mewled a plea. Its voice was full of fear and pain and despair.

Ten-Wolves felt as if he'd been stabbed by that voice. He paused, swaying before the shape. He recognized it. The mummy from the banks of the Rio Grande. The girl child who'd probably been murdered and transformed long before he'd been born. She still wore her turquoise mask with obsidian eyes, but now it seemed she could see through those eyes. They followed him as he slid slowly to his knees before her.

"What?" he began. "What do you want?"

The child answered. Her words whispered and belled, murmured and roared. They came from all around him, poking out of the darkness like needles into his ears.

"Rest. I only want to rest. To rest. Please!"

"I'll find you," Concho said.

A slender hand grabbed his wrist. It wasn't skeletal like a mummy's; it wasn't cold like the dead. It was fleshed and warm. And somehow, that was worse. He groaned and leaped backward to his feet.

He came awake in his own bed with a cry from out of the past ringing in his thoughts. He sat up. Maria slept on the other side of the bed, her breathing soft and steady. Concho remained still while his pounding heart slowed. A dream. Only a dream!

But many Kickapoo did not believe dreams were meaningless things. Concho's friend and mentor, the tribal elder Meskwaa, would likely call this dream a sending, a communication across time and unfathomable distance. He would say a child of the past had called out for aid.

Concho knew he had to give it. Even if Meskwaa was wrong and it meant nothing to the dead, it would mean something to him.

CHAPTER SIXTEEN

As the power of his strange dream receded, Concho checked the time on his phone. 4:00 AM. Early, but he wasn't going to be able to sleep again. He got up, moving silently to avoid waking Maria. Shutting the bedroom door behind him, he headed for his home office at the other end of the trailer and switched on his computer.

He fixed himself a hot tea and microwaved a sausage and egg biscuit, then sat at the computer. He had to do some thinking on a subject he'd prefer to avoid: just who on the reservation could have been the target for the delivery he'd intercepted on the Rio Grande? He opened the file he'd already started on the case and began to make notes, which he'd found to be a good way to organize his thoughts.

Roberto had mentioned the tribal council members as potential suspects. True, the five members of the council had power on the Rez, but did that extend outside the local Native American sphere? To move the kinds of items the Ranger had confiscated would require powerful connections and lots of money. To his knowledge, none of the council members had either of those in abundance.

The richest person on the reservation was likely Melissa

Nolan, who ran the tribal casino and was well paid for it. She also—by virtue of her position—had connections all over Texas and beyond. But, while Concho didn't think Nolan was any saint, he couldn't see her for something like smuggling counterfeit money and black market human organs. He'd ignore the child mummy for the moment; it just didn't fit.

The next two richest families on the Rez were farmers who sold their products even outside the Rez. Sam Whiteheart and George Night-Run. The Night-Runs had cattle, and friends in the powerful Cattlemen's Association of Texas. But the family had experienced a recent catastrophe when the mother, Delores Night-Run, had been arrested for a decade-old murder of a young woman who'd seduced her son. Concho had made that arrest. Her husband, George, remained a broken man, surely not capable of the calculating nature needed for this particular crime. If he'd ever been.

Sam Whiteheart, on the other hand, was shrewd, calculating, and—from Concho's perspective—rife with greed. He owned a vegetable farm and sold to most of the local markets in Eagle Pass and the surrounding area. He was also on the Tribal Council and had a history of throwing his weight around on his and his family's behalf. He and Concho had butted heads plenty, and Whiteheart had a similar history with Roberto Echabarri.

Although Concho tried to keep his personal feelings out of his investigations, it wasn't completely possible. He just didn't like Sam Whiteheart. Nor his son, Pete, who he'd also butted heads with. And he knew they weren't completely above board in their dealings with the tribe. But, something like smuggling, counterfeiting, and organ trafficking seemed a bit of a stretch.

The only other suspects Concho could imagine were those related to the late Daniel Alvarado, who'd once been on the Kickapoo Tribal Police Force and had been as crooked as a sidewinder's trail. In fact, Alvarado had been killed to keep him from talking about the gun-smuggling business of Jacob Drake, who Concho had put in jail a few months before.

Two of Alvarado's older sisters still lived on the Rez—Leticia, sometimes called Letty, and Francisca. Letty was married to a man named Henry Garcia, who Concho rather liked. But Letty herself had a vicious temper and could carry a grudge better than Sisyphus could push a rock.

Letty's son, Cisco, and daughter, Selena, had been involved with Pete Whiteheart in the NATV Bloods, a Native American gang operating surreptitiously on the Rez, mostly dealing drugs. Cisco and Selena, at Pete's urging, had even tried to assassinate Concho. He and Roberto had arrested the bunch of them but had eventually dropped the charges for a variety of reasons.

Afterward, Pete moved back to the Whiteheart compound on the Rez, a virtual fortress, and had kept his head down of late. Cisco and Selena had been sent south by their mother to stay with relatives near the town of Múzquiz in Mexico, where many Kickapoo lived, though he'd heard rumors of them visiting home.

Concho sighed. He picked up his tea and finished it. A plethora of suspects but none who quite fit the bill. It was time to dig deeper, and maybe rattle some cages. The law officer grinned to himself. He rather enjoyed rattling cages.

* * *

MONDAY. TENISH. AN ORANGE FIREBIRD PULLED INTO THE parking lot of the Lucky Eagle Casino on the Texas Kickapoo Reservation. Two women got out. Zoe deSaint and Liana, who used a variety of last names but was currently going by Spencer.

Since the women had dual citizenship in the USA and Mexico, it had proven easy to cross the border. Of course, they'd left their two prisoners behind, in the capable hands of Zoe's friends. They'd also left their weapons behind, although almost as soon as they came into Texas they stopped by a friend of Liana's and purchased more.

As the two women strolled casually toward the casino, Liana commented on the weather. "This is why you live in the south," Liana opined, lifting her arms out and turning her face up to the sun. "Sunny and sixty-two degrees in January. Save me from the cold hells of the north."

"How would you know?" Zoe asked. "You've hardly been past the Mason-Dixon Line in your life."

"I don't know what the Mason-Dixon Line is but it sounds like you're insulting me. What about the year we spent in Chicago? Surely you remember that?"

"Year! We were there for three days. Two years ago."

"Three days in December. Which equals a year in Texas time."

Zoe shook her head. "Come on," she said, as the casino's electric doors slid open.

They were here primarily on a scouting expedition, to get the lay of the land. This was Ten-Wolves' turf and you never went to war on someone else's territory without having mapped it out beforehand.

Also, before they'd left Mexico, they'd allowed Jorge Gonzales to make a phone call while they listened in. He'd called his cousin, Leticia Garcia, on the Eagle Pass reservation and set up a meeting between the three women. Garcia had been willing, even eager. She'd had plenty to say about Ten-Wolves. None of it good. The promise of making an ally on the Rez was well worth the risk. The enemy of an enemy and all that.

As the two women entered the gambling area on the first floor of the casino and hotel, the cacophony struck them like a surprise hailstorm. Voices shouted. Machines clicked, clacked, murmured, rang, and buzzed. Zoe made a face; Liana blinked, then smiled.

"This is more like it!" the blonde said. "Some action and excitement."

"All yours," Zoe said. "I'm going to find a place to get breakfast."

"Uh oh," Liana said.

"What?"

"To the right. At the money-changing window. Someone we know."

Zoe looked where Liana had indicated. "Crap!"

CHAPTER SEVENTEEN

At 6:30 AM, Concho entered the kitchen and plugged in the coffee pot. He then took a shower. As he was drying off, he heard the sound of Maria's cell phone alarm from the bedroom. He quickly slipped on jeans and a T-shirt and met his girlfriend in the kitchen.

She was naked but Ten-Wolves had learned some time ago not to take such as an invitation for any kind of play. Not before coffee. He stood out of the way as she padded past him like a sleepy lioness, her hand drifting out to tap his chest absentmindedly before she reached the coffee pot. Concho had set out her favorite cup and she poured, blew across it, and drank with nary a wasted motion.

As usual, Concho marveled at her ability to handle the scalding liquid without screaming. He started counting down silently to himself from twenty. Maria took a second sip at "ten," sighed at "six," and turned to face him at "one."

"Morning," she said.

"Morning, beautiful."

"Meh."

"You look ravishing."

"And you look like a man flirting with disaster."

Concho swallowed a grin. "Would you like some breakfast, dear?"

Maria made a face. "I would not." She replenished her cup, then walked back past him toward the bedroom to get dressed. He watched her go and considered a wolf-whistle, but that would indeed have been pushing his luck.

Shortly after 7:00, Maria left and Concho got ready to head out on patrol, and to shake some trees in hopes of knocking down evidence he could work with. His phone rang as he stepped out of the house. He checked the caller ID and recognized the name, though it wasn't someone he expected to hear from.

"Hello Miss Teshigahara," he said after swiping to answer. "What can I do for you?"

Tessa Teshigahara was a woman of mixed Kickapoo and Japanese heritage who had recently moved to the Texas Rez from out of state. She was interested in literary matters, mostly from the publishing side. He'd been introduced to her at a casino function, and she'd given him a small booklet of poems by Native Americans that she'd edited and printed. He'd only had time to glance through it so far.

Teshigahara had also told him of her plan to start a reservation newspaper. She had some local backing for it, but so far nothing in print form had materialized. He couldn't imagine why she was calling him.

"Hello Officer Ten-Wolves," Tessa said. "Glad I caught you. I'll get right to the point. I'm sure you're aware of my newspaper?"

"Yes, I've heard the plans."

"Well, we are going to be coming out with our first issue soon. Both online and in print. And I would *love* to interview you for it. I just read the article on you in *Texas Monthly*, and I noticed they didn't actually speak to you directly. Great stuff but all of it was secondhand. It would be wonderful for us to get your actual thoughts and words."

"Well, I—"

"I can assure you I won't waste your time. Just basic stuff and—if you like what we do with it—we can have you back again later."

"I'm not much for interviews."

"Of course, I understand. And I know you're a busy man. But, like it or not, you're the closest thing the Rez has to a celebrity. It would go a long way toward getting our first issue off to a good start."

Concho sighed inwardly but kept it out of his voice. Over the past six months he'd refused at least thirty requests for interviews, including from *Texas Monthly* magazine, who'd done an article on him anyway. He didn't feel comfortable talking to civilians about the life of a law officer. He seldom knew what to say, or even what was expected of him. And it was risky. Any wrong word could be pounced on and cause havoc in the ranks.

"Ma'am, if you're looking for a piece about me to sell papers for you, I have to tell you it could backfire. Plenty of people around don't much like me."

"Please call me Tessa and let me continue to be honest with you. The people who hate you will buy more papers than the people who love you. But…I also don't want to embarrass you or the Texas Rangers. I'd like to record our session, then play it for you, and whatever quotes you don't want, I'll erase them. And if you can't stand any of it, we can ax it before it ever sees print. That's a no-lose situation, isn't it? It's nearly unprecedented. But that's how bad I want you."

"Ma'am—"

"Please call me Tessa."

"Tessa, do you know how many requests for interviews I've turned down of late?"

Tessa chuckled. "You're just making me want it more, Ranger Ten-Wolves. I want to do more than fluff pieces on reservation life. I *need* to do more. Native Americans need an independent voice. The Kickapoo especially. And again, like it or not, you're in a position to speak for your people. For *our* people."

Concho fought back a sigh and knew he wasn't completely successful. He was beaten, with only one card left to play.

"I'd have to clear it with Texas Ranger headquarters."

"Of course," Tessa said. "I think they will. I spoke last evening with Dalton Shaw. I believe he's the commander of Company D of the Texas Rangers. Your direct boss. It took some convincing, but I believe he sees the merit for both sides in an interview. I'm sure you'll want to corroborate, though, so I'll let you speak to him about it. I'll call you in a couple of days?"

Concho almost appreciated the way he'd been outmaneuvered. "Remind me, Tessa, never to play chess with you."

Tessa laughed. "Poker is a better analogy. I'll call you. Thanks for your time." The woman hung up before the lawman could say more.

So, Concho thought, *the day is off to a great start.*

* * *

THE MAN LIANA HAD NOTICED EXCHANGING MONEY FOR TOKENS at the casino window was named Bearfoot. He was Kickapoo, lean and stringy, with a tangled strip of long dirty hair hanging down his back. Bearfoot was a drunk, a drug addict, and an inept gambler. He lived on the Texas reservation but was known on occasion to visit below the border.

On one such trip to the south, he'd met Zoe and Liana. And before long, he owed them money. However, considering that getting it from him would be more hassle than it was worth, the two women had decided to write off the debt.

But now!

"He hasn't seen us yet," Zoe said. "Give me a minute to get in position, then approach him from the entrance side of the casino. Let him see you."

"Gotcha," Liana replied.

The blonde Liana drifted off while Zoe circled around a row of slot machines and positioned herself carefully behind a display of Kickapoo cultural items. Bearfoot was leaving the money window when he caught sight of Liana surging through the crowd with a grim look on her face. As Zoe knew he would, the thin drunk turned immediately and scurried in the opposite direction.

Zoe stepped out of her hiding place as Bearfoot scrambled by and hooked his elbow with her arm, dragging him to an abrupt stop. "Bearfoot!" Zoe exclaimed. "Imagine running into you here. So good to see you."

Bearfoot made a halfhearted attempt to tug free, then gave up. He tried to smile but couldn't hold it. Zoe noticed he'd lost a few teeth since the last time they'd met. Liana arrived and hooked his other elbow. Terror creased the skinny Kickapoo's face.

"Don't make a scene," Zoe said quietly, "and things will work out."

The thin drunkard licked at his overly red lips and nodded. With the two women guiding, the party of three headed toward the rear of the casino, toward a hallway leading to the elevators. They passed these by and reached an emergency exit. Zoe positioned herself in front of the exit while Liana pushed Bearfoot up against the wall and pressed her butterfly knife against his throat. If any camera was observing, it should record nothing more than their backs.

Bearfoot gave a few quick huffs of fear and froze. He dared not call out with the knife so close to his throat, and he knew anyone coming down the hallway to the elevators wouldn't be able to see the blade, only a man and two women talking close together.

"How…how did you find me?"

Liana grinned, and she could put a lot of evil into a grin. Bearfoot wilted a little more.

"You don't think you're smart enough to elude us, do you?" Zoe asked softly.

"Wasn't…tryin' to elude you. I just needed time. To get the money."

"You got it now?" Zoe asked.

Again, Bearfoot licked his lips. "Uh, well, not…with me. Not here."

"Tsk tsk," Liana said. She pressed the razor edge of the blade a little harder against the man's throat.

"Wait, wait!" Bearfoot protested. "I promise I can get it. I *will* get it."

He was looking at Zoe rather than Liana, knowing he'd find no mercy in the blonde's eyes. Zoe studied him as if he were a piece of dog crap on her shoe, but then let the man see her relent.

"All right, all right. Lord knows I'm a soft touch. We'll give you a little time to get the funds together. In the meantime, there's something you can do for us."

"What? Bearfoot asked, without enthusiasm. He had to know it wasn't likely to be something he could feel good about doing.

"Oh," Zoe said, waving her hand around. "I don't know yet. But we'll tell you."

Liana pulled the knife away from the short Kickapoo's neck and stuck it in her jeans. She slid her left hand into *his* front pocket and felt around. Bearfoot's eyes got big. Liana chuckled and pulled the man's phone out. She swiped it on, typed her cell phone number into his contacts, then showed it to him.

"Beary, don't lose that number," she said. "It's the only one you want. And if you get a call from it, you pick up pronto. Understand?"

Bearfoot swallowed and nodded. "Right."

"And if you try to run out on us again," Liana added. "Well…" she tucked the phone back into his pocket and patted it, "we know where you live. And where your family lives." She offered him a dazzling smile full of bright white teeth.

"Yes, yes, of course."

The three stood quietly together for a moment, as if they

were indeed old friends. Liana finally shook her head and frowned. "Well go!" she snapped.

Bearfoot fled. Liana looked at Zoe and laughed.

"Don't imagine a threat to his family will do much good," Zoe said, "but a nice touch anyway."

Liana shrugged. "Now let's get that breakfast you were talking about. Threatening pissants always makes me crave pancakes. I noticed they have an IHOP here."

CHAPTER EIGHTEEN

Concho climbed into his Ford F-150 and raised dust across the Rez to Sam Whiteheart's place. The Whiteheart farm lay farther from Kickapoo Village than even the Ranger's trailer. It had always been isolated but he saw now the rumors were true. It resembled a military encampment.

A six-strand barbed wire fence stretched tautly all the way around the Whiteheart land. At least four wooden towers were visibly spaced out behind the fence. From what Concho had heard, these were supposed to be for spotting wildfires. They looked like sentry towers to him.

He arrived at a closed and locked gate of barbed wire strengthened with metal poles. No one would be bursting through that gate in less than an armored vehicle. A guard stood behind the gate. He held a shotgun. All the defensive measures seemed like overkill. Or maybe paranoia.

Concho stopped in front of the gate and rolled his window down. The guard with the shotgun approached.

"You have an appointment, señor?" the guard asked.

The man was Hispanic, but not Kickapoo. Concho didn't recognize him, which was unusual. He thought he knew everyone on the Rez, but this fellow must have been imported recently. Might be worth looking to see if he was registered with the Kickapoo sheriff's office.

"My name is Concho Ten-Wolves. I'm a Texas Ranger investigating a case. I don't need an appointment."

The man's black eyes sparked but he smiled and nodded, looking totally at ease. This was no common laborer. More likely a hired gun.

"Of course, señor. Just let me call the house and I'm sure I'll be able to open the gate for you in a moment."

"Make it snappy!"

The guard nodded. He drew a cell phone out of his pocket and turned away to make his call. A moment passed. The man hung up and returned to the gate without a word. He unlocked it and pulled it open, offering a short, almost insolent bow as he waved the lawman through.

The Ranger threw the truck into drive and powered through the gate and up the dirt road toward Sam Whiteheart's big house. Things were starting to get interesting.

* * *

At 10:23 AM, Zoe and Liana left the IHOP in the Lucky Eagle Casino complex and headed for the elevators. They took a ride to the fourth floor and strode down to Room 414. Promptly at 10:30, Zoe knocked on the door.

Both women wore jackets with guns holstered beneath them at the small of their backs. Both had the distinct impression of being stared at through the spyhole before the door in front of them opened.

A young man of seventeen or so stood in the doorway. He was tall, almost six feet, and thin, but with the promise of muscles showing under the tanned skin. His long, dark Kickapoo hair flowed freely. His features were even and handsome, his teeth white and straight.

This lad would break some hearts when he was older, Zoe imagined, as she watched Liana give him the once-over from head to toe as if he were a candy bar she wanted to devour. The youth flushed and stepped backward.

Zoe stepped forward, though not pushing it. "We're here to see Leticia Garcia."

The boy nodded. "She's…she's expecting you." He pulled the door open wider and moved to the side.

Zoe strode through, with Liana trailing. Zoe heard Liana say something under her breath to the boy, and when she turned her head to see, the youth was flushing hard enough to bead sweat on his face. Zoe dropped her hand on the blonde's shoulder and gave a tug. Liana smiled like a wolf.

They were all standing in a short hallway leading to the actual room. A television played ahead, with canned laughter sounding hollow. The boy skirted around them, staying as far away as possible, and called into the room, "Mom, they're here!"

"Well, bring them in," a voice called.

The youth beckoned the women to follow him and went on ahead. Zoe hardly bothered to glance at the decor as she stepped into the main room. It was a hotel, like any other hotel, with much the same trappings.

Instead, the brunette's gaze passed slowly over two men who sat impassively at a table in front of the window with the curtains pulled wide. She didn't like either of the men nor the exposure. Nor was her first impression a favorable one of the woman who sat propped up on the bed with her back against the wall.

Leticia Garcia was not quite as tall as her son, perhaps five-seven or five-eight. She looked to be in her forties, though fit and athletic. No gray in her black hair, yet, though perhaps she plucked such when they appeared. She was as handsome as her son, with aquiline features and skin a smooth tawny brown. But there was a...meanness evident in the sharp lines of her face.

Leticia did not rise to greet her visitors but did press a button on a remote control to switch off the TV. "My son, Francisco," she said to the two women, gesturing a hand almost dismissively toward the boy. To Francisco she ordered, "Go to the door. Keep watch."

The youth nodded, then fled for the hallway after a quick glance at Liana, who was studying him like a hawk studies a morsel of potential meat on the loose.

Zoe gestured toward the men at the table. "I thought this meeting was going to be kept small," she said to Letty Garcia. "Some of the things we discuss are likely to be sensitive."

Letty waved her hand about in dismissal of Zoe's words. "Do not worry about them. They know well to keep their mouths shut. Now, who are you?"

"I'm Zoe and this is Liana," Zoe replied. "Thanks for seeing us."

"Cousin Jorge mentioned on the phone that it was about Concho Ten-Wolves," Leticia said, practically spitting the name. "Got my attention."

"Seems he's an unpopular fellow in a lot of places," Zoe said.

"Deservedly so. He's a betrayer of his own people. A lap dog for the whites."

"It's surprising a determined foe hasn't gotten to him."

Leticia shook her head. "I do not say he will be easy. He has pulled the wool over many eyes. He is lucky and has his own lap dogs. Our *sheriff* is one such. Roberto Echabarri. You will have to play smart to isolate him."

Zoe nodded and tried to speak calmly. "I believe Jorge spoke to you about our initial meeting. We're just here to get information. From what we've heard, you're the person to talk to. What can you tell us about this Ranger? Anything about his habits, where he lives, who he hangs out with, what he does for fun?"

"You pay me, of course."

Zoe nodded. "Of course. We pay well."

"And afterward, you will kill him?"

Zoe blinked. Was this woman stupid? This was not the forum to say such things so openly. And in front of far too many potential witnesses. But they still needed the information Garcia could give; she had to be handled with care. Zoe hesitated a moment as she tried to think of how to reply.

Leticia Garcia suddenly threw her head back and laughed. "You think someone might be recording this conversation? There are no bugs here. I have checked." Her face wrinkled in a hard frown. "Unless you brought them in with you? Perhaps you are undercover police agents?"

"This isn't working," Liana said. Her eyes were darting every which way.

Zoe nodded. "Seems we've made a mistake," she said to Garcia. "We'll show ourselves out."

Leticia looked startled. "Wait," she said, as she saw the prospect of money about to flee.

"No harm, no foul," Liana replied. She turned and started toward the door, her gaze seeking and finding Francisco Garcia, although not with interest this time. She watched the youth for any suspicious movement.

Zoe lifted her hands, palms out in a calming gesture, and backed toward the door, her eyes on Leticia but taking in the two men by the window, who suddenly looked froggy.

"Wait, we can talk!" Leticia said. "I have all the information you could want."

"We'll be in touch," Zoe said. "Another meeting later. On neutral ground. With fewer people. But not here and now. You can still get paid. It'll just be a little longer."

Leticia started to rise in frustration. The men at the table started to stand as well. But Letty saw Zoe's hand slip under the hem of her jacket and immediately signaled the men to sit again. She slid down on the bed with a sigh. Francisco was smart enough to quickly open the door for the two women and stand aside.

Neither Zoe nor Liana spoke until they'd cleared the hotel and returned to Liana's Firebird. Once they were in the car, Zoe sighed and relaxed. "That went well. I heard Jorge go over the protocol for the meeting with her on the phone. I wasn't expecting her to be such a loose cannon."

Liana's tension began to bleed away as well. "I don't like dealing with amateurs."

"Hazards of the craft," Zoe replied.

Liana abruptly chuckled. She glanced over at Zoe and gave a low whistle. "But dayum, you could feel the hate for Concho Ten-Wolves jumping off her like bugs. I feel like I should have a flea bath."

Zoe laughed, too. "Don't worry. I'll buy you a collar."

Liana winked broadly, but then added, "Seriously, though, that woman is wound a lot tighter than is safe. You really want to set up a second meeting? We could probably get a lot of the same information from Bearfoot. He lives here. He's bound to know this Ten-Wolves."

"Maybe we could," Zoe agreed. "We'll keep our interactions with Leticia Garcia to a minimum. But there's a couple of good reasons not to cut her out completely."

"Oh?"

"One, if she doesn't get paid, she's liable to go off half-cocked. No telling what she might do or who she might tell. And that'll make our job harder."

"And the second good reason?"

Zoe smiled. "She'll make a helluva fall guy if we need one."

Liana chuckled. "Amen, sister. That's why you're the boss."

Zoe arched an eyebrow. "First time you've ever called me boss."

"Zoeita!" Liana protested. "Doesn't mean I don't recognize it. Just remembered one thing."

"What's that?"

Liana grinned like the Cheshire cat. "Francisco is mine. All mine!"

CHAPTER NINETEEN

THE WHITEHEART HOUSE WAS THE BIGGEST ON THE reservation—a two-story wood frame farmhouse, painted white with green trim. Porches on two sides. A shingle roof. Two brick chimneys. There were many like it in the southern United States—some as well maintained, many others not.

Concho pulled up the circular gravel driveway and parked in front. Three freshly painted barns created a rough pyramid behind the house. Off to the right, fields spurted dust into the blue sky as tractors plowed them. To the left stood an open field holding a small herd of cattle. The bull was a big Angus, and the Ranger did a double take. He'd seen the animal before. A month ago, it had been the primary bull on George Night-Run's cattle farm.

Wondering what else he was missing about Whiteheart's new cattle herd, Ten-Wolves slid out of his Ford. Two Hispanic men stood on the porch to either side of a wide set of cement steps. They each held a semi-automatic shotgun, not pointed exactly at him but not pointed at the ground either.

Concho started toward the porch. The two men stepped forward; the door to the house opened and Pete Whiteheart exited. Pete was a big young man, at least six feet and over two hundred pounds. His long hair was tied behind his head. He held a cigar, though it didn't appear to be lit.

"What do you want?" Pete demanded, his voice full of both anger and arrogance.

Concho paused at the bottom of the cement steps. "To see your father," he said. "Not you."

"Any concerns you have with my father, you can share with me. We run this place together."

Concho shook his head. "Not how it works." He glanced at the two shotgunners, making sure of eye contact with each. "You two gentlemen point those weapons at me and I'll have the Rangers, the FBI, and half a dozen local law enforcement agencies here in fifteen minutes. You'll be arrested for threatening an officer of the law with a deadly weapon, held for days, interrogated, and," he let his shark smile show, "deported."

Without giving the men time to think, Ten-Wolves started up the steps toward Pete Whiteheart. The gunmen hesitated, glancing toward Pete and then at each other. The shotguns wavered in their hands, but neither of them swung toward the Ranger.

By that time, Concho had reached Pete. The younger man took a step backward, then stiffened as he realized he'd shown fear in front of his men. A sneer crossed his lips, and he lifted his arms into fighting position, balling his fists.

Concho's hands leaped upward, blurring with speed. He grabbed Pete's fists, enveloping them, and shoved with about a third of his strength. The younger man stumbled against the wall. The lawman stepped past him. The door and screen to the house opened with a snap and Sam Whiteheart stood there.

"What's going on?" Sam demanded.

"You and I are going to talk about the law," Concho replied. "Alone. Either inside or outside. Either here or at the jail. Your choice."

* * *

Earl Blake, the coroner for Maverick County in Deep South Texas, shut off the MRI machine in his lab and listened to the whine die away. Not many coroner offices had their own MRI setup, but Blake had been an academic researcher working in a medical school before becoming coroner. He knew how to write a grant. The one that funded this machine had already paid dividends in other cases.

Walking over to the MRI, Blake stood looking down at his subject. It wasn't a normal cadaver. This was a mummy, the preserved remains of a long dead human girl who'd been about nine years old at the time of preservation. A stab of empathy for the child passed through him. What she must have suffered!

He pushed those thoughts aside as unprofessional as he carefully picked up the body and moved it to a wide plastic tub on one of his worktables. Flipping on a light, he bent to examine the form. A chime rang from down the hall, indicating that someone had entered the front office.

He was expecting Timothy Wiese, from the University of Texas campus in San Antonio, who'd agreed to drop by and have a look at the mummy. Tim was an old friend and an anthropologist who specialized in Mexican and Central American tribes like the Aztecs and Mayans. If anyone could tell him more about this child, Tim could.

"I'm in the lab, Tim!" Blake shouted. "Come on back!"

A long moment passed. No voice answered his call. Blake frowned and looked up. He couldn't hear anyone coming down the hall. With his frown deepening, Blake walked around the table toward the door.

The figure of a person stepped abruptly into the doorway, startling him. They wore a ski mask, a balaclava, and Blake's first thought was that it must be getting colder outside for Tim Wiese to have worn such a thing. Then he saw the object hanging in the shape's left hand.

A gun!

Blake threw up his arms as something hit him in the chest. He felt a needle-sharp stab and a burst of fiery current turned his bones and muscles to cooked spaghetti. He stumbled backward, hit the table where the mummy lay, and fell. His body arched and his mind went white and blank.

He awoke to someone shaking him. When he opened his eyes, Tim Wiese bent above him, a look of mixed fear and concern on his familiar face. "Earl! Earl! Are you OK?"

Blake pushed Tim's hands away and sat up. "I'm...I don't know yet. What happened?"

"Tim's voice verged on the shrill. "Happened? I have no idea. I found you lying on the floor. I was about to call an ambulance."

Blake's memory returned. His hands dropped to his chest. It hurt. He smelled a hint of ozone in the air. "A Taser! Someone hit me with a Taser! Help me up."

"A Taser!" Wiese repeated. He looked confused but grabbed Blake by the proffered arm and pulled the coroner to his feet. Blake gasped for breath as he took hold of the corner of a lab table for support.

"You sure you're OK?" Wiese asked. "You want to go to the hospital?"

But Blake didn't answer. He was too busy looking at the empty lab table where the child mummy had so recently lain.

CHAPTER TWENTY

For a moment, it looked as if Sam Whiteheart was going to choose conflict instead of communication. The old familiar feeling of impending action swept over the lawman. His muscles tightened against the bones. His mouth dried; he was ready.

But, while Whiteheart was arrogant with money and power, he wasn't stupid. Right here and now, on his porch, he had the numbers. But four against one wasn't enough for absolute confidence. Not against a Ranger who'd taken on more enemies in the past and won. And, of course, even if you beat one Ranger, more would come.

Whiteheart turned and pushed open the door to his house. He stepped through, beckoning Ten-Wolves to follow. Pete Whiteheart moved to join them, and Sam held up a hand to forestall him.

"Check on the fields," Sam ordered.

Pete's face twisted with anger, but he nodded. He glanced at Concho, who ignored him and entered the house behind Sam. Pete stomped off, his boots thumping on the porch's planks.

Concho closed the door behind him as he gave the place a

quick once-over. It was functional inside, not fancy. But there was a certain elegance. The floors were red cedar, the walls covered with a white wallpaper dappled with magenta roses. Sam was already striding down a hallway and turning right into a living area.

Concho followed, taking an instant to study the framed family photos on one wall. Sam and his wife were in the center —Sam at fifty plus, graying, looking every bit the patriarch. His wife made a contrast. She wasn't Kickapoo. Some claimed she was Choctaw, although from looking at her, the Ranger thought there was more to her heritage. She was still slender and raven-haired at fifty.

Ten-Wolves had only spoken to Tallulah Whiteheart a few times. She'd been gracious but aloof, intelligent but laconic. She was creative, many said. She wrote songs and played a variety of instruments. He'd read a bit of her poetry and found it lovely if inscrutable.

Next to Sam hung a picture of Pete Whiteheart, the eldest and only son, who was in his late twenties. On Tallulah's side were photos of two daughters. The elder daughter was probably nineteen here, although she'd be older now. She was dark complexioned, as lovely as an arrowhead of smoky quartz.

Concho had seen her fewer times than he'd seen her mother, and only when she was younger than this photograph. He wasn't sure he'd recognize her today. About all he knew was that her name was "Isi," which meant "deer" in the Choctaw tongue, a name intended to reverence the Kickapoo sacred animal. Rumor had it she'd gone off to school in Mexico City, though he didn't know for sure.

The younger daughter looked to be eight or so in this photograph but was surely a few years older now. She looked almost ethereal, like the ghost image of a child. Reservation scuttlebutt suggested there was something "wrong" with her, though no one could say what. To his knowledge, the Ranger had *never* seen her. She was being homeschooled and Concho wasn't asked over for dinner much at the Whitehearts'.

Continuing on, the Ranger walked into the room Sam Whiteheart had disappeared into. Though it had only been seconds, the Kickapoo farmer had already taken a seat in a large brown recliner next to an unlit fireplace. A look of impatience carved his face.

The room appeared to be a living room. A TV faced the recliner, its face black. A flower-patterned couch sat at a slight angle to the television set and Sam gestured toward it. The Ranger remained standing. From elsewhere in the house came the hum of a woman's voice, perfectly pitched but a little overly controlled for Concho's taste. Perhaps some of the homeschooling he'd heard about.

"Why do you come here?" Whiteheart snapped.

Concho considered. He hadn't been sure he'd get this far. He had no plan other than to shake things up. To do that, he needed to keep Sam Whiteheart off balance. "I need your help," he said calmly.

Startled, Whiteheart blinked and seemed at a loss for words. Maybe he was wondering what kind of *Twilight Zone* he'd suddenly found himself inhabiting.

"Are you making a joke? Help you? With what? You said you would talk about the 'law.' What was that?"

Concho sat down on the couch, leaned forward, and rested his elbows on his knees. Ideas began to churn in his mind. "Look, you don't like me, and I don't like you. But I'm sure you don't want to see the reservation go back to how it was before the casino. The poverty, the alcohol, the dead eyes of hopeless people."

"You are making no sense."

Concho nodded. "Because you don't know what I know. We've got a smuggling problem on the Rez. A new kind of problem."

Whiteheart shrugged. "What is new about smuggling?"

"What's new is they're smuggling money. Counterfeit money! I just broke up an attempt to deliver four hundred thousand dollars in counterfeit twenties onto the Rez."

"I have nothing to do with that."

Concho shook his head. "Didn't say you did. Though I can't rule out some of your…employees. But that's not why I'm here. Whoever is behind bringing in that kind of cash will need to launder it in some fashion by mixing it in with regular money. Other than the casino, you're the only operation on the Rez that handles a lot of cash. I know you pay your workers in it. Have you noticed any suspicious twenties around? Among your people, or being moved through your money stream at all?"

Whiteheart continued to frown. "I don't usually handle the money directly. I have an…accountant who does that."

"Who's your accountant?"

"I do not share information about my employees."

"I just want to ask him the same question. Or her."

"Or perhaps accuse them of counterfeiting as a way of attacking me."

Concho drew in a big breath and released it again. "I can see why you'd suspect such. And I don't imagine there's any way I can alleviate your fear on that point. But you have to understand I'll find out. On my own if I have to."

"Then on your own!" Sam snapped.

"It's Pete, isn't it?" Concho said, acting on a hunch. "Your son? You wouldn't be so protective if it weren't a family member."

Sam surged up from his chair. "You will leave now!"

Concho rose. Inside he was elated. His trip out here had merely been a fishing expedition, but it looked like he'd hooked something. Now to reel it in, though, that would likely mean a fight.

"All right," he said. "But keep in mind, if there's any movement of counterfeit money in or out of your coffers, you'll pay the price. Look into it. You know how to contact me if necessary."

"Get out!" Sam roared, pointing toward the hallway.

Concho tipped an imaginary hat and strode out. He'd done

enough for today. He'd left Sam Whiteheart full of questions and doubts the farmer wouldn't like. It would irritate him the way a burr under a saddle irritates a horse.

"Trees shaken," the Ranger murmured to himself as he climbed in his truck and wheeled away.

Taking out his cell, he made a call to Earl Blake at the coroner's office, figuring he might stop by for a talk about the case. The phone rang and rang. As he started to frown in concern, a voice answered. It wasn't Blake. It was a woman.

"Ten-Wolves, that you? Della Rice here."

"Agent Rice! What's going on? Blake OK?"

"He's alive. We're having him checked. But something has happened. Get over to Earl's office!" She hung up.

Concho punched the gas.

CHAPTER TWENTY-ONE

Concho whipped his Ford into the parking lot of the L-shaped building at 1995 Williams Street in Eagle pass. This was the office and lab of Earl Blake, county coroner. An ambulance sat parked right near the office.

Flinging back his truck door, the Ranger piled out and rushed toward the building. A bell chimed as he entered. Six people turned to stare at him. Two were FBI agents—Della Rice and Will Bolin. Two were paramedics standing to either side of Earl Blake, who sat in a desk chair with a blood pressure cuff on his arm and a look of irritation on his face. The last man stood fidgeting against the wall. He was tall and slender, dressed in a suit and tie. He looked to be an academic-type.

"Before you ask, I'm fine!" Blake snapped. "Everybody needs to stop fussing."

Concho nodded. He straightened and took a deep breath. "Oh, did something happen? I came over because I heard there was a giveaway at the coroner's office. Everything free. I wanted to get this collection of coprolites he's been talking about. Supposed to be something special in the way of fossilized poop from what I hear."

Della Rice exploded with a bray of laughter he'd never heard from her before. Earl Blake rolled his eyes. The paramedics looked confused, and the academic-type frowned and turned to Blake.

"Earl," he said. "I didn't know you had any coprolites. What species are they from? I'd like to see them."

Concho joined Rice in laughter and even Blake cracked a smile, though it looked like it might break his face.

* * *

THE PARAMEDICS FINALLY LEFT, GRANTING EARL BLAKE AN ALL clear with a warning to take it easy. Concho had been mostly brought up to speed, including being introduced to the academic. He was Timothy Wiese, an anthropology professor from the University of Texas branch in San Antonio. Wiese had come to study the missing child mummy; he was out of luck.

"So," Concho said to Blake, "you didn't get any details on the man who Tased you?"

Blake shook his head. "Not absolutely sure it *was* a he. Could have been a tall woman. The clothes were bulky, and the ski mask hid the face."

"No sign of hair underneath the mask?"

"None!"

"We covered all this," Rice said.

"Never hurts to cover ground twice," Concho replied. "And he/she didn't say anything? Or make any sound at all?"

"No, he/she was like you, Ten-Wolves. They let their Taser do the talkin'."

"Good one. Not as funny as stone poop, of course."

"What is?" Rice agreed.

The Ranger turned toward Tim Wiese. "What about you? Did you see anything suspicious when you came in?"

Wiese looked startled. "Me? Uh, no. I don't…think so. I came in, called for Earl. When he didn't answer I went back to his lab. I've been here before. I found him on the floor. He came around when I shook him. I called the ambulance."

"It wasn't necessary," Blake muttered.

"Maybe not," Wiese said to Blake, "but you need to be sure." He glanced at Concho. "The mummy was gone, of course. Though, I didn't know."

"There's something else gone, too," Blake added. "I'd just completed an MRI scan on the thing when the...thief came in. They deleted that data from the computer. Deleted the whole computer, in fact?"

"Deleted the computer!" Concho exclaimed. "What?"

"They magnetized the hard drive," Della Rice explained. "The whole system is wiped."

Concho frowned. "MRIs use magnets, right? Could that have caused the problem?"

"No," Blake said. "The computer is shielded from that. This was deliberate sabotage."

"Do we know if the thief made a copy for himself?"

"Impossible to tell."

"And, the perp must have worn gloves," Rice added. "So, no fingerprints."

"As soon as I realized the mummy was gone, the MRI recording was the first thing I checked," Blake said.

"While the ambulance was on the way and he should have been resting," Wiese added, giving his friend an accusing glare.

Blake shrugged. "Told you, I was OK."

Concho glanced over at Della Rice. "Can your FBI computer geeks do anything with it?"

The woman shrugged. "I'll have them look into it, but the perp knew what he or she was doing."

"Someone with technical expertise then."

"Yep."

"Shouldn't there have been more security?" Tim Wiese asked. "*Some* security at least. I mean, you have criminal evidence here. Why was Earl alone under those circumstances?"

"Good question," Concho said. "Who'd be in charge of that? The state?"

"We've never needed it before," Blake said.

"Well, you should have had it," Wiese said.

"I don't need a babysitter!" Blake protested.

Concho interrupted. "I'll talk to Isaac Parkland about it. He's the local sheriff. He'll be able to track down whose jurisdiction the coroner's office falls under. But, in the meantime." He glanced toward Wiese. "When you arrived, Professor Wiese, did you notice any vehicles in the parking lot that aren't there now?"

"I…don't know." With his mouth forming a determined line, Wiese headed for the door. The others followed. Once they were outside, the anthropologist studied the scene for a couple of minutes. "Nothing. No, there wasn't."

Did you pass anyone on the road coming into the building?" Concho questioned.

"I…don't remember. Maybe."

"Think carefully."

A long pause followed. Wiese turned to study Williams Street, the road running past the coroner's office. "There was something," he said. "Not far down the road. A man...a driver, was riding the center line. I was getting ready to swerve when whoever it was realized and pulled back to the right."

"Anything memorable about the driver?"

Wiese shook his head. "Just a blur in the sunlight."

"What about the car?"

"Might have been an Accord. I'm not completely sure. New-looking model. Mid-sized. White. No, not white. Ivory or pearl."

Will Bolin pulled out a pad and wrote the information down.

"You have a good memory for cars, Dr. Wiese," Concho remarked.

"Ex-Eagle Scout there," Earl Blake said, pointing at Wiese. "He notices that sort of thing. It's obnoxious."

"Well, it could be very helpful," Concho said.

"I hope it will," Wiese added.

"I'll call in the description," Bolin said, as he strode toward the white SUV that Della Rice habitually drove.

"Thanks," Concho said. "Let's hope we get a break. Now, much as I hate to, I guess I'm going to have to glance at the crime scene." He stared over at Earl Blake.

A moment of silence followed. Blake caught on. "Hey!" he protested. "You're a real dick, Ten-Wolves!"

CHAPTER TWENTY-TWO

ZOE DESAINT SAT AT ONE OF THE BARS IN THE LUCKY EAGLE Casino and Hotel complex. She wasn't drinking. Not alcohol. But sometimes she liked looking at the stacked bottles of liquor in all their bright shades of venom. She even liked the smell of such places, all the scents of spilled liquor, disinfectant, and loneliness—what she often thought of as the odor of human desperation.

She was also thinking about an article she'd just read in the magazine *Texas Monthly*. She'd spotted a wire rack full of the magazine and had immediately recognized the face on the cover—Concho Ten-Wolves. The article painted him as a hero. Ten-Wolves wouldn't be the first supposed hero with feet of clay, but the story certainly painted a very different image of the Ranger than she'd been building in her head.

Liana slid onto the stool next to her, distracting Zoe from her thoughts. The blonde took a small handful of peanuts from the bar bowl. She crunched them while Zoe looked at her with distaste.

"All the diseases known to man cluster in those bowls," she said.

Liana grinned around a mouthful of peanut shards. "Good

thing I'm a woman. Besides, I've got an immune system that could choke a Tijuana donkey."

"And the personality of said donkey as well."

Liana grinned. "Why, Zoeita, you always say the sweetest things."

Zoe shook her head and took a sip of her Coca Cola. "You have something to report?"

"There's another player in this game."

"What are you talking about?"

"So, we're here for Aquila. Then there's this Concho dude, with the tribal police on his side. There's Leticia Garcia and her delicious son on the outskirts. And…there's someone else."

"What makes you think so?"

"Someone watching everything around them."

"Casino security?"

Liana shook her head. "They're easy to spot."

"Bearfoot's people?"

Liana laughed. "Bearfoot has no people."

Zoe laughed too. "Yeah, I know. But who, then?"

"The only possibility coming to mind is whoever Jañega's smuggled 'supplies' were meant for?"

"If so, we best leave it alone. Aquila wouldn't want us prying into that."

"Yeah, sure. Let's leave it *alone*."

Zoe sighed. She drained her Coke, then stood. "All right, what's your plan?"

Liana grinned. She reached up and tossed around a few strands of her long blonde hair. "It's a guy."

"Gotcha."

* * *

CONCHO RETURNED TO THE SCENE OF THE CRIME. HE DROVE to the Rio Grande and parked on the little ridge above where the smugglers had off-loaded faux cash, black market organs, and a child mummy from their flatbottom boat. The scene had been cleaned. No bodies or strange loot remained.

As he stepped out of his truck, his boot kicked up a piece of black plastic. Part of the spy drone he'd shot. He considered that drone and wondered where its camera footage had been sent. Somewhere in Mexico, he imagined. But no way to know exactly.

He walked downhill to the river's edge. What passed for winter in southern Texas was on the run today. Heat from the sun prickled on his shoulders and sent glints of diamond light dancing off the silt-brown river. The dark blue sky stretched out forever, marred only by a passing flock of starlings. It was quiet.

Concho could smell the water. He glanced down and saw his own muddied reflection. His friend, Meskwaa, elder and naataineniiha—medicine man—of the Kickapoo Traditional Tribe of Texas, always said that everything was connected and time was a myth. The little bit of physics he'd taken in college had claimed the same.

While Ten-Wolves the Texas Ranger stood along this river, another Concho sat in a classroom in another time and read of quantum mechanics and dreamed strange dreams, and yet another Concho trudged a desert much like this one in a foreign land where he carried a gun as a Ranger in the US army. It was the Army Ranger that took him now.

Afghanistan, 2010.

Another river. Even shallower than the Rio Grande. With only a few stagnate pools of water so murky only goats would drink from them. Concho's twelve-man ODA (Operational Detachment Alpha) moved along the mostly dry bed of the river, darting in and out of cover. Concho brought up the rear, a .50 caliber machine gun in his arms.

A single shot cracked from a rocky bluff ahead. Likely a sniper. In this rocky landscape, the absence of a ricochet meant bad news. Russ

Adelaide commanded the ODA. His voice shouted a warning, but Concho was already belly down behind a boulder.

The Ranger's gaze studied the bluff ahead. Sunlight glared down on the stone. A shallow overhang provided the only cover he could see for a gunman. He caught a glint of light from there. It could have been a bit of quartz, or discarded plastic. Or it might have been a belt buckle or the shine of a scope momentarily catching sun.

Rocks rattled ahead of him in the riverbed, other Rangers working their way forward, perhaps to a wounded comrade. They needed cover. Swinging the .50 cal up, Concho opened fire.

Lead slammed into the suspicious overhang. Rock shattered; ricochets whined away. The long feed of brass shells whirred through the gun, spitting out again as winking empties. Sound and smoke and dust filled the empty river like a strange, otherworldly water. Spent powder stung his eyes.

The gun ran dry; the trigger clicked, clicked, clicked. Concho reloaded but held his fire. Keeping an eye on the bluff ahead, he worked his own way forward. To tragedy. Only a few weeks ago, Concho's best friend in the army, David Lanoue, had been badly wounded in a gunfight. He'd been evacuated, and lived, but was being shipped home. Ten-Wolves would miss him but was glad his friend was out of the fray.

Lanoue's replacement had been a man named Jorgenson. Now, Jorgenson was going to be shipped home too. In a body bag. The left half of his forehead was only an open hole surrounded by spatters and shards of blood and bone. Concho winced.

Russ Adelaide duckwalked over to Ten-Wolves. "You get him?" he whispered.

"Don't know. Never actually saw him. Only a glint that might have been him."

Adelaide nodded. "Too close to call in air support," he said.

The commander turned to the others in the ODA and flashed a series of hand signals as orders. He glanced back at Concho and gave a nod. Ten-Wolves lowered the .50 cal to the ground and shrugged off the compound bow he'd been carrying since the fight where Lanoue was wounded. He pulled his M4A1 carbine into his fists instead.

At a signal from Adelaide, six men went over the top of the river-

bank and dove for the cover of the closest rocks. No shot came from the bluff ahead. Maybe a good sign the sniper was dead.

The six spread out and probed slowly forward, staying low enough to scrape their buttons on stone. Concho kept his head twisted upward, though, staring ahead. A study of the overhang he'd blown apart with the big .50 revealed no sign of a body, or even a bloodstain. His eyes shifted elsewhere, focused. He moved on.

Ten minutes passed. Fifteen. Concho reached the rocks at the base of the bluff. He rose to a crouch but froze as a prickling feeling spread across his scalp and down his back. A quick whistle warned his fellows to be still, that they were being watched.

The Ranger turned his head slightly. His dark eyes bored into the terrain, scanning rocks, a twisted tree, a flow of dust and scree down an otherwise flat and smooth stretch of bluff. And then a movement.

For an instant, a small fragment of the mountain came alive. It slid backward over the top of the ridge, like water flowing uphill, and was gone. The tingling in Concho's scalp went with it.

Concho rose. Adelaide hissed at him, but Ten-Wolves shook his head. "I saw him, sir. But he's gone."

Adelaide rose as well and slipped over to the Ranger. "You saw him! A Taliban fighter?"

The big soldier shook his head. "I don't know what he was. A ghost maybe. Or stone come to life. Or maybe just a man so good at camouflage that he could hide in plain sight."

Adelaide was used to hearing odd things from Concho. "Maybe don't mention the ghost or the living stone to the others," he said.

Concho nodded but his eyes never left the defile in the top of the bluff where the "ghost" had disappeared. He knew it wouldn't be the last encounter between them.

Concho's reverie faded. He stood staring down at the reflection of his own face in the Rio Grande. *Hide in plain sight*, he thought. Maybe that was what was happening now. Maybe the person he was looking for was close by. Close, but hidden without seeming to hide. Camouflaged. Invisible. And deadly.

CHAPTER TWENTY-THREE

Zoe and Liana had taken a room at the Lucky Eagle Hotel. Liana went upstairs to prepare while Zoe staked out the gambling floor and played the slots. She quickly spotted the man Liana had described. He was very good looking, with dark Spanish skin and long, dark hair worn loose to his shoulders.

A long time ago, Zoe might have thought this man was too pretty to be dangerous. She now knew such types were the *most* dangerous. This one sat at a blackjack table and appeared to be oblivious to everything around him. It was a clever lie.

Every once in a while, the man glanced up, sleepy faced, or he leaned back in his chair and stretched. And when he did so, his eyes became cameras recording every detail. Zoe immediately retreated a bit so she wouldn't be spotted. This guy wasn't going to miss much.

Liana came down the stairs rather than the elevator. More of an entrance, Zoe supposed. She'd exchanged her jeans for a knee-length purple skirt, and her T-shirt for a purple silk top that occasionally flashed a sliver of her flat midriff. She'd brushed and fluffed her hair, and put on a little lipstick, though she scarcely needed any. She had on heels and even carried a purse, a small white one with pearl beads on it. About the only thing in that purse would be her knife.

Liana could do whorish better than any woman Zoe had ever met, but that wasn't the look she was going for here. She was classy and yet naïve, sexy but reserved, unapproachable and yet…not. Almost every man in the casino looked at her when she came down the stairs. And it didn't matter if they were straight or gay. Most of the women looked, too, and for many different reasons.

The mark at the blackjack table didn't look. And a warning buzzer starting vibrating in Zoe's brain. She moved closer again as Liana approached the table and slid into a chair next to the man. The two exchanged casual greetings but Zoe couldn't specifically hear what was spoken.

After a few minutes and a winning streak, the mark must have offered to buy Liana a drink. He made a gesture for a waiter and two drinks arrived, one with a cherry in it for Liana and another of amber liquid in a square cut glass for the gentleman.

Liana said something and smiled prettily. The two clicked glasses and drank. Zoe almost laughed to see Liana sipping from her glass with apparent pleasure. There was little Liana hated more than "frou-frou drinks." She was a beer and whiskey kind of woman.

After ten minutes of flirtation, Liana flashed Zoe a discreet signal and Zoe headed for the women's first-floor bathroom. She slipped into a stall. Ten minutes passed before Liana entered. She stood in front of the mirror, fluffing out her blonde hair. The musk of her perfume zinged Zoe's nostrils even five feet away.

"Room 314" Liana said, as if to the air. She smoothed on a touch of lipstick and left.

Zoe felt the familiar thrum in her veins of impending action. She followed Liana out the door, then cut across to the elevators. Stepping into an empty car, she pressed three. The ride was silent, but her thoughts rang loud as gunshots.

* * *

As Concho drove back into Kickapoo Village from the Rio Grande, he decided to head to the casino and speak to Melissa Nolan. She seemed a long shot as a suspect in a smuggling operation, but she did have money and influence. And she knew a lot about what happened on the Rez.

He headed up Chick Kazan Street toward the police station, figuring to turn on Bishop Gracida Drive toward the casino. A running figure coming toward him caught his attention. The figure was a man, and completely nude.

As the running man swung onto Bishop Gracida ahead of Concho, the lawman recognized Nate Wronghorse. He waved and Nate waved back but didn't slow down. At the tribal police station, activity roiled around one of the department's SUVs. The two events were probably related. Turning onto Bishop Gracida himself, the Ranger sped up to pull alongside the runner.

Concho's windows were already down on a nice day, as was his habit. He leaned his head out of the truck and called to the unclothed and apparently unflustered man beside him.

"Hi Nate. How's it going?"

Nate kept running, his bare feet slapping loudly on cement. "Good, Ranger. Thanks!"

"You need a lift?"

Nate flipped his hand up to his forehead and offered a quick salute. "No sir, Ranger. All good here!"

Behind them from the direction of the police station, a siren blipped on and immediately off again. Safe to assume, someone from the office was headed their way.

Concho wanted to scratch his head. Instead, he said, "You know, I think there's an ordinance against being naked in public around here, Nate. What happened to your clothes?"

"Spring!" Nate said.

"Ah."

A Kickapoo tribal police SUV whipped around them both

and wheeled back into the lane in front of Concho and Nate. Nate stopped running. Ten-Wolves stopped driving.

Two Kickapoo deputies piled out of the SUV, Timbo Corbett and Nila Willow. Corbett looked like he was about to go all nightstick-up-beside-Nate's-head, while Willow looked mildly amused.

Concho stepped out of his Ford and got between Corbett and Nate. "I think everything's under control," he said to the light-skinned officer. He turned back toward Wronghorse. "That right, Nate?" he asked.

Nate sighed. He crossed his arms over his chest but made no effort to hide the lower part of his body. "Reckon so, Ranger."

Nila came around and took Nate's arm and led him toward the SUV.

"Put a towel down first!" Corbett yelled at her.

Concho almost laughed but thought better of it. Corbett looked pissed.

"What did he do?" the Ranger asked.

"Stealing eggs over at Estrella Deer-Run's place. Naked as the day is long. Estrella had an old coat I got him into for the drive over to the jail, but when we got here he tried to pee on me. While I was trying to avoid that, he grabbed the keys out of my vehicle and threw them into the grass, then took off running. Sans the coat."

Concho nodded. He walked over to the SUV where Nate sat on a blanket in the back. A strong odor rose from the man through the open window, some combination of oil, sweat, and urine.

"Why you stealing eggs, Nate?" he asked.

"Hungry, Ranger."

Concho nodded. "Well, they'll get you something to eat at the department. You go with them and don't give them any more trouble."

"All right," Nate said, smiling with tobacco-stained teeth.

"And maybe keep on whatever clothes they give you," Concho added.

"Spring!" Nate replied.

* * *

As Concho climbed into his Ford, he noticed Tessa Teshigahara standing across the road in front of the small building she'd taken over for her budding newspaper. She was holding her phone up in the air, which meant she'd probably been recording the Nate Wronghorse incident. Oh well, not a lot of hardcore newshound stuff there.

Two other young women stood beside Tessa. The first was sixteen-year-old Tamara Redvine. It made sense. Tamara was a literary-minded young girl and would naturally gravitate toward anyone else on the Rez who might want to talk about poetry and writing instead of family relations and the weather. She and Concho had spoken about books a few times. And her mother, Carmina, was a cook at the local daycare down the road.

The second woman was probably twenty-three or twenty-four and stood about halfway between five and six feet tall. She looked very lovely in jeans, a leather vest, and a fringed jacket. He realized he'd seen this woman twice recently—once in person at the casino talking to Melissa Nolan on the night of the bomb threat, and another time as a photograph on a wall. This was Isi Whiteheart, daughter of Sam.

Concho considered stopping to talk to Isi but that would mean being reminded by Tessa Teshigahara about his interview. Shifting into drive, he continued up Bishop Gracida toward the casino. He'd prefer to avoid the interview as long as possible. If he waited long enough, maybe he'd die and escape it.

CHAPTER TWENTY-FOUR

ZOE WAS LINGERING CASUALLY IN FRONT OF THE DOOR TO Room 315 on her cell phone when Liana and her Spanish dark companion came off the elevator. Liana had draped herself all over the man's left side and appeared to be sparkling drunk. Zoe didn't know how much it would take to get Liana actually drunk, but it would be a lot more than she'd consumed downstairs.

After the one to-be-expected glance, Zoe ignored the couple as they worked their way down the hallway toward her. "That's right," she said into the phone. "I've lost the keycard to my room, and I need someone to let me in." She paused. "Yes, it's 315. I really need to get inside."

Liana didn't even spare a glance at Zoe; she was too busy leaning in to nibble at her companion's neck. The man glanced at Zoe; Zoe glanced back and offered a preoccupied smile, then turned away and spoke further into the phone.

"Really! That long! But I…Oh, never mind, I'll come down to the front desk!"

She swiped at the phone's window and stuffed it angrily into her pocket. As she turned, Liana's beau inserted his keycard into the door slot. Zoe heard the click as the door unlocked. The man pushed it open. Liana laughed and danced through the door ahead of the man, then spun to beckon him coquettishly with a hand.

No one else was in the hallway. Zoe spun swiftly and shoved the man hard in the spine, thrusting him forward into the room. Liana, suddenly sober, whipped out a leg and tripped him. He sprawled forward onto the carpet, grunting as he hit hard.

Zoe leaped through the doorway behind the man and slammed the door. She drew a Glock Model 38 from under her leather jacket. But the mark wasn't about to call it a day. He twisted around like a cat and swept out his own leg, knocking Liana's feet from under her. The blonde sat down hard on her ass.

Lunging off the floor, the man hurled himself toward the bedside table, probably for a gun of his own. Zoe had her weapon drawn but didn't want to kill before they'd questioned. She threw herself forward and dove. Her left hand hooked an ankle and jerked. The man stumbled and fell across the bed, his hand merely slapping against the bed table.

The fellow rolled and came up standing by the foot of the bed. Liana had risen too. She'd lost one high heel and kicked the other at the man's head. He swatted it aside, then swung a roundhouse blow at Liana. The blonde dodged backward.

Zoe surged to her feet and swung the pistol in her hand at their foe's head. He tried to block, and she got only the shoulder but heard him gasp and saw him wince. Instead of falling back, though, he charged.

Zoe swung the pistol again, but he ducked under the blow and threw a punch at her midsection. She twisted to the side, taking the blow on her hip. But the guy was strong, and the punch sent her stumbling against the wall.

He lunged after her, one hand grabbing for the gun. Zoe snapped a punch from her left hand into his jaw, but she was off balance, with little strength behind the blow. The mark only snarled and swung hard for her midsection again. This time the blow connected.

Zoe's eyes bulged. Her breath fled. Reflexively, she curled her shoulders downward. The man grabbed for the gun again. Zoe jerked it away, but the fingers of his left hand wrapped around her wrist, pinning her arm above her body. He shoved his right forearm into her throat, driving her head back. His left hand slid up her wrist and latched onto the pistol barrel. He twisted and yanked.

Zoe's trigger finger dislocated as the weapon was twisted in her grasp. She tried to hold on but felt her grip slip. For only the second time in her life, she was about to be disarmed. A moment later she'd probably be dead.

But the man had discounted Liana. A mistake. Maybe because she was wearing a dress and had been flirting with him, he couldn't see the blonde as anything more than a simpering female, afraid of violence.

He learned differently when she put her butterfly knife into his side right at the level of the kidney and carved up. He screamed, but Liana had locked her free hand over his mouth and very little sound escaped.

Liana grunted, leaning into the man almost intimately from behind as she drew the razor-edged blade through the man's flesh. He let go of the gun; his hand slapped down, reaching for the fiery steel brand burning its way through his kidney. Liana grunted again and put all her considerable strength into driving the knife in and twisting it.

"Don't kill him!" Zoe croaked.

It was too late. Liana yanked the blade out of the man's side. Her other hand pulled the fellow's head back over his shoulder, and she cut his throat into a wide red mouth beneath his chin.

Blood frothed into the air, spraying across the carpet and furniture. Liana released her grip and shoved the man face-down across the bed where he sagged lifelessly into the becrimsoned sheets. She swiped the red blade across the man's jeans to clean it and stepped away with a snarl.

"So much for questioning him," Zoe said.

Liana sent a blazing glare in her friend's direction. "You'd rather be dead?"

Zoe reached with her left hand and took the gun carefully from her right. She lay it on a dry spot on the bed, then yanked her dislocated finger back into position with a groan. Shaking her head at Liana's question, she said, "No, but I'd still like to know who this guy is?"

Liana reached for the man's rear pocket and pulled out a thick wallet. She opened it and flipped through the plastic inside, then turned the open wallet toward Zoe and showed her an identification card. Zoe saw the name but barely registered it. Because next to it was a title.

"Wonderful!" Zoe groaned. "Mexican police."

CHAPTER TWENTY-FIVE

Zoe deSaint gazed down at the throat-slashed body of the Mexican police officer. What he was doing in the US at a Kickapoo casino was unknown, but that he'd been working on some kind of an investigation didn't seem to be in question. This was bad. In multiple ways.

"OK," Liana said. "Now what?"

Zoe huffed a heavy breath. She scratched at her ear. "Doesn't seem anyone heard the struggle or there'd be knocking at the door already. You stay here. Wipe down anything we might have touched."

"We didn't have time to touch anything."

"Well, wipe it down anyway. I'll go up to our room and get you a change of clothes. Some of my clothes. Without blood on them. The room is in my name, which is a good thing. People notice *you*. Me, not so much. People downstairs surely noticed you with him. Once he's found, the cops will come looking for you. So, *you're* going to leave. Get a room somewhere in Eagle Pass. Where you won't likely be traced."

"And what about him?" Liana pointed at the corpse.

Zoe looked around. "Give me a hand."

She leaned over and grabbed the policeman's arms. Liana grabbed the booted feet. They lifted together, both grunting.

"The tub," Zoe said.

They carried the man into the bathroom and dumped him unceremoniously in the porcelain tub. Zoe moved to the sink and flipped the hot water lever over with her wrist. As she rinsed off the blood, she said, "While I'm gone, put the bloody comforter and sheets in there with him. And clean up as best you can without getting the stuff all over you. We'll put the *Do Not Disturb* sign on the door and hope we get lucky for at least twenty-four hours."

"And then?"

"The storm breaks. But, with any luck, we won't be caught in the wind shear."

"So poetic," Liana said.

Zoe made a face. She pointed toward one of the storage bags that hotels provide their guests for dirty clothes and such. "Put your stuff in one of those. And take his wallet with you. It'll cloud the investigation. But throw it away as soon as you get off the reservation. Someplace it won't be found."

"I know the drill," Liana snapped.

Zoe sighed but nodded. "Of course you do." She grabbed a couple of hand towels from the rack beside the tub and headed for the door. She used one towel to turn the knob and tossed the other to Liana.

Peeking out into the hallway and seeing no one, she used the towel again to hang up the *Do Not Disturb* sign, then closed the door behind her and headed quickly for the stairs to the fourth floor, where their room and a temporary and inadequate solution to a serious, long-term problem lay.

* * *

AFTER LADY LUCK DEALT HIM A PARKING SPACE RIGHT NEAR the front of the Lucky Eagle Casino, Concho exited his Ford and entered the building. The place was busy in the late afternoon; the recent bomb threat didn't seem to have discouraged any visitors. Gamblers were apparently a tough lot. Or at least a committed one.

A man passed by the Ranger carrying a serving of nachos and his stomach growled. It had been a long time since breakfast with nothing more than a couple of granola bars to stave off the wolf. As soon as he finished talking to Melissa Nolan, he'd have to grab a bite.

Nolan's office was on the second floor. Concho started up the stairs. He met a woman coming down. She wore baggy jeans and an untucked work shirt in blue that couldn't quite hide the curves beneath. One hand held the strings of a white plastic hotel bag. He gave her a brief smile and nod, but her eyes had caught his and didn't pass on.

Despite the blonde hair tucked under a baseball cap, the woman had brown irises, almost a gold color that complimented her tanned skin. Her pupils were dilated, although he was pretty sure it wasn't from drugs. She smiled, and it was like someone had turned up the wattage on a lamp.

"Ma'am," he said, nodding.

"Ranger," she replied. There seemed to be a lot of meanings packed into that word.

He kept walking; she did too. But after another few steps Concho glanced back. The woman had stopped as well and was staring after him. Her gaze now held the same heavy mystery as her use of the word, "Ranger."

Ten-Wolves felt his skin flushing from being caught looking, but the woman's face revealed no 'knowing smile,' no disdain, no smug superiority. Her gaze was focused, intense, almost carnivorous. Then her features relaxed and became dreamy. She sighed and turned away.

Concho turned as well and continued up the stairs. But his spine prickled. The urge to look around again began to pound in his temples. He fought it away and was grateful to see Melissa Nolan's frosted glass office door ahead.

The door was shut but it opened into a waiting area, so he

stepped through without knocking. A thin young man who appeared to be new to shaving sat behind a computer on the administrative assistant's desk. He startled as Concho entered, then immediately looked flustered. He and the Ranger had a history of not getting on well together.

"Officer Ten-Wolves," the man said, trying to appear calm although his voice cracked a little. "I will…will tell Director Nolan you're here. If you'll…uhm, just have a seat."

"No problem." Concho offered the young fellow a limited edition of his shark smile. "I know it won't be long, so I'll stand."

The young man nodded, without making eye contact. He pressed the intercom on his desk and leaned forward to speak softly into it.

"Ms. Nolan. You-know-who is here to see you. He…uhm, doesn't have an appointment."

"Maybe I should have a standing one. Don't you think?" Concho offered.

"I'll…I'll…don't know—"

The buzz of the intercom saved the man further consternation. "Send him in," Nolan's voice said.

Concho opened the inner door and stepped through. Melissa Nolan sat at ease behind her desk. She wore a black linen jacket over a blouse of deep satin blue. Blonde hair purled across her shoulders; her hazel eyes were large and artfully enhanced with a touch of shadow. The manager of the Lucky Eagle Casino was a very beautiful woman, but somehow, at the moment, the law officer's mind flashed back to the gold-eyed woman in the baggy clothes on the stairs.

No doubt, his distraction was because of the different ways the women had looked at him. The other woman's focus had all been on him. At least, a passing attraction had been in evidence. To Melissa Nolan, with her lips curved into a faint moue of irritation, he appeared to be mostly a nuisance.

Laughing inwardly at himself, he sat in the chair across from Nolan without being invited. It was a sturdy piece of furniture, perhaps put in for just such visits. No use standing anyway. Unlike many potential suspects he interrogated, this woman wasn't intimidated by his size. Not that he wanted to intimidate anyone at the moment. It *wasn't* an interrogation. He was here on a fishing expedition. Nothing more.

Yet, it wouldn't hurt to keep her off balance. "New perfume?" he asked.

Nolan's eyes flashed wider. Her slender right hand drifted up to touch her sculpted neck. "You can smell it?" Her voice was soft, feminine. For the moment. "I didn't think I'd used that much."

"Lilac," Concho said. "It's not too much. I just have a sensitive nose."

Nolan's gaze narrowed again as she realized what he was doing. "What is it you want, Ten-Wolves?" she asked, her voice brusque and professional now.

Concho grinned as normal of a grin as he could manage. "I love our little fencing matches. I'm just trying to be friendly."

"Right. You're well-known for your friendliness. Why are you bringing it into my office, though? That's the question."

"Counterfeiting," the lawman replied.

Nolan blinked. Again, she was off guard. "What? What are you talking about?"

Concho let her think about the word for a moment, then continued. "I interdicted a recent shipment of counterfeit cash onto the reservation. Enough to cause serious problems for an operation like the casino. But maybe an earlier shipment got through. I need to hear if you've seen any signs of counterfeit bills flowing into your coffers."

She leaned back in her chair, which gave a faint crackle of fine leather. Again, she recovered quickly. "I've got people for that. But I check samples myself at least once a week. I've seen nothing suspicious and had no reports of such."

Concho nodded. "You might want to triple your checks for a while. And make absolutely sure of your 'people.'

Needless to say, what I've told you doesn't go beyond these walls."

"Of course."

"If you were a suspicious sort, is there anyone at the casino, or anywhere on the Rez, who you think might be involved in such a scheme? Maybe even anyone close to you?"

Nolan's armor was fully on now. She didn't even blink. "No one I can think of. But I'll give it some thought and let you know."

The woman's words were clearly a dismissal. Concho was ready to be dismissed. He'd dangled the bait. Quite possibly in front of the wrong fish. But now all he could do was wait. Climbing out of his chair, he moved to the door, but glanced back. "The lilac suits you," he said, grinning.

"Goodbye, Ten-Wolves!"

CHAPTER TWENTY-SIX

As he left Melissa Nolan's office, Concho noted the time—5:29 PM. The day had gotten away from him. He'd done a lot of things, but it felt like he'd accomplished little. He called Maria, only to find out she had a late meeting and wouldn't be back to his house until 9:00 or later. That meant dinner on his own.

He stopped by the Red Sky Grill and ordered two burgers and fries to go. His stomach was growling like an angry mountain lion by the time he reached his truck in the parking lot. He was trying to decide whether to eat one of the burgers on the way home when a voice interrupted his thoughts of food.

"Ranger Ten-Wolves! May I speak with you?"

He turned. Surprise gave him a little slap. Isi Whiteheart stood staring at him, wearing the same outfit he'd seen her in earlier—jeans, a leather vest over a white cotton shirt, and a fringed jacket of buckskin. Cowboy boots on her feet completed the look. She was tall and lovely. And, unlike every other Whiteheart he'd run into recently, she wasn't glaring at him with hatred.

"Ms. Whiteheart," he said casually.

Ruminating on the pleasures brought by the mere sight of

beauty, he opened the door of his Ford and put the food bag on the passenger seat before turning fully to face the third beautiful woman he'd seen in the last half hour. This was the youngest of the three at twenty-three or twenty-four.

Isi Whiteheart had the same attractive dark complexion he'd seen in the photograph at the Whiteheart home but was considerably more lovely in person. A silver clasp held her black hair away from her forehead, but the sides fell well past her shoulders like two sable banners. Her eyes were very deeply dark, enough to make him think of the Apache tears he'd collected once on a trip to Mexico.

"You know me?" Isi asked, surprised.

"I've seen your picture. At your father's house."

"Ah, yes, of course. You came to see him earlier today."

"I did."

"And apparently it didn't end well."

"It never does."

Isi nodded and sighed. "I would very much like to change that."

Now it was Concho's turn to show surprise. "Why?"

Isi considered her answer and finally replied with, "The Kickapoo are not a large tribe. What few of us there are need to work together. Not be at odds with each other."

"Your father doesn't think of me as Kickapoo. Nor does your brother, Pete. My skin's not the right kind of brown."

"I know," Isi said. "And they're both wrong. I may be able to change such things over time. But it won't be easy. I saw you…helping the tribal police with Nate Wronghorse. Your kindness was in evidence."

"Nate's a good guy."

"Yes. He used to work for us."

"Until?"

She shrugged. "My brother says he was stealing. He probably was. But maybe only because he was hungry."

"And he's one of us after all. A Kickapoo."

Isi's gaze sharpened. "I hope you are not mocking me, Ranger."

He shook his head. "No. Absolutely not." He smiled. "Perhaps I was teasing a little."

She laughed, and it was a good one, firm and open and full of an awareness of life's absurdities.

"You've been gone for a while," Concho continued. "Away from it all. Perhaps the problems between me and the Whiteheart clan are unfixable."

"Yes, I've been away at university. In Mexico City. But my dream of united Kickapoo is no college student pipe dream, as they say. It is a necessity. More so each day. And it must begin with me. And perhaps with you. Whether some of our elders agree or not."

Concho nodded. "*I* agree."

She took a few steps forward and held out her hand, then started to pull it back as she noted the buddy splint on the outside two fingers of his right hand.

"It's all right," he said. He took her hand and squeezed it gently with his three free fingers. He liked the strength and warmth he felt there.

"Perhaps we have made a start," she said.

Once more, he grinned. "I feel better about the Whitehearts already."

Her laughter came again, and he enjoyed hearing it.

She turned as if to go, then spun back around. Her hand reached out and patted the hood of his F-150. "By the way," she said. "Did you know that ninety-five percent of all Fords ever sold are still on the road today?"

Concho blinked. "That…seems unlikely."

"It's true, though." A sly smile crossed her lips. "The other five percent made it home."

Her laughter rang behind her as she sauntered away toward the casino.

* * *

ZOE HAD JUST GOTTEN OUT OF THE SHOWER WHEN HER CELL phone rang. It was Liana.

"You found a place?" Zoe asked as she wrapped a barely adequate towel around herself.

"I did, and I paid with cash, and I handled a couple of other tasks you assigned me. I'll hang out here until you get in touch with fresh *orders*."

"Good." She started to say more, maybe even apologize for snapping at Liana earlier. But the words wouldn't come. "Good," she repeated.

"Hmm," Liana grunted. "By the way, I saw our Ranger."

"What? I hope he didn't see you."

"He did. We passed each other on the stairs. He was coming in while I was going out."

"Not good. You couldn't avoid him?"

"Didn't realize who it was until I got close. It would have looked suspicious to turn around then. But I think you can relax. Pretty sure he was looking at my tits rather than imagining handcuffing me as a murderer." Liana laughed. "Not that I'd be averse to the handcuffs mind you. He's quite a specimen of Texas manhood."

"Don't let your imagination run wild. We might well have to kill him before this is all through."

"Can we handcuff him first and have our way with him?" Liana teased.

Zoe hung up without responding.

* * *

CONCHO HEADED HOME, IN NO HURRY, MUNCHING FRIES FROM the bag on the seat beside him. Soon, the lights of Kickapoo Village fell away and he drove slowly through a gathering darkness toward his trailer. It had been dry for a while, as it usually was here. His wheels spun up dust that lingered in the glow of his taillights.

The air had cooled as the day ended but he kept his

windows down, enjoying the solitude both inside and outside the vehicle. An early possum rambled across the road ahead of him and he slowed. An early coyote yipped in the distance. He relaxed for the first time in several days.

A flash in his rearview mirror caught his attention. A glance behind him showed a single headlight coming fast. Relaxation dissipated like water on a hot griddle. This was not a well-traveled road. In fact, he was the only one who lived out here, although others sometimes drove this way to hunting or fishing sites, or for other reasons.

Slowing a little more, he stuck his head out the window into the chill air and listened. One headlight might mean a motorcycle, but if so he should have been able to hear the whine of a sport bike or the thud-rumble of a Harley or Harley clone. He didn't. That meant it was probably an automobile with one headlight. He tried to think of anyone he knew with one headlight burned out. He couldn't recall.

The light switched off suddenly. Someone had killed it. But did that mean they'd stopped, that they weren't following him? Or, were they still coming and trying to hide it?

He had a bad feeling it was the latter.

CHAPTER TWENTY-SEVEN

ZOE WENT DOWN TO THE GIFT SHOP IN THE CASINO AND bought a burner phone. She'd already checked her room for bugs, but she checked it again before she placed a call on the new cell.

The phone began to ring, then abruptly cut off as the call was shunted by software to another number, and another. Finally, a woman's mechanical voice answered.

"Que numero por favor?"

She gave the number she really wanted, the one for Doctor Gutierrez Aquila. It rang through and Aquila answered immediately.

"Zoe deSaint. I was not expecting to hear from you quite so soon."

"Most everything is going according to plan," Zoe replied. "We've identified our target and made connections with two people who've provided us with information about him. But there's something I need to check with you."

"What is that?"

"Another player. About six feet tall. Two hundred pounds. Shoulder-length dark hair. Very handsome. Don't know his name but he's a Mexican cop."

"A Mexican police officer," Aquila said. It wasn't a question. "Interesting. And what is your take on this...man?"

"Well, he wouldn't be working with Texas law so that leaves three possibilities. He's yours. He's working for whoever your delivery was meant for. Or he's independent. I seriously doubt the last."

"Yes, I can see why you would. Well, let me assure you he's not mine. I would have told you if such were the case. I should have imagined you would understand that."

"I felt pretty confident of it, sir, but I don't like working off assumptions."

"Reasonable." A pause, and then, "I will attempt to find out if he's employed with certain...individuals. Call me tomorrow evening. Around this same time. I may have an answer for you."

"And in the meantime?"

"Work around him."

"Gotcha."

Aquila hung up, leaving Zoe listening to the hollow sound of an empty line. She closed her phone as well and removed the sim card, which she'd crush and flush. She considered Aquila's order to "work around" the Mexican police officer. She hadn't told Aquila the man was already dead. She reckoned she could work around a corpse easily enough.

As soon as Concho reached his long driveway and turned in, he sped his pace. The truck jounced across past ruts but in a couple of minutes he pulled into his front yard and slid to a stop. Grabbing the hamburger bag and the night vision goggles from his extended cab, he locked the truck and set its alarm, then ran for the door.

Once inside, he flipped off the porch light and flipped on lights in the kitchen and living room to make it look like he was home for the night. He tossed the food bag on his counter but kept hold of the goggles. He also pulled a shotgun off the gun rack against one wall in his den and stuffed his pockets with extra shells from the box beneath it. His next move was to slip quickly out the back door.

Circling the side of the trailer, he crouched in darkness against a grove of mixed juniper and mesquite that shaded the corner of the house. A few early stars winked overhead in a mostly ebon sky. He pulled the night vision goggles over his head. The goggles recreated the night in green, revealing a strange world he'd become used to during his years in the army.

His truck glowed with heat from the slowly cooling motor. An owl with gleaming yellow eyes sat on a limb of the big mesquite across from him, where he'd built his firepit. He could even see the three lawn chairs scattered around beneath the tree. Nothing else revealed itself to him but he wasn't quite sure the night was empty.

Concho's army training had never left him. Right after he'd moved in here he'd prepared some bolt-holes in case of danger. And it had come, forcing him to use them more than once.

Cradling the shotgun across his arms, he went to his belly and worked his way into the front yard toward one such sanctuary. This was a small depression in the ground that looked natural. It wasn't. He'd dug it out and surrounded it with rocks covered with soil. He'd also strategically planted a few mesquite bushes that helped hide him while still providing a view in three-hundred-and-sixty degrees.

Now, he practiced the patience he'd learned through many violent encounters. Fifteen minutes later, patience was rewarded. A shadow crept from the road into his yard. It darted to the rear of his truck and paused there. The figure wore a coat with the collar turned up. He thought it was a man but couldn't identify him, even though he could follow the figure's movements well through the goggles.

Concho scanned slowly back and forth across the yard but saw no more than the one figure. That suggested they weren't here for a frontal assault against him. They'd have brought more men. But it could be this visitor had come to plant a bomb.

The figure finally moved in a crouch down the side of the pickup and paused again where it could study the front door of the officer's trailer. The face was still hidden by the coat collar.

The distance from Concho's bolt-hole to the truck was nearly thirty yards, a little far for best effect with the shotgun. Besides, the shape had made no overt threatening moves yet and the Ranger wasn't ready to shoot him. Moving quietly, the big officer eased out of his hiding place and began taking panther steps toward the figure, which had its back to him. He was halfway to his target when the man stood up from behind the truck.

Concho had his truck keys in his pocket. Through the denim, he pressed the button to beep the alarm. The sound startled the figure by the pickup. The shape recoiled, leaping back as if struck at by a snake.

"Freeze!" the lawman shouted. "Or I'll cut you in half."

The figure startled again, crying out. It spun around, arms flinging into the air. "Don't shoot! Don't shoot! Please!"

Concho recognized the voice. And with the man's arms up, he could see the face. He took three quick steps forward. The man could see only the alien, insectile shape of the night vision goggles. He quailed, flinging himself back against the truck. The alarm went off for real.

"Quiet!" Concho yelled.

But the man dropped to his knees and stuck his face in the dirt. His hands were out in front of him, pleading along with his words. "No, no, no!"

Concho grabbed for his keys and pressed the button to turn off the alarm. "Quiet!" he yelled again. "It's me!" The figure looked up. Concho pulled off his goggles and let them dangle in one hand. "Bearfoot!" he snapped. "What are you doing here?"

Tears left shiny streaks down Bearfoot's face, but his eyes were suddenly hopeful. "Ten-Wolves! Is it really you?"

Concho did not like Bearfoot. The man was a drunk, a poor husband to his wife, Estrella Deer-Run, and a poor father to his children. But the Ranger had never thought him to be dangerous.

"You can see it's me! Get up!"

Shaking, Bearfoot rose to his feet. His hands were still stretched out in front of him, and he slowly lowered them to his sides and wiped the palms on his dirty canvas pants.

"I'm…sorry," he said.

Concho took another step toward the thin Kickapoo. "Why…are…you…here?" he repeated. "Sneaking around in my front yard is a good way to get yourself shot."

"I'm sorry," Bearfoot said again. "I just…just…came…"

"Came to what?"

"Warn you!"

CHAPTER TWENTY-EIGHT

"Warn me of what?" Concho asked Bearfoot.

Still shaking, Bearfoot gazed around, as if afraid some devil were about to appear and eat him.

"You're sure…sure we're alone?" the man asked.

Exasperation deepened in the lawman. "I've been out here watching for nearly half an hour. You're the only person I've seen skulking in my yard."

Bearfoot nodded. "It's just that, I couldn't know if they were watching your place. And if they found out I told you. They'd kill me."

"Who?"

"Zoe and Liana." Bearfoot shook his head. "I mean, that's their real names but I don't know what names they're under here. And you don't know them and I don't know their last names."

"You're not making sense. Start at the beginning."

Bearfoot took a deep breath. He'd finally stopped shaking, though he continued to look around for whatever devils had so terrified him.

"This morning. These two women. They came in the casino. They cornered me, threatened me."

"And their names are Zoe and Liana?"

"Yeah."

"And you owe them money?"

Bearfoot lowered his head. "Yeah."

"Go on from where they cornered you."

"They…made some threats. But then they said I could maybe do something for them and that might…help with my debt."

"Help them with something to do with me?"

Bearfoot shook his head. "Not directly."

"Then why are you warning me about them? What makes you think they mean me harm?"

"I don't know, for sure. It's maybe a feeling. They work for various people. Usually in Mexico. And they're dangerous. They're here for a reason. At the casino. I thought at first it was because of the money I owed them. But that can't be it. I'm not that important to them. They've got another reason. Bigger. I think maybe it's you."

Concho scratched his cheek where the goggles had rubbed. "I'm not seeing how you've connected these criminals to me."

"They're not criminals. Not really."

"What are they?"

"Enforcers. They threaten people who need threatening. And sometimes they…"

Bearfoot's words trailed off, but Concho knew what the man had been about to say. This Zoe and Liana were contract muscle, and killers if the contract called for it. And they were connected to Mexico. If they were really here for him, then it had to be related to the smuggling operation he'd busted.

"What do they look like?" the lawman asked.

Bearfoot sighed. "Zoe is tall. Like, taller than me. She's muscles all over. She loves the gym. She wears baggy clothes to cover them, though. So no one will know. She's got dark hair. Not quite to the shoulders.

"Liana is...well, she's beautiful. Like a...a copperhead snake. Or more like a...puma. She's blonde. Not quite as tall or big as Zoe. But she's a lot scarier. She doesn't like guns, though she uses them. She likes knives. I don't know about Zoe for sure, but I'm pretty sure Liana has killed people."

Liana, Concho thought. That had to be the blonde woman he'd seen on the stairs at the casino, the one who'd looked at him so intently. She'd been wearing baggy clothes, but maybe they were Zoe's clothes. For reasons unknown. But this still didn't mean they were here for him.

The big Ranger took in a long breath and let it out. "OK, you've warned me." His voice softened a touch. "I appreciate it. You better get going."

He unlocked the Ford and stuck the shotgun and goggles into the crew cab area, then locked the vehicle again. Bearfoot hadn't moved.

"Is there something more?" Concho asked.

"I just...hope you're taking this seriously."

"I take all potential threats on my life seriously."

Bearfoot nodded. He turned to go, paused, and looked back.

"By the way," Concho said, "when did you get a vehicle? I saw you following me. Before you switched off your headlight. You know it has only one front light, huh?"

Fear surged back into the slender Kickapoo's face. "I...I don't have a car. I rode my bicycle. Hid it in the ditch to come up here on foot. In case they were watching. It must have been someone else. Maybe…"

A chill coursed up the law officer's spine as Bearfoot's words trailed off.

* * *

AFTER BEARFOOT LEFT, CONCHO REENTERED HIS TRAILER. THE clock on the microwave read 7:52 PM. Still early. But that reminded him. Maria would be on her way over soon. And, given the potential that someone other than Bearfoot had followed him home, he couldn't let her risk it.

An attempted call went to her voice mail. She'd said she had a meeting. He left a message to phone him when she got out. Opening the food bag on his counter, he took out a Styrofoam container holding two burgers from the Red Sky Grill. His stomach growled and he ate the first burger cold, finishing it in five big bites, though he hardly tasted it. He took a little longer with the second burger. Halfway through, he tossed it in the microwave but that didn't help his taste buds much. He was too wound up to enjoy eating.

Filling a stainless steel travel mug with tea, he headed for his truck. He figured to drive into Kickapoo Village and scout for any sign of the one-headlight vehicle that had followed him at least part of the way home. As he climbed into his Ford, his phone chimed. He swiped to answer Maria's call.

"Whatcha need, lover?" she asked.

Concho took a deep breath. He and Maria had just passed a few very good days together after a long period of either being apart or having to deal with potential threats on their lives. All such threats had come about from his job as a Texas Ranger. He hated to spoil any potential good times, but he didn't want to put Maria at risk by having her come to his place when someone might be waiting who could hurt her.

"Baby," he started. "I'm sorry but I think it's better you don't come over tonight."

Maria's voice changed instantly, from intimate to cold. "Why?"

"I…uh…well, someone followed me from the casino tonight. At least part of the way home. And they turned off their headlights so I'm not sure exactly where they might be. But maybe on the same road you'd take to get here. I was about to go see if I could spot them, but if there's a problem I don't want you in the middle."

"Are you sure you're not being paranoid?"

Concho sighed. "Bearfoot also told me there were two… uhm, people at the casino who were looking for me. Dangerous people."

"Bearfoot told you?"

"Yes."

"And you believe him?"

"I'm not sure. But better to err on the side of caution, I think. I love you. I wouldn't want anything to happen to you."

The anger seeped out of Maria's voice but hurt seeped in, making it much worse.

"Is there ever going to be a time when we get a little peace?" she asked.

"We had a good week. It felt…so right."

Maria huffed a response, and the anger returned. "A week! Hardly a happy little family life in the making."

"I'm sorry!"

"Stop apologizing! It doesn't help."

"I'm…I understand."

Maria sighed, and the hurt slipped back in. "I keep telling myself things will get better. But they don't."

"I'm…I know." He tried to make a joke because he didn't have any idea what else to do. "Smugglers, am I right. No regard for a couple's home life."

"Don't! Just don't!"

"I'm…"

Maria took in a long breath and exhaled. "Call me in the morning to let me hear you're still alive." She hung up.

Concho stared at his silent phone for a long moment, then laid it down on the seat. He was alone, and the night felt hollow.

CHAPTER TWENTY-NINE

PULLING OUT OF HIS DRIVEWAY, CONCHO TURNED TOWARD Kickapoo Village and drove slowly, scanning both left and right for any sign of the vehicle with one headlight. He passed several turnoffs, to either gas wells or what had once been homesteads but saw no sign of any hidden automobile.

The moon began to rise, in an almost autumn red. The light seeped like watermelon blood across the landscape. Concho stopped. Although it was difficult to be sure, he thought he was almost to the place along the road where the light had disappeared earlier. He flipped off his lights, killed his truck, and got out. He listened.

Temps had dropped into the fifties. A sharp breeze sniffed around him. He heard it rustle among the roadside brush but there weren't any other sounds. He did smell a very faint odor of exhaust, but it might have been from his own truck.

As a kid, he'd often walked this road on summer nights toward town, with the blinking embers of firefly hordes lighting the darkness. There weren't nearly as many fireflies anymore. He didn't know why, unless it was the spray used along the roads in mosquito abatement programs.

Climbing back into his truck, he started it and pulled

forward. His headlights flashed ahead. Dirt and rock in front of him. Dry brush and brown grass to the sides. He had his windows down. A whirring struck his ears.

A nightbird?

Something swept across the road in front of him. Flying. Almost at the upper edge of light cast by his headlamps. He caught only a glimpse, but it was big. Bigger than the bats you might expect to be out at this time. Eagle or buzzard sized. But neither eagles nor buzzards hunted at night.

He slowed a little more. Maybe he'd seen an owl. The whirring returned; it teased his thoughts. He just about had it when a shape came swooping out of the darkness and dove violently into his windshield.

The Ranger slammed on his brakes and startled backward in his seat. The window didn't break but cracks spiderwebbed across it. He saw the gleam of plastic. A drone had smashed into him. Even as he realized the event was no accident, a single headlight flashed on in the road ahead.

Concho's hand darted toward the gear shift and yanked it into reverse as the darkness ahead ripped open with sound and streaks of light. *Gunfire!* Bullets punched through the windshield where the drone could not.

Concho ducked and stomped the gas. His tires spun in the dirt and the big Ford lurched backward. More lead ripped into the front of his truck. He dared not look up; he couldn't see where he was going but the road ran straight here. He tried to keep his wheels between the ditches.

The gunfire died away as he backed out of range. Concho sat up and tapped his brakes. The Ford slid to a stop. The window was Swiss cheese. One of *his* headlights was shattered now. But the engine chugged on.

Ten-Wolves could see nothing in the road ahead. But something was there, just beyond the edge of his lights. He snarled. His big hands clenched on the steering wheel, the joints creaking.

He flipped off his remaining headlight and slapped the

shift into drive. His foot punched the gas pedal to the floor. The Ford lunged ahead, picking up speed. In the darkness, the Ranger hurtled down the road toward whatever obstacle lay in his path.

* * *

A KNOCK ON ZOE DESAINT'S DOOR BROUGHT HER TO HER FEET, her hand filling itself with the Glock from the bedside table. She'd been lying in bed, fully dressed, back against the headboard as her thoughts worked through an event-filled day. She was starting to feel a little paranoid and a knock where there shouldn't have been a knock didn't help.

She padded to the doorway and took a look through the peep hole. A frown crossed her face but she slid the pistol into the waistband of her jeans at the small of her back and unlocked the door, opening it slightly to peer out.

"Señora Garcia. I'm surprised to see you here."

Leticia Garcia offered a smile that looked more ghastly than friendly. "I assume that in your own room, you've swept for bugs. Perhaps here we can talk more openly?"

"How did you find my room number?"

"Please," Leticia said, smirking. "This is a small reservation. I know half the staff who work in the hotel. Some are relatives."

Zoe nodded. "I guess so." She opened the door and motioned Leticia inside.

The woman came in and walked down the short hallway into the bed area. She turned and leaned against a wall beneath a painting of an Indian chieftain in full feathered regalia. Zoe had been calling the painting "Geronimo," though she had no idea who it really was. Or even if it was supposed to represent an actual historical figure.

"I did not take my cousin Jorge's phone instructions regarding our first meeting seriously," Letty said. "It did not seem a big thing to me. But I realize the instructions must have come directly from you. And that you had your reasons."

Zoe figured this was about as close to an apology as she was going to get. "Thank you for acknowledging that." She motioned the woman toward one of the room's two chairs and sat on the edge of the bed herself.

Letty remained standing. "I can give you the information you want about Ten-Wolves. What you do with it will be up to you."

"All right. Go ahead."

"You don't want to...write it down?"

"I'll remember. I *always* remember."

The "always" must have sounded a little like a threat to Letty Garcia. It was meant to. The Kickapoo woman began to talk swiftly. And completely. Zoe listened and kept her hand on the bed within easy reach of the pistol behind her back.

As the Ford F-150 snarled down the road with its lights off, Concho kept his injured right hand on the steering wheel and used his left to draw one of his Colts. He raked the gun barrel through the shredded windshield in front of him, knocking out a gaping hole to stab the pistol through.

His enemies must have heard him coming. Their engine started; their one headlight flashed on. The outline of an old pickup appeared, seeming almost to float in the air over the ruts of the road. An instant later, gunfire sleeted again from that direction.

This time, Concho fired back. Against the glare ahead, all he could see for a target was a dark, human-sized shadow limned with light standing next to the passenger side of the truck. He didn't *aim* at the shadow, only pointed at center of mass and pulled the trigger. Twice.

The big pistol kicked in his hand once, then again, spitting hot brass onto the floorboard. The shadow target lurched and fell. The stream of shots speeding in Concho's direction ceased as if hacked off by a knife.

The Ranger shifted aim to the front windshield of the other truck, above the one headlight. Twice more he fired. If he got a hit, it didn't stop whoever was driving the vehicle. They shifted *their* truck into reverse and lurched backward trying to escape the oncoming juggernaut of steel racing in their direction.

They didn't make it. The F-150 ate the ground, closing the distance in an instant. The left side of the Ford's bumper blasted into the grill of the smaller pickup. Metal crunched. The blow sent the other pickup slewing to one side. The driver still had his foot on the gas and his truck plunged backward into the ditch with a bone-shaking bang.

Concho hit the brakes and twisted the steering wheel of the Ford. The truck slid to a stop across the road in a cloud of white dust. Ten-Wolves threw open his door and lunged out, drawing his second Double Eagle.

A dark figure clawed its way out of the other truck and swung what looked like a long stick of metal in the Ranger's direction. Concho double-actioned the trigger on his second Colt. The recoil sent pain rocketing through his broken finger, but the figure cried out and fell away, the shotgun in his hands discharging into the dirt.

The engine of the smaller pickup lurched and died. Its driver and passenger were flat on the ground. It wasn't clear if they were dead or alive. Ten-Wolves loomed alone in the glare of two headlights. The last man standing.

CHAPTER THIRTY

In the aftermath of violence, Concho's mind flashed back to army days.

Afghanistan, 2010.

Concho's Army Ranger ODA stumbled upon a scene of turmoil and tragedy. They'd been on routine patrol, coming down a mountain held by the Taliban into United States patrolled territory. Gunfire ahead informed them of a battle in progress. The sound of American weapons against Russian and Chinese identified the parties. From the roar, the Americans were outnumbered.

Commander Russ Adelaide signaled orders with both hands. A rocky defile in front of them led toward the battle. They took it, moving with both speed and control. Concho swung the M2HB .50 caliber machine gun he carried into position by his hip. It was like holding a chainsaw, but one that could reach out and cut you at a hundred yards.

As the twelve members of the ODA exited the defile in a crouch, they glimpsed a dirt road snaking through the desert ahead. An American convoy of trucks and armored vehicles—sans tanks—were pinned down behind a wildly burning vehicle that must have struck a mine.

The regular army troopers from the convoy had piled out of their sitting duck vehicles and were returning fire toward a field of boulders ahead of them. Even heavier fire stabbed from the boulder field back toward the soldiers. The smoke trail of a rocket-propelled grenade twisted toward the convoy but hit to the side of the road, exploding with little damage to the Americans. The next RPG might be on target and claim lives.

Concho's squad had come out of the defile on the flank of the attacking Taliban fighters. Boulders and a shallow ravine provided them cover. Adelaide gave the signal; Concho opened the game with the big .50. The rest of the squad followed suit with M4s.

A lead scythe hacked into the flank of the Taliban formation. A complete surprise. Guns roared. Bullets shrieked, pinged, whined into rocks, into flesh. Men cried out. With their ambush undone, the rebel fighters whirled and ran. Adelaide signaled a cease fire.

Concho let the .50 cal cycle to a stop but did not rise from his crouch. At the convoy, a lieutenant in sweat-darkened khakis stepped from behind the door of his sand-colored Humvee.

Too soon!

Even as Ten-Wolves watched, the lieutenant staggered backward just as the hollow boom of a distant shot echoed down the long hills. A sniper! *Concho swung his .50 cal around in the direction of the shot. No target. All he could see was the empty side of a desert hill.*

"Where is he? Where is he?" Adelaide shouted.

"Don't see him!" Concho shouted back.

But then he did. Right at the top of the hill, a good eight hundred yards off, a tiny movement, a shifting of sand in the sunlight. A shape that looked like it was made of rock and dirt slid upward over the top of the hill before anyone could swing a weapon to bear. The sniper was gone. As if he were vapor on a hot day.

"The same shooter," Concho muttered to himself. The one he'd seen before. Had to be. A ghost. Or near as.

Concho returned to the present, to a different dirt road in a different landscape and different time. His reverie had taken barely a second. The air around him hung thick with the smells of gasoline and gunpowder. The two men who'd tried to kill him still lay in the dirt. One moaned in pain. Proof of life. The other didn't make a peep and could be dead or playing possum.

Keeping his guns handy, the Ranger moved toward the silent would-be assassin. It was a man, a stranger, Hispanic looking in the glow of his own vehicle's headlight. The fellow wasn't faking. He wasn't dead either. A bullet had grazed his skull, knocking him unconscious.

The second man was also Hispanic. Ten-Wolves didn't recognize him either. This one was gut-shot, with his lower body saturated in blood. He moaned and writhed in pain. Concho fished for his cell phone to call for backup and an ambulance. The phone wasn't in his pocket. He recalled laying it on the seat in his truck and found it on the floorboard next to an empty brass casing.

After making the calls he needed to make, Concho grabbed the first aid kit from the extended cab area of his truck and tried to do what he could to stop the conscious man's bleeding. He had a small vile of WoundSeal powder and emptied the whole thing on the man's injury, though he doubted it would help much.

The fellow didn't fight him but muttered the whole time in rapid Spanish. The Ranger was able to make out most of the man's words, but they made little sense. They seemed to consist of various mixed-up prayers to God and Mary, the holy mother.

Concho finally pushed away from the man and rose. He'd done what he could. Sirens snarling in the distance and the flash of blue lights off the few clouds in the dark sky indicated help coming.

Ten-Wolves wondered why his mind had taken him to Afghanistan in the moments after the shooting. He hadn't thought of the sniper he and others had called "the ghost" for a long time. Why now? There had to be a reason why his subconscious had generated that memory. It was telling him something. He just wasn't sure what.

After the lieutenant's shooting at the convoy, Concho had scouted up the hill where he'd seen the sniper. He'd found little more than a few scuffs on the rocks and in the dirt. By the time he'd gotten back to his ODA, the squad had mixed in with the other US troopers and the conversations centered around the mysterious rifleman, who'd apparently appeared out of nowhere about a month earlier and racked up a dozen confirmed kills, mostly against the Afghan allies of the US.

Concho remembered the chill he'd gotten, even in the blistering heat of an Afghan day, as he listened to men tell increasingly wild stories about the ghost sniper who moved in and out of American-controlled territory at will and struck with silent but deadly success.

The chill had not been from fear, at least not mostly. It had been from an anticipation of conflict. He'd understood that this was not the last time he'd meet the sniper. Eventually there'd be a confrontation between them. And he couldn't know what would happen, though blood would flow.

The Kickapoo tribal police arrived in a flurry of blue lights and sirens. Thoughts of Afghanistan would have to wait. Concho turned his attention toward the now, toward identifying the men who'd just tried to kill him and figuring out who'd set them on his trail.

CHAPTER THIRTY-ONE

CONCHO STOOD BESIDE SHERIFF ECHABARRI AT THE SCENE OF the shooting. An ambulance had finally arrived, and paramedics worked over the two wounded men. The one with the head wound still hadn't regained consciousness; the belly shot one had finally stopped crying out as the paramedics poured morphine into him.

One of Roberto's deputies checked the truck and various dropped weapons for fingerprints or other clues. Another bagged up pieces of the wrecked drone that had flown into Concho's windshield.

"I checked for wallets but neither of them had any ID," Concho said to Roberto. "You recognize either of them?"

The young sheriff sighed. "Afraid I do. At least the one with the head wound. Came up from Mexico recently. Last I knew he was working as a field laborer for Sam Whiteheart."

Concho groaned. "Not Whiteheart again!"

"Does it make sense, though?" Roberto asked.

Ten-Wolves considered. "Not logically," he finally said. "Sam would have to know we'd trace the fellow to him. But he and I recently had a…disagreement. And Sam isn't the most patient of people."

Roberto nodded. "Agreed. But he's not stupid. This just seems…questionable."

The Ranger nodded. "Yeah, it does. But it's a place to start."

Roberto grunted assent. "Let's do it now." He looked over at the banged up and bullet-ridden F-150 parked in the middle of the road. "Your truck drivable?"

"It was running until I shut it off, but I'd like to have it looked at before I put many miles on it."

"Right. I'll have a tow truck called. They can take it to John Gray-Dove's garage."

"Sounds good."

"You're with me then."

Roberto gave some quick orders to Nila Willow, his second at the scene, then climbed into his SUV. Concho joined him after grabbing a couple of items from his truck. They headed toward Kickapoo Village so they could pick up the road running to the Whiteheart farm.

"Been meaning to ask," Concho said, "what's going on with that kid from the casino? Deke Cooper? Did you get in touch with his mom?"

"Yep. Finally got hold of her this afternoon. At that place you mentioned. *Fatty's*. Her first words were, 'keep him!' but after a few minutes she calmed down and said she'd come and get him tomorrow."

"She say anything about the death of her husband?"

"Just one word. 'Good!'"

Concho shook his head. "Feel bad for the kid."

"You can't save everyone. Tell you the truth, from my interactions with him the kid seems pretty much a lost cause already."

"Was a time when plenty of folks considered me a lost cause."

"I see your point. So what do you want to do? We can't fight her for custody."

Concho sighed. "I don't know. I guess, just call me when she arrives. And give some excuse to stall until I get there."

"All right. What about tonight? At the Whiteheart's? How do we proceed?"

"Don't ask me. I'm making it up as I go."

* * *

GUTIERREZ AQUILA LEFT HIS HACIENDA AS THE MOON ROSE. Carrying no weapons, followed by no guards, he walked the desert with long strides under luna's silver light. The land lay quiet and peaceful, a contrast to his thoughts, which churned with chaos.

Just when plans were coming to fruition. Just when desires seemed about to be quenched. Disruptions had occurred. Perhaps he'd planned badly. Or perhaps it was only terrible luck.

It felt comforting to blame the Tejano Ranger, Ten-Wolves, for his troubles. And the man *would* be punished. But truth be told, his luck had been bad ever since he'd taught a few semesters at university. He'd arrived as royalty, expecting to be granted all the perks he'd earned as a successful physician and wealthy man. Instead, he'd stumbled into a mine field of interpersonal politics that revealed his weaknesses.

And he'd made the worst mistake of all. He'd fallen in love.

"Princesa," he'd called her at first. An affectionate joke. A tease at her sometimes-regal attitude.

The humor had faded over time. Initially, he'd been master of the situation. Or so he'd convinced himself. He knew now he'd never been master. In heartless moments directed inwardly, he called himself "marioneta," a puppet.

And yet, still he loved, though that emotion had gotten far more complicated over time. And still he had a goal, one built from all his thoughts, experiences, and actions over the past two years. A visit to the United States. Guest lectures at selected universities. A job offer and a move. A new life where he'd have a chance to win the woman. And beauty in it all.

He stopped and leaned against the bole of a big mesquite tree. His fists clenched.

"And beauty in it all," he murmured to a world that wasn't listening.

* * *

ROBERTO ECHABARRI PULLED HIS SUV UP IN FRONT OF THE barbed wire gate leading into the Whiteheart farm. The same shotgun-wielding guard that had greeted Concho before greeted them both now. By the time Echabarri rolled to a stop, the man was already calling the house.

The guard spoke into the phone for a moment, then lowered it and said, "The family is in for the evening. They ask for you to come back in the morning."

"Can't," Echabarri replied. "This is official business. If we have to come back, we'll bring a warrant to search the premises."

The guard's eyes brightened in the glow of the SUV's headlights. He returned the phone to his ear and spoke in rapid Spanish. Both Roberto and Concho translated the man's words on the phone. "They say it is official why they are here. They will get a warrant to search if they have to come back tomorrow."

Another moment passed while the man listened to instructions. He finally tucked the cell phone into his pocket and quickly opened the gate, waving the lawmen through.

Raising dust in the moonlight, they tooled up the long dirt road to the farmhouse. Roberto pulled into the circular driveway and parked directly in front of the door to the Whiteheart home.

The only person on the porch awaiting them was Isi Whiteheart. She'd changed her jeans of earlier for a heavy blue cotton dress, and her tennis shoes for a set of low heels. Roberto glanced over at Concho and raised an eyebrow. The Ranger shrugged. They climbed out and approached the porch.

"Good evening, gentlemen," Isi said. Her glance crossed Concho's and shared a flash of concern with him, then shifted back to Echabarri and took on a sterner expression—not exactly adversarial, but no-nonsense. "How can the Whiteheart family help you?"

Roberto got right to the point. "We need to ask your father about one of his employees."

"Oh! Who?"

"Perhaps, if Sam would—" Roberto started, and was interrupted.

"I've been fully involved in the hiring on the farm recently and I know everyone who works here," Isi said forcefully. "I'm sure I can help you."

Roberto flashed an eyebrow but nodded. He drew his phone from his pocket and swiped to a picture he'd taken of one of the wounded men at the scene of the shooting. The porch light was on. Stepping underneath it, Echabarri blew up the picture and held the phone out for Isi to look at.

"Don't know his name," Roberto said. "But I've seen him come and go with your other employees in the village."

Isi stepped into the light, revealing a faint flush in the sheen of her dark brown skin. She tucked stray strands of crow-black hair behind her ear and took the phone, wincing as she saw the face of the unconscious man in the image.

"Is he dead?"

"No," Concho said. "Just knocked out."

Isi nodded. She studied the picture carefully.

"Turo," she said after a moment. "At least that's the name we had on him. I'd have to look up the last name. He worked here until about a week ago."

"A week ago?" Echabarri asked.

"We hired him on the recommendation of his cousin,

David Flores. That was a few months ago. But both of them were fired last week. I believe Tuesday."

"Fired for what?" Concho asked.

Isi studied the Ranger. "Is that relevant?"

"Very," Roberto said.

Isi drew in a deep breath and let it out. "My brother, Pete, hired them. He was shown citizenship papers on Turo but when I went through those files last week it appeared as if the papers had been forged. We immediately let both men go."

"But you didn't report it to immigration?" Roberto asked.

Isi's gaze focused intently on the Kickapoo sheriff. "Would you?"

Roberto sighed. "Possibly not." He swiped to another picture on the phone and showed it to Isi. "The second man involved in tonight's assault. You know this one?"

Isi didn't wince this time, though the fellow in the picture was more clearly in pain than the first man. She also didn't have to look as long at the photo. "That's David Flores. The cousin."

"Did you realize the two men hadn't left the reservation?" Roberto asked.

Isi shook her head. "We assumed they left immediately. Out of fear we might call ICE."

"I'm going to need whatever paperwork you have on the two," Roberto said.

"Of course. I'll pull it tonight and bring it to you first thing in the morning. If that's all right?"

Roberto glanced over at Concho, who nodded.

"OK," the sheriff said. "I'd like a statement on the matter from Pete, as well. If he could swing by the office."

"I'll tell him," Isi said. "And I'll make sure he gives you a statement. One way or another."

"You the new Whiteheart family publicist?" Concho asked suddenly.

Isi relaxed and grinned. "Publicist, advocate, troubleshooter. Don't you think they need one? Especially," she gestured at both officers, "in dealing with the local authorities."

"I think something needed to change," Concho agreed. "The old way wasn't working for anyone."

Isi nodded and put on a serious look. "I'll be honest with you both. My brother Pete's actions have not reflected well on the family lately. The reservation is a very small place and gossip is like currency. Reputation means much to the Kickapoo. For some, it is all they have. I intend to repair the Whiteheart reputation here. And my father supports me. He knows he's not the most suited by temperament to do so himself."

"I think that's a good idea," Concho said.

"Agree," Roberto said. He tipped his recently acquired Stetson to her. "Thank you, Miss Whiteheart."

"The men," she said. "Are they…going to live?"

"We hope so. They're being treated. I'll call the hospital tonight and give them the names. In case it helps them."

She nodded. Roberto turned and led Concho off the porch.

Back in the SUV, as Echabarri started it up and slipped it into drive, he glanced over at the Ranger. "So, you know Isi Whiteheart?"

"Officially met her today. She spoke to me outside the casino. Seems she wants to bury the hatchet her family has been trying to whack me with for a while."

"And not bury it in your skull, I take it?"

"That's my understanding. How do *you* know her?"

"She came into the office a few weeks back to introduce herself. She'd been in Mexico for several years. Going to university there. Since I wasn't chief when she was here before she wanted me to know she was no stranger."

"I see."

"Quite a lovely young woman," Echabarri ventured.

"I hadn't noticed."

Roberto laughed. "Right!" Then he sobered. "You believe her?"

"About what? Burying the hatchet? Repairing the White-heart reputation? Or what she said about the two men who attacked me?"

"All three."

"I don't see any reason not to at present, but I'm not going to make a bet on it."

"You're a suspicious sort, Ten-Wolves."

Concho glanced over and smiled. "You, too."

Roberto nodded. "Learned it from the best."

CHAPTER THIRTY-TWO

In the army, Concho had learned to sleep even in the face of danger. So, it wasn't the danger he'd just survived that kept him awake once he got home from the Whiteheart farm. Nor was it any fear inherent in not knowing who wanted him dead. It was thoughts of Maria that kept him tossing and turning in fitful slumber much of the night. He was up well before his usual 6:00 AM.

After a quick breakfast, he had a morning workout, which he'd neglected for too long. Exercise and weights distracted him at least. He wrote up a report of his minimal progress so far on the smuggling case for his superiors in the Texas Rangers, including last night's attack. At 8:00, he called John Gray-Dove's garage, where his truck had been towed. John told him to check at 11:00.

He phoned Maria, who'd be at work. She answered on the fourth ring.

"Hi." Her voice sounded down, and Concho winced inwardly.

"Hi, baby. You said to call and let you hear I was OK."

"Glad you are. Anything happen last night?"

Concho took a breath. "Afraid it did. Two men ambushed me on the road."

The flatness fled from Maria's voice. "Oh, my God! Did you… Were you hurt?"

"No. My truck is a little worse for wear but I'm fine."

"And…the other men?"

"Alive and in custody. Looks like they might have been illegals working on the Rez under false papers. We're still checking into it."

"But why would *they* want to kill you?"

"I'm sure they were hired. The question is by who."

Maria's only reply was a long sigh.

"Listen. I was thinking maybe I could swing by the mall and take you to lunch today. Somewhere off the Rez. Some place nice."

"Maybe...maybe another time."

Concho's chest tightened. "Of course."

"And tonight. Well, I guess you won't want me to come out there again so I'll probably go over to Mom's and see how she's doing."

"All right. I'll call you in a couple of days. Hopefully everything will be clarified."

"That's good. I'll...talk to you." She hung up.

Maria's recent greetings and goodbyes had all contained some version of the "love" word. Not this time. Concho chewed his lower lip as he lay the phone on his computer desk. It was only a little after 8:30, too early for the things he needed to do today. Although he'd already worked out, he decided to have a run.

Stepping out on his back deck in shorts and moccasins, he took a few deep breaths of chill air. His inner world might be in turmoil, but the morning held its peace. The opening lines from one of his favorite books came to him. N. Scott Momaday's *House Made of Dawn*.

He recited them, almost as a ritual. "There was a house made of dawn. It was made of pollen and of rain, and the land was very old and everlasting." That book had begun with another dawn, and with a man running after having painted himself with ashes.

Concho didn't have the ashes, but he had the need to run. The eternal land beckoned.

* * *

TEN-WOLVES HAD BARELY ARRIVED AT JOHN GRAY-DOVE'S auto repair shop when the call came from Roberto that Deke Cooper's mother, Dana Angel, was here to pick up her son.

"She's at the casino," Echabarri said. "I'm sending someone to guide her here. It'll probably take ten minutes or so. You need more time? We can stall."

"No. I'll be there in ten. I'm down the road at Gray-Dove's."

"Gotcha." Echabarri hung up.

Concho glanced at Gray-Dove. "So, what are we looking at?"

John Gray-Dove was full-blood Kickapoo, but his irises were grayish rather than brown—no doubt an influence on the family name. Concho liked Gray-Dove. They were friends.

"Troubles," John said. "New grill, radiator, hood, left headlight, windshield, front and back. Got some hoses shot up. Not sure about the engine. Will pull it today to check."

"Any idea how long it'll take?"

"If the engine's OK, three days. Otherwise, five."

"Not bad."

Gray-Dove grinned. "Got a fellow can get me F-150 parts pretty easy. I keep him on retainer just for you."

Concho winced. "Yeah, I'm pretty hard on vehicles. Glad I can spread the wealth around."

The two shook hands and Concho headed for the police department SUV Roberto had loaned him. It was a basic Dodge Durango with added blue lights and sirens. Tribal police insignia marked the sides. He pulled down the road a few hundred yards and turned into the parking lot of the police station, a long, low, one-story wooden building at the corner of Chick Kazan Street and Nakai Breen Avenue.

Stepping into the building, he greeted Nila Willow at the dispatcher's desk—she nodded back—then strode through the open doorway into Echabarri's office. The Kickapoo sheriff was pouring over a medium-thick folder of notes but glanced up and waved his friend toward a worn and sweat-stained brown couch against one wall of the office.

Concho sat. "Those the documents from Isi Whiteheart on our would-be assassins?"

"Yeah. They were delivered about an hour ago. All sealed up for my inspection."

"Anything noteworthy?"

"Not yet."

"Where's the kid?"

"In the back with Ara." Ara was Araceli Espaderos, the second woman appointed to the Kickapoo tribal police. "I sent Timbo to fetch the mother," Roberto continued, "but I thought it best to talk to her before bringing the boy in."

"Good idea."

At that moment, the outside door to the police department slammed open and a gale swept in. A woman's loud voice rattled the whole office and footsteps stomped across the wooden floor. Concho heard Timbo Corbett's exasperated voice.

"Ma'am! If you'll wait."

"Ain't got time to wait," the woman's voice returned. "Things to do. Where's this sheriff of yourn? And where's my boy?"

Roberto started to rise but froze as a woman suddenly filled his doorway. Concho leaned forward a little on the couch. Timbo's lanky frame hovered over the woman's substantial shoulder. The light-skinned officer wore a consternated look.

The woman, who had to be Dana Angel—Deke Cooper's mother—had brilliant orange-red hair that must have come out of a bottle. Her lipstick was bright scarlet and her cheeks rouged to the maximum. She was maybe five feet two and weighed about two-forty. She was attractive, the way a storm front is attractive when it's not coming right at you. Unfortunately, Dana Angel was coming right at Roberto and the sheriff dropped into his chair again and pushed back a foot from his desk.

"You the sheriff?" the woman demanded. "Echobarry?"

Her accent wasn't Texan. More of a Midwest twang. Concho had an ear for such; he thought she might have been an Arkansas native, though she'd been gone from there long enough to be influenced by other accents.

"Echabarri," Roberto responded automatically to the woman's question. "You must be Dana Angel."

Dana snorted. "Your powers of observation amaze." She glanced over at Concho, who sat very still on the couch, afraid his eyes were going to start watering from the powerful perfume the woman had carried into the room with her. "And who the hell's this?" she asked.

"This is Concho Ten-Wolves," Roberto began. "He's—"

"Right, right!" Dana said, "the Texas Ranger what killed my husband."

Concho stood up. "I'm...very sorry, ma'am."

"I ain't. He weren't worth the spit you'd use to shine your shoes."

Concho had no idea what to say so he held his tongue. He'd been expecting someone a bit like this woman, although the intensity level was incredibly high. She was also younger than he'd imagined. He'd figured Deke Cooper at about fourteen and this woman looked to be in her early thirties, which meant she'd had her son as a teenager.

Dana turned back to Roberto. "So where's my boy? I need to get him and get going. Ain't makin' no money standing around."

"He's in the building, but I…well, *we* wanted to ask you some questions first."

Dana frowned. "There some criminal thing going on here? Because if there ain't, you've got no right to ask me anything."

"Well," Roberto said. "Your son *was* involved in an attempt on Concho's life." He nodded toward the Ranger. "He's not pressing charges, but we still have some questions."

Dana's hands found their way to her hips. Her voice calmed, which Concho figured wasn't a good sign. "You didn't mention that on the phone. Only that my husband—ex, I guess—had been killed in an attack on a Texas Ranger. How was my son involved?"

Roberto cued his fellow lawman with a look.

"I was attacked on the roof of the casino," the Ranger said. "Your son was there. Your husband used him as a distraction. I'm not sure Deke even understood what was happening, and that's why I'm not pressing charges. But I'd like to know that, if we release him to your custody, he's not going to pose a danger to himself or others."

Dana glanced back and forth between the two men. Abruptly, her face fell, her shoulders slumped, her lower lip began to tremble. Concho felt stricken. He took a step toward the woman. "Ma'am!"

Dana threw back her shoulders and laughed. She winked at Roberto, then glanced at Concho. "Acting," she said. "Strippers have to be the greatest actors in the world. But do we get nominated for an Academy Award? No!"

Abruptly, the woman sobered. "Sorry. Couldn't help myself. You two are so earnest. Boy scouts even. My son's fourteen. His *father* has been there for him maybe a total of two years in that time. He comes and goes. Or he used to. He'd drop by for a few days, take Deke to the zoo or out for ice cream, or maybe just ride around in whatever fast car he was driving at the time. Then he'd disappear. Off on a job. Or maybe in jail. He spent time in prison twice."

The woman's voice gained a tinge of bitterness. "But Deke always believed one day Myron would come home for good. That the next visit would be permanent. That they'd be father and son like you see on TV. He loved his dad. And he resented me because, I guess, Myron told him *I* was the reason they didn't get to spend more time together. So this time when Myron got out of prison, I told him to take Deke and raise him. I figured Deke would finally find out for himself what his father was like. Harsh, I know. But I was at my wit's end."

Concho nodded. Echabarri too. Roberto rose from his chair. "I'll fetch him." He walked out.

Ten-Wolves faced Dana Angel alone. He fidgeted. A deep breath calmed him. He opened his mouth, not sure what he was going to say.

"Don't apologize," Dana Angel interrupted. "Something like this has been coming to my husband for a very long time. Only the fact that he was so big, so tough, saved him. I know he's hurt a lot of people." She glanced toward the doorway to the office, as if to make sure the sheriff wasn't already returning with her son. Her voice dropped. "Sad as it is to say, it may be the best thing ever happened to Deke. Though I'm sure he wouldn't thank you for it."

"I reckon not."

They both heard Roberto's bootsteps, accompanied by a smaller and lighter pair of feet. Deke Cooper stepped through the doorway with Echabarri at his shoulder. The youth looked exhausted, though he would have been fed and allowed to shower and sleep if he wanted. He didn't even glance toward Concho but kept his eyes glued to his mother. After a few seconds, his gaze dropped.

In a gentler voice than any Dana Angel had used before, the woman asked, "Are you OK, son?"

Deke nodded his head manfully, but then gave it up and threw himself across the room into his mother's arms. He was as tall as his mother and buried his face against her shoulder as he burst into tears. She hugged him with one arm and patted his back with her free hand.

"Shhh," she said. "Let's go home." Glancing at Roberto, she asked, "I have to sign anything?"

Echabarri shook his head and stepped out of the doorway to let her pass. She tugged on her son's shoulders and he turned with her. A glitter of tears clung to his eyelashes but his unfocused gaze found Concho.

"I'm sorry," he said.

"It's all right," the Ranger replied. "I am, too."

Deke looked back down and walked out with his mom. Roberto glanced at Concho and shrugged. "Tough!"

Concho nodded. A virtual hole had formed in his belly. Too many kids of late had been getting hurt. And there was the mummy of the young girl. He still had no idea who she might have been or where she belonged. He wanted to find out; he needed to.

"Maybe Deke Cooper will turn out OK," he said.

"Maybe," Roberto agreed.

CHAPTER THIRTY-THREE

After leaving Echabarri's office, Concho headed home, then abruptly made a U-turn as he decided to question David Flores and his cousin Turo about their attempt on his life. The two men had been taken to an Eagle Pass hospital to be treated for the wounds. Echabarri knew the hospital, but Concho had forgotten to ask.

Both men would be under guard, of course, with the manpower supplied by the Maverick County Sheriff's Department, under the head of Isaac Parkland. Parkland was an old friend who Concho hadn't spoken to in a while. He called him.

"Ten-Wolves," Parkland said when he answered. "Seems like I heard you were gonna take me fishin' after I helped you out on a case. When is that supposed to happen? Next year or never?"

"Sooner than that. I just gotta dip down below the border and pick up some of that good Dos Equis beer you like."

"Promises, promises. I sure hope you aren't gonna break my heart."

"Never."

"I suppose you're calling about those two boys who tried to off you."

"Yeah."

"Pretty stupid of them. They're at Fort Duncan Medical Center. Guarded twenty-four seven, of course."

"They make any statements?"

"The one is still unconscious. They say he's in a coma. The other one hasn't given up anything as far as I know."

"Thanks, I appreciate it. By the way, I wanted to touch base with you about security over at the coroner's office. You heard about the assault and robbery case, I guess? I wasn't sure who to call about getting a guard over there."

"Yep, heard about old Earl Blake getting Tased. I'm looking into a guard."

"Thanks again. I haven't forgotten the fishing."

"And the Dos Equis," Parkland added. "That way, if the fish aren't biting we can still have a good day."

Concho chuckled. "See you soon."

The Ranger hung up and headed into Eagle Pass, to Bob Rogers Drive and Fort Duncan Hospital. Pulling into a busy parking lot, he found a space off to one side. He had no idea who'd designed Fort Duncan. It didn't look much like a hospital from the outside, which was maybe the point. It looked more like a construction of Lego blocks, with sections painted in different bright colors.

Striding beneath the US and Texas flags, he passed through the doors of the main entrance. After seeing his badge, the lady at the information desk provided him with some. The man called Turo—no documented last name—was in a coma from his head wound. The doctors could not say when or if he'd wake. The man named David Flores was awake, however, and could be spoken with.

The woman directed Concho to the elevators and the second floor. As soon as he stepped off the elevator, he knew something was wrong.

* * *

LIANA, WITH HAIR CUT SHORT AND FRESHLY DIED BLACK, PICKED up Zoe at the casino in a non-descript rent-a-car. They called Bearfoot and he did indeed answer the call, as he'd been ordered. He met them at the casino and guided them to the GPS coordinates on the Rez that Zoe had gotten from Jañega's phone, the coordinates where Doctor Aquila's smuggled supplies were supposed to have been dropped off.

Zoe didn't know what she expected to find. Probably nothing. But it needed checking out. They headed southwest on the reservation but would never have found the place without Bearfoot. There were few roads, all dirt and all rutted. Bearfoot finally pointed them onto what looked like an overgrown farm trail.

Tall, dead grass and lots of stunted trees and bushes lined each side of what purported to be a road. Ruts bounced them around. Reaching limbs and briars scratched the car's paint job.

"Good thing I didn't bring the Firebird," Liana said. "I'd have been pissed."

"How much farther?" Zoe asked their skinny guide.

"Just there," Bearfoot replied, pointing ahead to a small meadow bordered by a stand of oaks mixed with juniper and mesquite. "The tree where the sacred deer are born."

"What?" Zoe asked.

Liana pulled the rental to a stop at the edge of the meadow. Dry, seared grass thrust upward all around them. About fifty yards ahead stood a large, twisted oak tree. An arroyo ran behind it.

"What?" Zoe asked again.

Bearfoot looked at her. He was sweating and flushed. He looked nervous. "It's...it's a story. One my wife wrote in high school. About this big oak and how it gave birth to all the sacred deer."

Liana laughed. Bearfoot's face flashed with anger, but he didn't say anything.

"Why are you nervous?" Zoe asked.

Bearfoot shrugged.

"I don't think he likes it here," Liana said. "Reminds him of the little woman, I guess. She probably beats him at home."

Bearfoot's eyes flashed dark but again he said nothing.

Zoe sighed and pushed open her door, climbing out into the meadow. "Looks like the coordinates are right on the oak." She started in that direction.

Liana climbed out, too, and motioned Bearfoot to join her. She shoved him along after Zoe. The three reached the tree, gazed around, and glanced into the arroyo, which was dry at the moment. However, rushing waters had undermined the oak in places, leaving skeletal roots stabbed out of the bank into the open air above a dark hole.

"Down there," Zoe said. "That's where they would have hid it."

"Hid what?" Bearfoot asked.

Zoe ignored him and dropped off the bank to land a few feet down in the red sandy bottom of the arroyo. Liana and Bearfoot joined her. Strange tracks marred the dry soil.

"Cloven hooves," Liana said, raising an eyebrow. "You got little devils running around out here?" she asked Bearfoot.

"Wild pigs," Bearfoot explained. "They're all over."

Liana suddenly looked unsure of herself. "They dangerous?"

Bearfoot smirked. "Not unless they see you. Or smell you."

Liana's gaze narrowed. "You get smart, and I'll slap the snot out of you."

Bearfoot's gaze dropped.

"Enough!" Zoe snapped. She'd taken out her phone and turned on the flashlight app. She shone this into the hole under the bank.

A savage grunt answered the beam of light. Eyes flashed in the dark. Zoe cried out in shock and stumbled backward. Liana grabbed for her Glock as a chorus of squeals racketed from the hole and half a dozen small shapes and one much larger one burst out of the darkness into the day.

"Pigs!" Bearfoot shouted.

The large sow at the head of the wedge of pigs hooked her muzzle and canines at Zoe, who fell backward on her rear trying to avoid it. Liana opened fire with her Glock, three shots that hit nothing. However, the explosive crack, crack, crack, split the small sounder of feral hogs and sent them rushing in separate streams around the cluster of three humans. The animals disappeared down the arroyo.

Zoe rose shakily to her feet. Liana muttered curses under her breath as she glared after the mother hog and her offspring. Bearfoot laughed.

"Just a mother and babies," the slender Kickapoo said, before he howled another laugh.

Liana shoved him. "Shut up!"

Bearfoot sobered.

"Shut up, both of you!" Zoe snapped. She was shining her light into the hole, making sure no more pigs inhabited it. As her eyes adjusted, she saw something much more disturbing.

"Dios mío!" she said, reverting to Spanish in a moment of shock.

"What is it?" Liana demanded. She turned on the flashlight of her own phone, then squatted beside a very still Zoe and peered beneath the undercut tree.

"Damn!" she said.

"What?" Bearfoot exclaimed. "What do you see?"

Liana glanced up at the Kickapoo. "Two bodies. Those pigs were eating them."

CHAPTER THIRTY-FOUR

ON THE SECOND FLOOR OF FORT DUNCAN HOSPITAL, CONCHO unsnapped both his holsters to free his Colts for a quick draw. The elevator had deposited him in a short corridor that extended only one direction. He was looking straight down it and seeing no one. He should have.

At the corridor's end was a desk meant to block off the two rooms behind it from any easy approach. According to the info lady downstairs, those were the rooms where Turo and David Flores were housed. There should have been a cop sitting at that desk.

The Ranger could move silently when he wanted. He started down the hall, not yet drawing a weapon but with his hands hovering close to the hilts. The left side of the hallway had windows opening to the outside. He could see the parking lot and a few of the palm trees planted around the building. The right side of the hall contained hospital rooms, all with closed doors.

He reached the desk and moved around it. A few steps ahead on his left, an exit sign marked a door leading to a stairwell, but it had been chained off temporarily. No one had come or gone through there. He couldn't smell anything unusual, nor did he hear anything other than the standard beeps, clicks, and thumps of a working hospital.

With two splinted fingers on his right hand, he felt more confident of his left-hand grip and drew that pistol. He used his right hand to ease open the first door. The sound of beeping grew louder, the smells of alcohol and cleaning agents and the indelible odor of sickness that abides in every hospital grew stronger.

Except for a man lying still in a bed, the room was empty. Concho recognized the face of Turo. His chest rose and fell with shallow breathing. Pressure bandages around his legs contracted and relaxed to stimulate blood flow to his extremities. Two monitors showed green waves slithering across their screens.

The Ranger had been hooked up to enough hospital equipment in his day to recognize the heart monitor. Turo's heart beat steadily. The other monitor showed a sine wave, which surely represented a brain measure and indicated that Turo was still in a coma.

Easing the door closed, Concho moved to the second room, where David Flores must be housed. Again, he gently opened the door with his right hand. About halfway, the door caught on something. A chill leaped down his body. He pushed harder and the obstruction fell away. He stepped inside—gun ready.

A man lay on the floor dressed in the dark brown shirt and pants of the Maverick County Sheriff's Office. Parkland's guard. Concho didn't know him. It was his feet the door had caught on. But at least the man was breathing; the Ranger could hear the rasp of it.

A quick glance found the bed. David Flores lay on his back, his face a rictus and his fists clenched as if he'd been clawing at something. Bloody foam flecked his lips. His heart monitor showed a flat green line, but no alarm was sounding, which meant someone had turned it off.

Concho twisted left and right, scanning the room for intruders. No one behind the door. No one behind or under the bed. The curtains were flat against the window, hiding no shapes. Whoever had done this had come and gone.

Or!

There was another door into this room. The bathroom, which was shared by Flores and Turo. Concho moved toward it. As he did so, he heard a loud bang on the other side of the door, and a click. He grabbed the door handle and pulled it down. It was locked. That must have been the "click" he'd heard.

Running footsteps sounded from the direction of Turo's room. Concho spun and raced out the main door into the hallway. Well down the corridor, a slender hooded figure in a dark coat darted past the elevators and slammed open the door to another stairwell. The lawman tore after them.

It took him a few seconds. He threw open the door and leaped through, then paused. The stairs went up and down, but he heard no sound of fleeing footsteps in either direction. And he'd heard no other corridor door open. Whoever had been here had disappeared.

Like a ghost.

* * *

"So, who you think they are?" Liana asked Zoe, pointing at the hole under the tree where two half-eaten bodies lay.

"Were, you mean," Zoe replied.

"Yeah."

"Two men. Probably middle aged. Can't tell much more."

Bearfoot snapped his fingers. "I bet I know who they are." The two women looked over at him.

"Spill it!" Liana demanded.

"Ten-Wolves," Bearfoot said. "Rumor is he busted some smugglers on the Rez a few days ago. He shot some but supposedly two escaped. This must be them."

Zoe startled. The skinny drunk had it. It felt right. "You think Ten-Wolves killed them?"

Now, Bearfoot looked startled. He started shaking his head. "No! He wouldn't have. Not and put them here. Someone else did it."

"Who?" Liana asked.

"Whoever the delivery was intended for," Zoe said. "I'll bet. They don't seem to like failure very much."

Liana nodded. She motioned Zoe over. The two women walked a little way down the arroyo to escape Bearfoot's ears.

"You thinking what I'm thinking?" Liana asked.

"That Mexican cop from the hotel," Zoe said. "The one we took out. I bet he's the one did this."

"Most likely."

"Which means the people who were supposed to get the delivery are pissed."

"And ruthless!"

"Your kind of folks," Zoe remarked dryly.

Liana grinned. "I wonder what they're paying?"

"Since you killed their boy, I don't imagine they're looking to reward you."

"Good point! So what do we do?"

Zoe shook her head and strode away without saying anything. She returned to Bearfoot and stared at him a long minute. He wilted under the directness of her gaze.

"So," Zoe said, "you like this Ten-Wolves, don't you?"

"Can't stand him! He's an arrogant SOB."

"And you admire him for it! He's everything you want to be."

Bearfoot shook his head violently back and forth.

Zoe slipped an arm around Bearfoot's shoulders. He flinched. "Walk with me," she said, as she led him down the arroyo in the direction taken by the fleeing sounder of wild pigs.

CHAPTER THIRTY-FIVE

Concho spared a few seconds to search up and down the stairwell for any sign of where the dark figure had gone. He found none. And, he had to worry about the deputy who lay unconscious in Flores's room. The man had been breathing, but very roughly. He might need help.

With frustration clawing at him, the lawman stepped out into the hospital corridor and rushed toward the room where the deputy lay, dialing the front desk as he ran to let them know what was happening. Pushing open the door to Flores's room, he dropped to his knees beside the officer.

A strong heartbeat met the fingers he pressed to the man's neck, but the breathing had shallowed even further. He was struggling. Concho was about to roll him over and begin mouth-to-mouth when the door burst open and medical personnel flooded in.

"He's not breathing right," the Ranger said, pointing at the deputy as he leaped to his feet and backed away to give the arriving nurses room.

Two male nurses bent toward the deputy while other medical personnel converged on the bed and its clearly dead occupant. Concho found a gap in the crowd and slipped out into the corridor. A quick peek in at Turo showed the man's heart monitor still beeping. So, the shadowy figure hadn't killed him, too. Was that deliberate or a result of having been interrupted before completing the act?

Pulling out his cell phone, Concho placed a call to the Maverick County Sheriff's Office to report the incident. Then he took a moment to breathe. Something he'd barely noted about the fleeing assassin finally registered. Their legs, below the knee. Beneath the dark coat they'd worn, he'd caught the pale green of hospital scrubs. By now they could have discarded the hood and coat and walked freely past him without recognition. They could even have been one of the nurses who'd responded to the emergency.

The lawman shook his head. He felt helpless. A flash of Afghanistan darkened his vision for a moment. For some reason, his mind kept trying to connect the ghost sniper he'd dealt with in Afghanistan with the current situation. It could be a spurious thread of memory that had nothing really to tell him. Or it could be more. He needed time to think about it.

He wasn't going to get that time right now. Out the window, he saw blue lights flashing and heard sirens screech as more Maverick County police responded to his call. It had already been a long morning and was about to get longer.

* * *

Zoe kept her arm draped over Bearfoot's shoulders as they walked down the arroyo. She felt the lean Kickapoo's muscles tremble, felt the mix of tension and weakness in his whole body. He must be expecting her to kill him.

"Listen," she said. "I'm not going to hurt you. I don't harm valuable assets."

"I'm…I'm…valuable to you?"

"Yes. Certainly for now. And I also reward those who help me."

"I don't want to…help you…kill anyone."

Zoe chuckled, trying to put the man at ease. "I wouldn't ask you to do anything like that. For one, Liana likes to take care of those matters when they arise. And they haven't arisen here. Yet. And two...well, I doubt you'd have it in you anyway."

"So what do you want from me?"

"I need you to tell me what you know about Ten-Wolves."

"And you're not…going after him?"

"I'll be honest with you. He's a person of interest for us. But that doesn't mean we want him dead. It's usually a mistake to go after law-types. Too much chance of their colleagues retaliating. It's not good business."

This was all true from Zoe's perspective. She just failed to mention that Concho's death had already been ordered by the man paying her and Liana.

Bearfoot nodded. He started speaking. "He's…well, I *don't* like him. Not really. He *is* arrogant. He doesn't care much for me. But he does care about…the tribe. Even though many of them haven't treated him well."

"Because of his mixed blood?"

"That and…"

"What?"

"Gossip, maybe. His mother was a drug addict. She went off with a...non-Kickapoo and abandoned him to *her* mother. As a kid, everyone said Ten-Wolves never knew his place. He fought all the time. Made enemies."

"Like I said," Zoe replied. "Sounds like you admire him."

"Maybe. For some things," Bearfoot admitted. "He doesn't take...any crap. And he doesn't tread lightly."

"From what I've heard, he's got his fingers in a lot of corruption on the reservation."

Bearfoot shook his head. "I don't…think so. He's about as straight as they come. And maybe that's why some don't like him. He won't bend the rules for them. Even for Kickapoo. And maybe people here think he should."

Zoe *hmmed* to herself. "A very different story than I've been hearing about him."

"Hearing from who? Probably Letty Garcia? Or maybe Pete Whiteheart? They hate him because they've either been involved in corruption themselves here or had family members who have. And Ten-Wolves busted them. He doesn't care about who your relatives are. Or how much money or influence you have. If you cross the law, as he sees it, he'll take you down. He's not one to cut people slack."

"People like you?"

"Yeah, like me. And a lot of others."

"So, he's got a lot of enemies who'd like to see him taken down?"

"Yes."

"Good to know," Zoe said. She glanced up as Liana called her name.

"Something here you better see," the blonde turned brunette said.

Zoe joined her colleague, with Bearfoot trailing behind. Liana had continued to use her phone flashlight to examine the bodies in the hole beneath the tree. She'd moved from one angle to another to get the best view, and now she shone her flashlight at the bodies from an angle that revealed something new.

"An arrow!" Zoe exclaimed. "He was shot with an arrow through the throat!"

"Both of them," Liana said. "You can see the other one too if you look close."

Bearfoot gasped. Zoe glanced at him with a frown. "What?" she demanded.

"Ten-Wolves! He…he…he often uses a bow and arrows."

"But you didn't think he'd have killed these men like this?"

"I didn't…think so."

"Those enemies of his," Zoe continued. "Would they frame him for something he didn't do?"

Bearfoot looked almost relieved at the thought. "In a heartbeat," he said.

Zoe straightened. Her mind clicked over these new developments. An idea occurred. An unpleasant one. "We need to get the hell out of here," she said. She took off running for their car.

* * *

A WHIRLWIND SWEPT INTO THE SECOND FLOOR OF FORT Duncan Hospital and decided to hang out. Medical personnel, law personnel, worried hospital administrators, and a local reporter who was quickly ushered downstairs—all of them moving and talking and sharing doubts and opinions.

Isaac Parkland himself showed up, the Maverick County sheriff. Parkland was a short, stout fellow wearing a white ten-gallon hat and a western-style shirt with new jeans. Except for his height, which was about five feet seven, he looked more like your traditional Texas Ranger than Concho did. The two men stood talking in the corridor when a doctor approached.

Parkland doffed his hat. "Ma'am," he said. "What can you tell me about my officer?"

"He's been placed on a ventilator but is going to be all right. Should be fully recovered in a couple of hours."

"Great news! Thanks!"

The young woman nodded. She appeared to be of Vietnamese descent but didn't look old enough to have finished medical school.

"What happened to him?" Concho inquired.

"Curare, I believe. Or something very similar."

Parkland frowned and glanced at Concho.

"That's…" Concho began. "I've read about it. Some kind of paralyzing poison used by Amazonian tribes for hunting, isn't it?"

"Yes," the doctor replied. "It paralyzes the neuromuscular junctions. Prevents muscle movement. But it doesn't affect the heart specifically."

"That's why the deputy's heartbeat was strong," Concho said.

"Yes, but it's a good thing you called when you did. Curare paralyzes the diaphragm, too. That's how it kills. By asphyxiation."

"Is that how David Flores was killed?"

The woman shrugged. "We're not sure. Some elements seem consistent with curare poisoning. Others don't. We'll have to get a toxicology report to know for sure."

"How was it delivered?" Concho asked. "As I understand it, the tribes who use it for hunting smear it on darts."

The doc nodded. "And that's what was used here. We found a dart in both the deputy and the dead…in David Flores."

Parkland shook his head. "Not enough we have to worry about guns and knives. Now we've got poison darts."

Concho's cell phone rang. He pulled it out and checked the caller ID. "I need to take this." Stepping away down the hall, he swiped to answer. "Della," he said. "What can I do for the FBI?" He recognized the sound of rotors in the background. "Are you in a chopper?"

"I am. And this is a courtesy call. I'm on my way to the reservation. We've got two dead bodies. Perhaps involved with that smuggling operation you recently busted. We've already cleared our involvement with Sheriff Echabarri. He and his people are on their way as well."

"Good. And you called me because of the possible smuggling connection?"

"More than that."

"Oh?"

"Apparently they were both killed with a bow and arrows."

Concho swallowed a groan. He wished he'd never gotten out of bed this morning. "Where's it at?"

"I've got the GPS coordinates," Della Rice said.

"Give them to me and I'll be there as soon as I can."

The FBI agent read them off. Concho knew the location immediately. There wasn't a good map to the place. GPS was the only way to find it unless you'd been there. The coordinates were centered on the tree where all the sacred deer were born.

Can't be a coincidence, the Ranger's thoughts murmured. "I'm on my way," he said into the phone.

CHAPTER THIRTY-SIX

Liana had driven out here and left the keys in the ignition. Zoe piled in behind the wheel now and yelled for Liana and Bearfoot to hurry.

"What's going on?" Liana snapped as she leaped into the passenger seat.

"In a minute!" Zoe snapped back.

Bearfoot slid in the rear. Zoe had the car started. She glanced behind her. The road they'd come in on wasn't wide enough to turn around in. Although she didn't like to leave the tracks, she pulled forward into the meadow and made a U-turn, then accelerated down the dirt road away from the bodies, not worried about scratching the paint on the rental.

The car rocked from side to side in the ruts. Liana clung to her arm rest as she swayed back and forth. "What's going on?" the newly minted brunette repeated, louder.

"I think they're trying to frame Ten-Wolves!" Zoe responded. "And if so they might have already called the cops. We don't wanna be found there."

Bearfoot gasped in the backseat. Liana frowned. "You should let me drive."

"No time!" Zoe replied.

Liana's window was down. She leaned her head out and listened, then jerked back inside. "I hear a helicopter!"

"Cops!" Zoe said. She braked to a stop. "We've gotta hide!"

Liana reached for her gun. "There's no place here to hide and there'll be more pigs coming along this road."

"There *is* a place!" Bearfoot shouted. "Up the road. About a hundred yards on the left. There's a turnoff to an abandoned homestead. It's almost invisible."

Zoe didn't waste time asking questions. She slammed the car into drive and sent it lurching forward. Her eyes scanned the landscape to her left—trees, brush, tall grass, dirt—but she would have missed the side road without Bearfoot's warning shout.

"There! Right there!"

Zoe hit the brakes and had to back up to reach the turnoff. It looked barely passable, a narrow dirt and grass stretch between two half filled-in ditches. She pulled into it and bulled ahead, sending grass heads and pollen scattering wildly. Rocks pinged off the undercarriage. A small sapling was dragged beneath the car and raked roughly along the metal.

Zoe had thought the main way behind them was a poor excuse for a road; this hardly warranted the name. Seventy-five yards along they pulled up to what had once been a house. Only a pile of rotted wood and a half-fallen chimney remained. But a thicket of juniper crowded close and there were several big oaks whose stretching limbs would partially hide them from above.

"We can't go any farther here!" Bearfoot exclaimed as Zoe slid the rental to a stop and killed the engine. In the resulting silence, they all heard the rumble of other vehicles moving along the road they'd just abandoned.

"The pigs!" Liana hissed, pushing open her door and sliding out with her gun in her hand.

"Relax!" Zoe snapped. "You can hear them. They're not turning in here."

Liana took a deep breath and slowly calmed. "They might when they come back this way. If they have half an eye, they'll see the trail we left. The smashed down grass."

"Then we need to be gone before they return," Zoe replied. "Or when more come along the road. Or when that chopper flies over us."

"What do you want to do?" Liana demanded. "Walk out?"

Zoe glanced at Bearfoot. "What about it? Can we get out of here on foot?"

Bearfoot nodded. "Yes. I can show you. It's a few miles but I know the way."

"I don't trust him," Liana said.

Zoe considered. "I don't think we have much choice. We wipe down the car, leave it and hike out. If they *are* cops, they'll be at the scene in the meadow for a while. We'll have time."

Zoe quickly began following her own instructions. She got out and flung open both car doors on her side. Bearfoot slid free of the backseat, then stood looking uncertain.

"Get a sock, a rag, whatever," Zoe snapped at Bearfoot. "Get to cleaning off any surface you may have touched and left prints."

The Kickapoo rushed to obey. Zoe had a clean bandana in her pocket. She yanked it out and began wiping down the steering wheel, dashboard, gear shift, and door handles.

Liana glared for a moment, then joined in with, "We oughta just torch it."

"And bring that helicopter right to us?" Zoe snapped. "Keep working."

In ten minutes, they'd cleaned everything they could. "All right," Zoe said, looking at Bearfoot. "Get us outa here."

Bearfoot nodded. Liana suddenly grabbed the little man by his shirt collar and slammed him against the car. "You try to lose us," she snarled, "and I'll put a bullet in your spine and leave you to crawl."

Bearfoot nodded, terrified. His nose dripped. He looked to

Zoe in appeal but the big woman only watched. "I promise, I promise!" he said.

Zoe tapped Liana on the shoulder. "All right. Let's get going."

Liana stepped away from Bearfoot, jerking her head toward the nearby bush. In another moment the three were lost to sight while the abandoned rental car ticked and cooled behind them.

* * *

Concho bade a quick goodbye to Isaac Parkland and ran for the Dodge Durango he was driving. He peeled out of the hospital parking lot and headed for the reservation. It would typically take him half an hour to get from here to the tree where all the sacred deer were born. He pressed the gas pedal harder to the floor. Maybe he could shave off a few minutes.

Pulling onto the Rez, he powered down a dirt road into the heart of the land, and from there turned onto a rough trail leading toward the GPS coordinates Della Rice had provided. It was after midday. His stomach growled for lunch, and he told it to shut up. No time to worry about food now.

Old ruts bounced his SUV from side to side, but he could see the crushed grass and crumbled dirt indicating the recent passage of other vehicles before him. Echabarri and his deputies, no doubt. He was halfway to the meadow where he'd find the crime scene when an anomaly on his right caught his attention. Concho hit the brakes; the SUV slid to a stop. He shifted into reverse and backed up.

To his right ran an old, overgrown road that hadn't been used in a month of Sundays. It led to a long-fallen-down house built years before, even before the Kickapoo had purchased this land for their reservation. Concho had been to the site several times; there was nothing much of interest, although deer occasionally came to nibble the grass that had once been part of a well-tended yard.

The anomaly now was that someone had recently traveled the road. It wouldn't be Echabarri or any of his people. They would have gone on to the crime scene, which lay ahead another three-quarters of a mile. So, who had taken this side road and flattened the grass and shrubs?

On impulse, Concho turned onto the road and accelerated toward the site of the fallen house. The limbs of mesquite and juniper whipped along the sides of the SUV, leaving deep scratches in the white paint.

Almost unconsciously, the Ranger unsnapped the thongs holding his Colt Double Eagles in their holsters. He slowed at a glint of light ahead, which reflected from something metallic. The metal proved to be a car, a light-brown Toyota Corolla. All four doors were open, but the engine wasn't running.

"A rental," Concho murmured to himself as he pulled to a stop.

He got out slowly, drawing his left-hand Colt, keeping himself shielded behind the door of the SUV as much as he could. His ears took in every sound—a whisper of breeze through the trees, crows calling in the distance, a songbird trilling in a nearby juniper. The songbird wouldn't be here if there were more people around. The car must have been abandoned. But when?

Stepping around the SUV, Concho walked toward the rental. He glanced inside. The keys dangled from the ignition. The vehicle was clean except for a little dirt and some dead leaves tracked in by the passengers. The dashboard looked smeared, indicating that whoever had been here had wiped the car down to erase any prints before leaving.

He rested the back of his hand on the hood. Warm metal. The engine had been running less than an hour ago. Moving around the car, he searched for tracks. Scuff marks on the ground attested to more than one person. Only one identifiable track was visible, a print of half a cowboy boot in a small patch of dirt. He estimated it as a size seven and took a photograph with his phone.

Other than the one track, all he could see were flattened places in the grass where at least two people had headed into the woods. The direction they'd taken would lead them to another road a couple of miles ahead. If they'd left an hour ago, they'd be there or be close by now, but what was two miles as the crow flies was at least ten driving the backroads.

Covering his hand with his shirt sleeve, Concho pressed the button on the dangling key chain to pop the trunk. A quick check revealed only empty space. The Ranger was debating his next course of action when his cell rang.

"Yes," he answered, recognizing Roberto Echabarri's number.

"You on your way?" Roberto asked. "You need to see this."

"Almost there," he answered. He explained the find delaying him.

'What do you want to do about it?"

"Della Rice had a chopper. It there?"

"Yeah."

"Can you send one of your people up with the pilot? Have them fly over Wild Dog Road and look for any sign of folks moving through there. I think that's where this crew is headed."

"Gotcha!" Echabarri said.

"All right, I'm on my way to you."

Concho hung up and started back to his SUV, then paused by the rental car again. The doors had been left standing open; a breeze had been blowing through. But maybe…

He leaned into the front seat of the car, took a deep whiff of the air, hoping to pick up some lingering scent of aftershave or perfume, something to give him a hint as to who might have been driving the vehicle. Nothing.

He tried again in the backseat. Something familiar teased his nostrils. He frowned and began running through possibilities in his mind. The answer came, arousing surprise, then anger.

He holstered his Colt and stalked to his SUV. Afternoon had arrived on an eventful day. Shadows were stretching across the land and night was coming. He didn't like to think of what the darkness would bring.

CHAPTER THIRTY-SEVEN

A FEW MINUTES LATER, TEN-WOLVES PULLED HIS BORROWED SUV into the meadow where Sheriff Echabarri and several FBI agents clustered around a very large oak tree. This, according to a story written many years before by a young Kickapoo woman named Estrella Deer-Run, was the tree from which all the sacred deer had sprung.

No helicopter squatted in the meadow, which must mean they were aloft looking for signs of the passengers of the car he'd found abandoned. Concho strode over to the gathered officers, all of whom nodded at him. None of them seemed comfortable; Echabarri's normal bronze-toned skin looked a little gray. Something had shocked him.

"Where are the bodies?" Concho asked.

Echabarri pointed to the dry arroyo that ran behind the tree and undercut some of its roots. Concho dropped off the bank into the arroyo, puffing up dust where his boots struck. A black hole under the oak drew the eyes, but what drew his vision more were two body bags lying on the sandy ground outside the hole.

Della Rice joined the Ranger, as did Roberto. Rice leaned over and unzipped the top of the body bags and pulled each one back enough to reveal the heads and upper bodies of the dead men inside.

Roberto turned and walked away. Concho made a face but moved closer to examine the men. One was of Hispanic origin, the other of Northern European descent. Both had been… gnawed on. The light-skinned man's eyes, nose, and lips were gone. The other had an empty hole where the left cheek should be.

"Pigs?" Concho asked Rice.

The tall African American woman nodded. "Yep. Least that's what Roberto claimed. Their tracks are all over here."

Concho nodded. He leaned a little closer to look at what protruded from the necks of each man. These were arrows, made of ash, with one fletched by wild turkey feathers and the other by the black flight pinions of a vulture. The heads of each arrow protruded from the necks. Both arrowheads had been knapped from local flint.

"They're mine," Concho said as he straightened.

"Any idea how they got here?" Rice asked. "Inside these two men?"

"Sure you don't want to arrest me for murder?" the Ranger asked.

Della offered a smirk as part of her answer. "I'm pretty sure you didn't do it."

"Why's that?"

"Because you wouldn't have been stupid enough to leave your arrows in their necks. Which returns me to my question. Any idea how those arrows got there?"

Concho flashed the agent a small, quick smile, then explained. "They're unfinished. Which means they could have come from only one place. John Gray-Dove's furniture workshop."

Roberto had approached again. "Gray-Dove!" he exclaimed. "You don't think—"

Concho shook his head. "John wouldn't have given those arrows to anyone. And he sure wouldn't have used them like this. Someone must have stolen them. Once we're done here, I'll swing by his shop and check."

Rice nodded. Roberto remained silent.

"You recognize either of them?" Rice asked. "They look like the two smugglers you said got away that day?"

Concho excavated his memories of the day, trying to mentally paint the faces he'd seen. But it had been very fast, with no time to study anyone. He sighed. "One of 'em I never saw up close, but pretty sure he was Hispanic." He pointed at the one body. "The ethnicity is right on that one, but I don't know about the face."

"What about the other?" Rice asked.

"A light-skinned guy drove one of the ATVs. He had sandy hair like this one." He pointed at the second corpse. "But the face?" He shrugged. "I hit him with a gun butt. Smashed his nose and maybe left a cut above his mouth. But those are the parts missing. I can't be sure."

"The fact those parts are missing is suggestive," Rice added.

"Maybe." Ten-Wolves glanced around at the floor of the arroyo. "I see some tracks here. What have we got?"

"Three sets of footprints," Roberto said. He walked away from the bodies. The others followed. The Kickapoo sheriff pointed out sets of human prints—two in tennis shoes and one in boots.

Concho studied the tracks, which were mixed in with the cloven-hoofed prints of feral hogs, most of them small enough to be shoats. "I saw that boot print around the abandoned car," he said.

"So, are these our suspects?" Rice asked.

"Not for murder," Concho said. "Probably not at least. Those bodies have been dead for a while. Twelve to fifteen hours maybe. The hood of that car was still warm so these three were here no more than an hour or so ago."

"Criminals revisiting the scene of the crime?" Roberto asked.

Concho shrugged. "Pretty unlikely. Though stranger things have happened."

"Then why were they here?" Rice asked.

"Maybe they got a tip, too," Concho said. "I assume that's where you heard of this?" He looked at Della Rice.

"Anonymous, of course," Rice agreed. "And no luck tracing it."

Concho used his phone to take pictures of the prints.

"Recognize anything?" Rice asked.

The Ranger shook his head. "Not on the prints. But there was something familiar at the abandoned car."

"What?"

"I need you to indulge me a little while. I want to look into something to make sure. Then I promise I'll share."

Rice looked as if she were going to spit out the word "No," but just shook her head and turned away. Concho glanced over at Roberto, who'd fumbled a roll of Tums out of his pocket and was feeding two into his mouth.

He placed a big hand on the sheriff's shoulder and squeezed. "A little ginger ale might settle your stomach."

"Not sure anything's gonna help after that," Echabarri replied, gesturing toward the body bags without looking that direction.

"Guess you won't be eating any pork sausage soon."

Echabarri groaned and responded with a glare. He stuffed another Tums in his mouth. "Get away from me!" he snapped.

Concho grinned and gave the younger man's shoulder another squeeze. "Sorry. I'm a dick, I know." He headed for his vehicle.

* * *

After checking with Della Rice and getting a report that the helicopter hadn't spotted any sign of the fugitives from the abandoned car, Concho told her how to locate said car for her investigation, then headed for Kickapoo Village. He made one call on the way, to Estrella Deer-Run, to ask if her husband was home. It was no surprise that Estrella hadn't seen her husband, Bearfoot, in a couple of days.

Concho tucked that piece of information away in the cluttered attic of his mind as he pulled up in front of John Gray-Dove's automotive shop. It was after 5:00 PM, but John greeted him as he stepped into the shop's work area where the mechanic was giving an old beater Chevy an oil change.

"Good truck news," Gray-Dove said. "Engine didn't get any serious damage. I can have it ready for you in a couple of days."

"Good. Let me know how much it'll be."

Gray-Dove nodded. "We'll settle up." The Kickapoo mechanic frowned then as he studied the officer. "Something wrong?"

"Seems so. I wanted to see if you've had any break-ins recently? Anything stolen?"

Gray-Dove looked startled. "I…well, I thought perhaps I did. But nothing was missing."

"What happened?"

"Yesterday morning. When I came to work. I went into my workshop. Something felt wrong. But I could find no sign of anyone. And nothing missing."

In addition to his automotive shop, Gray-Dove kept a smaller shop out back where he built furniture for local folks. He let Concho use his tools to make arrows for his bow and had even provided him a shelf to hold his raw materials.

"Did you check my bin?" Ten-Wolves asked.

Again, Gray-Dove looked startled. "Did not. Never thought to."

"Can we now?"

Gray-Dove offered a troubled nod. He led the Ranger out the repair shop's back door and toward a one-room wooden building painted an off-white. He lifted a key chain on his belt and selected a key.

"I keep it locked so tools don't walk away."

"Hang on!" Concho said. "Let me look at the lock first."

Gray-Dove nodded. The lawman stepped past him and bent to examine the lock. He didn't worry about fingerprints. John's would be all over it and if someone else *had* been here they'd almost certainly used gloves.

No rust speckled the lock, but it was old enough for the steel to be tarnished. Yet, several shiny scratches marred the metal around the keyhole—signs the lock had been picked. Concho pointed these out to Gray-Dove, whose eyes grew more troubled.

As they stepped into the building, Concho went straight to the big white plastic bin Gray-Dove had loaned him. He swung it down onto the worktable and popped the blue lid. Inside rested ten ash arrows in various stages of completion. There should have been twelve.

Gray-Dove was shaking his head. "I only looked for missing tools."

"No reason for you to suspect this."

"What would they want with your arrows?"

"They've already used them to try and implicate me in a crime."

"I am sorry."

"Not your fault. And it didn't work anyway. Have you seen anyone around acting suspicious?"

Gray-Dove shook his head.

"What about anyone new? Anyone come in who isn't a regular?"

Gray-Dove's face wrinkled in thought. "The only person who was unusual was Isi Whiteheart," he said after a moment.

"Whiteheart? Can I ask what she wanted?"

"She spoke about me working on their farm equipment."

Concho nodded. "And no one else?"

"The...Teshigahara woman stopped by. She wanted to interview me. For her newspaper. Something about profiles of local businesses."

"What did you tell her?"

He looked miserable. “I was caught off guard. I agreed.”

Concho winced and patted the older Kickapoo on the arm. “She got me too,” he commiserated.

“You think one of them…?”

Concho cleared his throat. “It seems unlikely,” he sighed. “Call me if you think of anything else.”

“Yes,” Gray-Dove said. “But you know, many people come and go here. Including strangers. With the police department so close.”

“It’s more the non-strangers I’m thinking about.”

Gray-Dove nodded and they parted, both troubled.

CHAPTER THIRTY-EIGHT

As Concho pulled away from Gray-Dove's, his stomach began to growl like a pair of dire wolves fighting over a fresh kill. He'd really eaten nothing all day and turned up the road to the casino to grab something to tame his belly. Getting a table at the Red Sky Grill, he ordered a whole fried chicken and proceeded to devour it while letting his mind work over the events of the day and the particulars of a very strange case.

A group of smugglers had landed on the reservation with hundreds of thousands of dollars of counterfeit money, an ice chest full of black market organs, and a young girl turned into a mummy in the Aztec tradition. Concho's presence at the scene had almost certainly been a complete accident. Most everyone who could have revealed the story behind the operation had either escaped or died. The only survivor was clearly nothing more than muscle.

Then, a man named Myron Cooper had tried to kill him at the casino, apparently having been hired or persuaded to do so by Wayne Quaite, a man Concho had put away and who was dying in prison. Later, two other men had tried again to kill him, and he wondered if the two attempts were connected, or independent.

He'd also been warned by Bearfoot that two women were after him, perhaps to kill him. How was that connected to the other two attempts? And how were these events tied to the smuggling operation he'd broken up? If they were?

Then, three more deaths had happened in close procession —the one man in the hospital who might have told Concho why he'd tried to kill the lawman, and two strangers who'd been murdered and used to throw suspicion in the Ranger's direction. Although he couldn't be sure, those men were likely the same two who'd escaped him on the banks of the Rio Grande when he'd busted the smuggling operation.

From what he'd heard from his commander, the Mexican Police weren't finding anything from their side to help. And what local clues did he have as to how these events knotted together?

Two of the men who'd tried to kill him had been tied to the Whitehearts, who had reasons to hate him and want him out of the picture. But supposedly they'd been fired before coming after the Ranger. The Whitehearts were one of the few families on the Rez who might have had the money and influence to move the counterfeit twenties and the black market organs, though it didn't seem the patriarch, Sam Whiteheart's, style.

Another clue was how his unconscious mind kept returning him to his days in Afghanistan and an enemy called the Ghost Sniper. His mind didn't throw up such events without reason, though so far he couldn't fathom it.

There was one other thing, the strongest morsel so far in a dish of mostly scraps. When he'd checked out that abandoned car, he'd smelled something familiar. Bearfoot! The skinny Kickapoo who'd warned him about two women enforcers had been in that car. He was sure of it. And he'd been with two other people, both with relatively small feet. Maybe women-sized feet.

Concho realized he was picking at bones on his plate, and his server was standing off to one side looking horrified at the damage the Ranger had done to the chicken carcass. He wiped his hands on his napkin, paid his bill, and left.

It was dark; he drove home with his mind roiling. As he pulled into his driveway, he realized his day still wasn't over. Someone awaited him. A car he didn't recognize sat in front of his trailer, the lights and engine off. His left hand dropped to the butt of his Colt.

* * *

FOR THE SECOND NIGHT IN A ROW, DOCTOR GUTIERREZ Aquila entered his home office a little before 8:00 and set up a cheap laptop loaded with special software in order to make a secure connection with a correspondent in the United States. For the second night in a row, he entered a web address and typed *a Good Evening* into the fresh blank screen that resulted.

For the second night in a row, he got no response. Not at 8:00. Not at 8:05 or 8:10 or 8:15. Not at 8:30. He shut down the system and pressed the lid closed on the laptop. Rage engulfed him, though he sat in an apparent frosted calm.

At 8:45, he activated his intercom and spoke into it. "Have Eduardo Diaz report to my office."

He didn't bother to listen to the reply but rose and walked over to a sideboard where assorted liquors were displayed. From a closed section of the cabinet, he pulled forth a bottle of Macallan 30 Year Old and poured a little of the expensive Scotch whiskey into a glass. He sniffed it, letting the sharp distillate tingle his nostrils, then sat it down to allow it to breathe a moment.

A knock sounded on his door. "Come in," he called, pleased his voice sounded calm and controlled.

Eduardo Diaz, the Mexican police lieutenant, entered. He looked terrified. "Yes sir? How can I help you?"

Aquila picked up his glass, took the tiniest of sips and let it roll across his tongue. He swallowed, then spoke. "I've decided to move up my trip to the United States."

Diaz nodded and relaxed a little as he realized he wasn't in trouble. "Yes, sir. To when?"

"Tonight! We'll take your vehicle. You'll drive. I'll want one experienced man with us. Your best. Have four others follow us in an additional vehicle. I'll need my assistant as well, but I'll take care of speaking to her. She'll ride with us."

Diaz's look of terror returned. "But sir. My superiors. They—"

Aquila interrupted. "If there's a problem, deal with it." He took a deep breath and another sip of Macallan.

Diaz's mouth hung open. He closed it, then actually snapped the heels of his polished shoes together. "Yes, sir!"

Aquila shooed him with a hand. As the door closed behind the policeman, the doctor threw back the rest of the whiskey and let it burn its way down his throat.

* * *

Zoe and Liana arrived back at the Lucky Eagle Casino Hotel and went up to Zoe's room. Bearfoot had led them across several miles of reservation land to a road where they were able to call Letty Garcia for a ride. She'd sent her son, Cisco to get them. Bearfoot had made sure to be gone before Cisco arrived.

Liana's threats for Bearfoot to keep his mouth shut, or else, seemed unnecessary. He'd appeared most afraid of Ten-Wolves finding out he was involved, although that seemed more a psychological fear than a physical one. Zoe filed that little piece of information away in the mental folder she was building up about the Kickapoo Texas Ranger.

Liana sighed with relief as they entered Zoe's fourth floor room. "I'm going to take a shower," she said. "Then grab a cab to my motel in Eagle Pass."

"Right," Zoe said. "Just let me get a towel."

While Liana fired up the shower, Zoe wiped herself down with the towel, removing the sweat and dust that might make her conspicuous to other patrons of the hotel. She slid on a long bathrobe to hide her dirty clothes, then slipped out into the hallway and went along to the stairs. There was something she'd been meaning to check on.

Stepping out of the stairwell onto the third floor, she strolled along as if she belonged. The hallway lay quiet. She slowed as she approached Room 314. A day earlier, she and Liana had killed a man in that room. And there'd been no uproar yet to suggest the body had been found. Surely it wouldn't be much longer.

Abruptly, something registered. The *Do Not Disturb* sign she'd hung on the door was no longer present. That meant someone had been in the room. But who? And why hadn't the police been called about the bloody body dumped in the tub inside? The casino couldn't have kept something like that completely bottled up. Could they?

The elevator dinged at the other end of the hall and two women got off. One younger, one older. They looked like a mother and adult daughter. Zoe passed them, then surreptitiously glanced at them from behind. They stopped in front of 314. The elder slid her electronic key in the lock, pushed open the door and stepped inside. The second woman followed. There were no screams.

Something was very wrong.

CHAPTER THIRTY-NINE

A strange car sat dark in Concho's driveway. He studied it briefly, then scanned his surroundings—the house and yard. No sign anywhere of an ambush. Drawing his left-hand Colt, he slid cautiously out of the SUV, leaving his headlights on and keeping his vehicle between himself and the other.

The dome light switched on in the car. He glimpsed a dark-haired head, and for an excited instant thought the figure was Maria Morales. When the face turned toward him, though, he saw it wasn't. He frowned.

Isi Whiteheart!

Isi opened her car door and stepped slowly out. A crooked smile carved her features. She raised her hands as if surrendering.

"Forgive me, Ranger," she said. "It didn't occur to me that in your line of work you'd be suspicious about an unrecognized car stopped in your driveway at night."

Concho took a breath; it wasn't cold enough for his breath to smoke. He holstered his Colt and stepped around the SUV to face the woman. "I wish I could afford not to be paranoid," he responded.

Isi nodded, then moved slowly toward him as she lowered

her hands. The glow of Concho's headlights limned her. She wasn't wearing her usual jeans tonight, but a long blue cotton dress speckled with white flowers. Whatever makeup or perfume she wore, it smelled like blackberries and cream.

"I...well," Isi said, "I hoped to continue the conversation we started the other night in front of the casino. I had some time so..." She shrugged and pointed at the car.

Concho nodded and relaxed. "Of course. You should come in." He reached into the SUV and turned off his headlights, then strode toward his front door. Isi followed.

A few minutes later, the two were seated at the bar separating Concho's small kitchen from his den. "Would you care for something to drink?" the lawman asked. "I'm afraid I don't have a wide selection. There's milk, soda, or water."

"Actually," Isi said, as she set her rather large purse on the bar in front of her and reached in, "I brought a drinkable gift." She drew out a tan, rectangular paper bag with the Spanish word "café" printed on the side. "This is a Mexican bean. You can't get it in the US. I fell in love with it when I was at Universidad Nacional Autónoma de México. Brought a good supply home with me. I thought you might enjoy it."

Isi handed the bag across the bar to Concho and he took it, blinking in surprise. "Thanks," he said. "I actually hardly ever drink coffee, but I appreciate it. And I'm sure Maria will enjoy it. When she's over." He smiled. "She's something of a coffee fiend. Would you like me to brew *you* a cup?"

Isi looked stricken. "Oh, no! I'm sorry. I guess I assumed all law officers drank gallons of coffee."

Ten-Wolves smiled to ease the apparent sting. "Don't worry about it. And thank you for the kind thought. It won't go to waste. A lot of officers do drink the stuff, of course. I'm rare in that regard."

The same smile from before quirked the left corner of Isi's mouth. It was certainly a charming expression.

"Rare in many regards, I'm told," Isi replied.

Heat flushed Concho's cheeks. "Uhm, well, you shouldn't

believe everything you hear," he muttered, and wondered if he could sound any more lame.

Isi's next smile was quirked a little more strongly. "Maria! Maria Morales, I guess. The mall manager. She's your…girlfriend?"

There might have been the faintest emphasis added to "mall manager" but Concho couldn't be sure. "She is," he said.

Isi nodded. Her smile deflated. "Well, I hope that's a happy thing. For you."

Feeling unaccountably embarrassed, Concho chuckled to cover it. "You know how it is. You take the good with the bad."

"Of course."

Ten-Wolves immediately wished he hadn't used the word "bad," but it was too late. "So...what did you want to talk about?" he asked, to switch the subject.

Isi shrugged. She stood up casually and came around the bar to stand closer to him. The scent of blackberries intensified. "Oh, nothing in particular. I just wanted us to get to know each other. The antagonism between my family and our local law officers is really counterproductive." She placed her right hand on the bar close to Concho's. The nails were painted red but carefully trimmed.

Concho felt his face flushing and considered the best excuse he could give to stand up and step away. Before anything reasonable occurred to him, Isi leaned over and gave him a quick kiss on the side of the mouth. He reflexively jerked his head back. Isi straightened abruptly. A whole series of emotions flashed across her face—shock, embarrassment, anger, and back to embarrassment.

"I'm…I'm sorry! I shouldn't have done that."

No, you shouldn't have, he thought. But he didn't know how to say it without sounding mean. "It's OK," he said instead. "You caught me by surprise. I...well, Maria and I. We're very close."

"You love her?"

"I do."

"And she loves you?"

"I think she does."

Isi nodded. She moved away, then abruptly swung around again. Her smile was back in place. Her eyes gleamed. "I still hope we can be friends."

"Of course. That would be nice."

Isi's smile flickered on and off, like electricity in a rising storm. "You know where I live." She reached in her purse again and took out a small square of paper. She placed this on the counter. "My cell phone number. If you ever want it. But I have to go now." She grabbed her purse from the bar and strode swiftly toward the door.

Concho let her go; it was a relief to be alone, until he suddenly started missing Maria. He took out his phone and swiped to Maria's number. His finger hovered over the call button for a long moment.

He didn't press it.

* * *

Zoe rushed to her room in the Lucky Eagle Hotel. She caught Liana fresh from the shower, dressed in a fluffy white hotel dressing gown with her new, short black hair wrapped in a towel.

"I'm this close to pulling out," Zoe almost barked at Liana. She held up her thumb and forefinger a quarter inch apart. "This is why I didn't want to do this kind of thing anymore!"

Liana frowned. "What's got your panties in a wad?"

"I went by Room 314. It's been rented. I saw people going in."

Liana pulled the towel off her head and scratched her cheek. "So? The hotel people found the body and kept it quiet."

Zoe shook her head. "No way. They would have called the cops. And even if the cops were circumspect, some kind of uproar would have happened. People would have noticed.

We'd have heard. Somebody else cleaned the scene. And did it professionally."

"You're thinking the people who were supposed to get the shipment from Aquila?"

"Gotta be. Leticia Garcia and her bunch wouldn't have done it. Or been so smooth about it."

"Maybe this Concho dude got it done. If he's crooked as they say. He's got allies here."

"That's another thing. I've been studying on this Ten-Wolves thing. Feeling people out. Letty Garcia's crew are the only ones accusing him of being corrupt. And we've both hung around criminals enough to recognize her for what she is. Everyone else around here either loves him or at least respects him. He's like a local hero. I'm not buying he's behind robbing Aquila."

Liana looked surprised. "You figure he was just at the wrong place at the wrong time? How many times have we heard that excuse from somebody? And how many times has it been true?"

"There's always a first time," Zoe said.

"I don't believe in coincidences."

Zoe shook her head. "I don't either. But seems like someone is very interested in setting this Texas Ranger up for a fall. And I don't like to be used in someone else's game."

"What does it matter anyway?" Liana said. "Even if we can't get the goods on the dude for stealing Aquila's shipment, we're still supposed to take him out."

"I don't know. We're paid to act in the best interests of our client. If Ten-Wolves really was in the wrong place at the wrong time, then it was just bad luck. And taking out an innocent lawman—a decorated Texas Ranger even—would stir up more hell for Aquila than it would be worth. Not to mention for us."

"Maybe," Liana agreed.

"You know it would."

Liana frowned. "You going soft on me?"

Zoe had been pacing. She froze and turned sharply on Liana. A retort formed on her lips, but she let if escape as nothing more than a breath. "You need to get dressed and get out of here," she finally said. "Get back to your room in Eagle Pass and get the Firebird packed for a quick departure if things go sideways."

"And go where? If we don't take out Ten-Wolves, we can't go back to Aquila."

"Let me handle Aquila. I'm going to call him tonight. As for Ten-Wolves, I didn't say we *weren't* going to kill him. I need more information first."

"How you plan on getting that 'more'?"

Zoe looked distracted. "Leave it to me."

CHAPTER FORTY

CONCHO STEPPED OUT ONTO HIS SMALL BACK DECK. THE MOON was rising, looking like an upside-down slice of watermelon on the horizon. The winter had been mostly mild so far and tonight was no exception. He didn't need a jacket.

He remembered his dream of a few nights before, when the moon had settled in his yard like a big glowing tent. First there'd been a woman inside the moon who reminded him of Maria, and an infant he'd thought was his. Then the child mummy appeared on the ground, in the shadows, grabbing at him, pleading for him to help her "rest."

He shook his head back and forth. He could not understand any message in that dream. If it had one. But there was something else here with him tonight—as he looked out over the dark landscape of southern Texas, alike in many ways to the landscapes in Afghanistan where he'd fought a war.

He remembered another night.

Afghanistan, 2010.

A sky of black, like you only see in places beyond the towns, beyond the reach of people. Or when people are too afraid to show the light because that's how the dark things will find them.

Concho wasn't afraid of the dark; as a child on the reservation, he'd spent many nights in the wilds, maybe with the moon for company, maybe just with the stars. Tonight, the moon was down. There were only *the stars.*

Concho sat in a nest of boulders, part of a moraine dropped here by some ancient glacier. A pair of night vision goggles amplified the ambient starlight and let him watch the world through a swimming green haze. Beneath the mask he wore warpaint of red ocher in streaks down his face. Tonight was a war within a war.

An M4A1 carbine leaned against a boulder next to him, but in his hands the Army Ranger held a much older weapon, or at least a modern replica of such a weapon. This was a black carbon steel longbow with a synthetic quiver containing fifteen broadhead arrows of silver and red.

Concho waited for someone. With bad intent. Where he sat lay in a valley between two rocky outcrops that would have been difficult to climb without making noise. And at the end of the valley, over a ridge, rested a big encampment of US military troops and their Iraqi allies. A perfect target for the ghost sniper. Or so the Ranger hoped.

Ten-Wolves had put together a mental portfolio on the sniper *from dozens of reports about the secretive killer and a few sightings of his own. The man liked to move and set up at night, with more than one easy withdrawal route handy. He'd strike and disappear. He'd killed more than a dozen officers, some of them American, some Iraqi. The encampment beyond the ridge had plenty of worthy targets for the huntsman.*

Concho had only one worthy target this night. He intended to kill the ghost sniper, and he'd gotten permission from his commander to try. So now he waited, a predator in the darkness.

Sometime around 2:00 in the morning, Concho became aware of a presence. It wasn't a sound he'd heard. It wasn't some scent his nostrils had detected. It was tactile, as if his senses were a spider web and something had brushed against a strand.

Every molecule of brain and muscle became alert. The urge to move was almost overwhelming but he fought it down. Too many hunters made that mistake. At the moment when the prey offered itself, the hunter shifted position to better prepare for a strike. And the prey fled.

If anything, Concho became even more motionless, not even allowing his head to turn or his nostrils to flare. Again came the flash of a presence. Closer now. The air seemed to eddy. Exultation set the Ranger's heart to pounding; he fought an internal war to calm it.

A boulder moved in the green light of his goggles. It wore a twisted bush upon its back. The boulder sprouted legs. It became a man. Slender. Wearing a turban of leaves rather than cloth. Covered with dirt and local seed pods. As Concho himself was covered.

Even the sniper's rifle resembled part of the natural world, like a long stick knotted with growths. But that, at least, was unmistakably a tool of death, the rifle of a long-distance killer.

The man moved again, perhaps two inches. In total silence. He wasn't quite on his belly but close. Ten-Wolves had picked an ambush spot with a lot of cover. And his enemy was using that same cover for himself.

Concho could see the sniper was going to pass about a dozen feet to his left. A gap in the rocks there gave the Ranger room. He wouldn't have much time but thought he'd have one shot.

But the sniper was not prey. He was as much of a predator as Concho. Perhaps more. His senses, too, were honed; they fed him something. Ten-Wolves saw the man stiffen, noting it only from a sudden quiver in the bush strapped to the fellow's back. The time to strike was now; in an instant it would be gone.

Concho drew his bow string and released. The broad headed arrow flashed forward, covering the dozen feet in less than an eye blink. Warned by instinct, the sniper was already rolling to one side. The arrow did not strike squarely but punched in beneath the man's shoulder. A low grunt followed the blow.

The man rolled into darkness; Concho heard a snapping sound. He moved instinctively, throwing himself out of his refuge through a withdrawal route he'd prepared.

Something hit inside the nest of boulders where the Ranger had crouched. It bounced off a rock and detonated. Concho was face down and burrowing; a blast of heat and shrapnel pummeled over his head. A grenade. A small one.

A glance up at the rocky nest he'd just abandoned showed the twisted remains of his M4A1 carbine. Didn't matter. He still had his bow, and a .45. He rose to a crouch and darted forward, his eyes scanning everything. The green world swam before his goggled eyes.

The ghost sniper was gone, but not without a trace this time. His rifle remained on the rocks like a dead snake. And there was blood—like splotches of metallic black paint on the stones.

Concho traced the trail as far as he could with his eyes. The man was beelining for one of the rocky outcrops ahead, where there'd be plenty of hiding places. Ambush ground.

But Concho had to go after him. The wound he'd inflicted likely wasn't fatal. Certainly not if the man got to someone who could help him. The Ranger had to follow, to finish the job—even though he knew the man would have at least one more gun besides his lost rifle. And, of course, wounded prey is the most dangerous of all.

CHAPTER FORTY-ONE

Concho's phone rang, interrupting his reverie. He swiped to answer when he saw the ID—Earl Blake, the coroner.

"Earl, you got another story about fossilized feces for me?"

"That joke's getting old."

"Eh, I don't know. Seems like it might have a little mileage left."

"Uh hmm."

"But what did you have to tell me of import?"

"Trying to put things together about that mummy. And why someone would steal it."

"I'm listening."

"The data I had from the MRI. All gone, of course. And I wondered why."

"Because it showed something the thief didn't want us to know."

"Exactly! And what could that be?"

"I've got nothing."

"All right. Bear with me here. Mummies don't normally have sentimental value. Not personal sentiment, I mean. It's not like they're the mother or the child of someone living. People care about them historically, or ethnically. But not individually."

"Makes sense."

"But what if someone *did* care about this mummy on a personal level?"

"Aren't you contradicting yourself?"

"I don't think so. I'm remembering little things I noticed when I was preparing the mummy for the MRI. And I've got a thought. I rejected it at first but it's growing on me."

"I'm way lost."

Blake pushed out a breath that rattled in the phone. "I don't think the mummy was old. It was convincing. I think it was made using old techniques but that it was, in fact, a recent death. Made to look old for either sentimental purposes or…"

"To cover a murder."

"Maybe!"

Ten-Wolves scratched his chin. "That changes a whole lot of things."

"Yes, I guess it does."

"How sure are you of the idea?"

"More and more all the time."

"All right. I've got to give it some thought. Thanks for the intel."

"No problem."

The two men hung up.

Concho felt the need to speak with Meskwaa, a Kickapoo elder who was his mentor after a fashion and the closest thing he had to family on the Rez. However, though he'd given Meskwaa a cell phone, the elder never kept it charged. And it was already nearing 10:00 PM. Meskwaa's place was a longish drive, and he didn't want to disturb the old man so late.

But maybe he didn't have to. Meskwaa had occasional visions that had helped solve mysteries, but, increasingly over the past year, the lawman had begun to have visions as well.

Both waking and sleeping. Some of them had made little sense; others had been helpful.

Meskwaa pinned all such visions on supernatural forces. Concho's rational mind still insisted it was the subconscious putting together vague clues the conscious mind had barely noticed. But did the source of the answers really matter? If they helped?

Maybe he could induce such an experience. He'd seen Meskwaa do it enough. Nodding to himself, he headed into his trailer to prepare.

* * *

GUTIERREZ AQUILA GOT OFF THE PHONE WITH ZOE DESAINT. He did not like what he'd heard, and as a result had not told the young woman he was already in the United States, currently staying at a friend's house outside Eagle Pass. Using the same burner phone he'd spoken to deSaint with, Aquila placed another call. A woman's voice answered.

"Liana Spencer," Aquila said.

"Yes, sir!" Liana replied.

"Can you be discreet?"

"I can."

"I just spoke with Ms. deSaint and am concerned."

"I am as well."

"Has she been compromised?"

"Not by Ten-Wolves directly. But she's convinced herself he's innocent of what he's been accused of."

"That seems highly unlikely. I don't know anyone over the age of four who is innocent."

"I told her much the same."

"Will she be able to do the job for which I'm paying her?"

"I hope so. But if she doesn't, I can."

"Potentially, that raises a much bigger issue."

Liana paused for a long moment before finally responding. "I realize."

"It may call for a more drastic solution than originally planned. Are you up to such a challenge?"

No pause this time. "I am," Liana answered. "Though such changes require negotiations."

"Of course. Should an additional one million pesos suffice?"

"Forty-nine thousand dollars. I believe it will."

"And, naturally, moneys previously determined to pay your colleague would accrue to you as well."

"I understand. But only if it becomes necessary."

"Of course. And one more thing."

"Yes?"

"Jañega!"

"I'll make sure you get him. Or I can take care of it for you at no extra charge."

"I'll want him delivered."

"I'll see to it."

"I'm putting my faith in you."

"It'll be justified."

"Good!" Aquila hung up. After dropping the phone into a trash compacter where it would be crushed and disposed of, he rejoined his friends for a late supper of grilled duck and a lightly chilled Bordeaux.

* * *

CONCHO HAD A FIREPIT IN FRONT OF HIS TRAILER. IT STOOD near a giant mesquite tree with several nylon lawn chairs scattered around. Sometimes in cool weather he'd build a fire and sit and read, or when Maria was over, they might char hot dogs and toast marshmallows. He'd imagined at times telling his children stories around the fire or teaching them to make s'mores. He'd never used it for anything like what he intended to use it for tonight.

Once he had a good blaze going in the pit, Ten-Wolves went back into his trailer and returned with several items. First was the medicine shield he'd made from local wood and the hide of a white boar. Meant for protection against spiritual rather than physical attacks, it bore marks of power in the center and around the edges at the four cardinal points. He hung this on a branch of the mesquite.

Next, he unslung his war bow from over his shoulder. He'd made this, too, from an Osage orange tree growing on the Rez, strengthening it with deer hide and buffalo horn. He placed this across two lower limbs of the mesquite.

He took the silver badge off his shirt, which was made—as all Ranger badges were—from a Mexican five-peso coin and stripped off the cotton shirt and tossed it across one of the lawn chairs. He'd already begun to sweat lightly from the fire, and shadows of light and dark flickered across his massive shoulders and chest.

Pinning the badge to the pocket of his jeans, Concho pulled one more object out of the pocket. This was a small silver tin of ocher, not the red he usually wore as warpaint, but white. He drew up fingerfuls of the pale mineral and smeared S-shaped streaks down from beneath his eyes to his jawline. He dashed a streak across his forehead, and thicker horizontal and vertical stripes down his chest.

When the tin was empty, he placed it on the ground. Taking down the medicine shield, he hooked it over his left forearm, where it was meant to be carried. He took the bow in his hands and knelt in front of the fire. On his hips he still wore the twin Colt Double Eagle .45s, which felt as much a part of his heritage now as the bow.

Closing his eyes, he composed himself. Deep breaths filled his lungs. His ears began to hum. He was Kickapoo; he was African. He had the lineages of Europeans and Asians within him. He was Texan. He was many bloodlines, some so ancient as to not even be human.

Out of nowhere, it began. Something began. Energy leaped from the mesquite tree to his medicine shield. Or so it felt. That energy twisted like snakes along his muscles. Fatigue dissipated. When he opened his eyes again, they gleamed a primeval red in the firelight. Acting on impulse, on instinct, he scooped up a small handful of dust and blew it into the flames.

The night erupted.

CHAPTER FORTY-TWO

THE NIGHT ERUPTED IN A CACOPHONY OF VOICES. THEY RUSHED in on Concho from every direction. They struck him, pummeling. Some loud, some barely murmuring. Some pleading, some belligerent. It was vaguely like the time he'd taken peyote in a Native religious ritual, but without the physical sensations—the stomach rumblings and nausea.

And now the voices weren't the only thing seeking his attention. At the edge of light and shadow, where the firelight flickered, amorphous shapes began to move. Scenes began to form and dance. Was this what Meskwaa experienced when he had visions? If so, how did he make sense of it?

The most rational part of Concho's mind insisted the voices and movements were mere personifications of his thoughts, of his subconscious. But a larger part of himself no longer cared about the explanation, only about the experience and what he might learn from it.

One scene gained strength, began to pull at him, to draw him in. It wasn't what he expected. It was something already begun. But Meskwaa had always told him to trust the vision. He let it take him.

Afghanistan, 2010. Hunt for the ghost sniper.

The sniper's rifle lay in the dirt in front of Concho. He could make it out through his night vision goggles as a long piece of blued steel framed in wood. How many men had it killed? How much blood had it spilled? A soldier of his own ODA was dead because of this thing. It didn't matter that he'd only met the man a few days before his death. They were brothers-in-arms.

Anger surged in the Army Ranger like a flood. He picked up the weapon. His hands began to twist at the barrel and the stock; the muscles in his arms and across the wide shoulders began to cord.

Anger built to rage; sweat burst from his pores. The wooden stock of the gun broke in his hands. He grasped the weapon by the barrel and swung it up over his head and brought it down onto a boulder. Pieces spanged off into the darkness. He brought it down again and again on the rocks, until it was a mangled obscenity barely recognizable as a gun.

He dropped it, turned, and looked into the darkness, his savage gaze following the faint glow of the wounded sniper's blood trail. It smelled like copper and iron. Rage congealed, grew cold. Hefting his bow, he slipped through the rocks and began to stalk.

The blood spatters were fewer and fewer. Until, abruptly, he found one more large splotch. Lying in it were the broken halves of the arrow. Concho bent close to study them.

The arrowhead must have punched all the way through the shoulder and the sniper had sawed away the aluminum haft of the arrow with a knife to rid himself of the thing. He had to have done so in silence. Concho had heard no moan of pain or grunt of effort. It was an almost superhuman act.

Beyond the gout of blood lay only a few more sticky droplets. The man had found some way to stop his bleeding, something to pack his wound with. But he'd lost a lot of vital fluid. He might have water with him in a canteen. Perhaps some simple pain relievers. But he wouldn't survive alone for long. He would be seeking help.

Concho studied his surroundings. The blood trail led directly toward a tall bluff, which would surely have nooks and crannies at its base to shelter in. It is the instinct of every wounded beast to find a place to hide. Of course, the sniper was no beast. He was a man. As Concho was a man. As a man, he'd know that sheltering would not help him replace the blood he'd lost.

The moon was down. Even with his goggles, the Ranger could see only the outlines of rocks and brush close to him. But he'd studied this landscape during the day. He called the memory up in his head.

The sniper was not a beast. Nor was he prey. He was a predator. And when predators are wounded, they may seek to escape but they always keep an eye out for a place to ambush whoever has hurt them. That's what Concho would do. He felt sure the sniper would do the same.

The mental image of this landscape snapped into clarity. He knew where the sniper must be headed. The man had a head start but blood loss would slow him. Turning at a right angle to the wounded man's trail, Concho began to run. If he were right, he'd have another chance to stop the sniper. If he were wrong, the man would certainly live to kill again.

Dawn was not far off; already a creeping gray had begun to tinge the blackness. Every instant, his vision improved. But that was a two-edged sword. What he could see, could see him. He crossed a short ridge separating this valley from the next and went to ground before the light revealed him.

Concho's vision altered. At first, it had been only a more emotionally intense version of the Afghanistan reveries he often experienced, with everything seen from *his* point of view and through the night vision goggles he'd worn at the time. But now it expanded. He looked down from above.

The green distortion of the goggles no longer affected him. A dim yellow-white glow suffused everything. Brighter than it had been at the actual moment. He didn't know what that meant. Would things continue to unfurl the way they'd really happened, or would there be changes? He'd find out; he couldn't stop this vision. Even if he'd wanted to.

A low, rocky ridge. Eroded. Crusted with a crop of boulders and a few leathery bushes. No curve of sun yet on the horizon but a wispy red-yellow line marks it as coming. The sky and land are graying. A figure moves in the wilderness, weaving in and out of stony outcrops. It strives to conceal itself, but weakness is evident in its gait. It stumbles.

The figure nears the top of a ridge and goes to its belly, crossing the highest point like a lizard, using only legs and a right arm to inch ahead. The left arm is bound to its side. Beyond the crest, the figure slumps down in a small hollow to rest. Clearly now, it is a man, dressed in desert camo and wearing wilted twigs and dead leaves glued to his uniform.

The man pauses for several minutes and sips from a canteen at his belt. He starts forward again, looking toward a distant blue mountain where he knows he'll be safe. He thinks of recovery. And of vengeance against the one who has hurt him.

Rising like a shark from the ground behind the man, a new figure appears, massive and dark against the gray rocks and tan desert. This man has lain for over an hour in complete stillness, covered with dust and fragments of stone, burrowed like just another boulder in the detritus.

Concho has his bow in his hands. As he rises, the sniper hears him and spins about, grabbing at a holstered pistol by his side. The big Army Ranger hooks the sniper's leg with the curve of the bow and yanks.

The man goes down and Concho steps forward and kicks the pistol out of the sniper's hand. He nocks an arrow and draws the bowstring back to rest beside his cheek. The scarlet and silver broadhead of the arrow is centered on the other man's chest.

"You can die here," he says softly. "Or surrender. I'll take you prisoner."

"Don't shoot!" the sniper says in English, with a New York accent. He fumbles at his throat and pulls a pair of G.I. dog tags from under his shirt. They wink in the early light.

Concho's vision ended as abruptly as it had arrived. His eyes refocused on the night and his fire, which was quickly burning itself to embers. The voices and images were all gone. The darkness felt lonely without them.

Churning the events of the vision over in his mind, Concho tried to make sense of them. Everything he'd seen had happened just as originally experienced, though seeing part of it from outside himself was new.

He remembered the shock of hearing the ghost sniper's voice—the New York accent coming from an Arabic-looking face he'd expected to speak in Dari. Turned out the man was an American citizen, an ex-solider and defector, which explained how he'd understood American military procedures so well.

But what did the story of the ghost sniper have to do with the problems on the Rez today? The sniper spoke English perfectly, though it had not been his first language. He'd been a mixture of heritages. Just as Concho and so many of his fellow Kickapoo were. Most importantly, the man had been able to hide in plain sight. If there was meaning here it must involve one of those three points. Or all of them.

Concho mulled over the information. Meskwaa said that understanding the meaning of a vision often took time. But he was out of time. He needed answers. Punching his leg with frustration, he pushed to his feet. He scanned his yard. His eyes caught and lingered on one specific spot—where Isi Whiteheart had parked during her visit.

A thought hit him like a douse of cold water. He hurried into his house.

CHAPTER FORTY-THREE

Concho strode over to the bookshelves in his living room. Several months previously, his trailer had been deliberately burned down. The most personal loss—for him—had been his bookshelves loaded with works ranging from the fictional worlds of Edgar Rice Burroughs and Jack London, to the naturalist essays of Loren Eiseley and Lewis Thomas, to the political and historical efforts of Dee Brown and W.E.B. Du Bois. With many, many others to boot.

As a somewhat lonely kid, books had served as excellent companions, ones that never deserted him. He'd still owned copies of books he'd bought at Scholastic Book Fairs when he was twelve and thirteen. His grandmother had preserved them for him until she died, and after she passed, Meskwaa had retained them until he came home from the army and joined the Texas Rangers. It had hurt bitterly to lose them.

He'd slowly been rebuilding his destroyed collection, though it was still depressingly slender compared to what he'd had before. Only one book had survived from that earlier time, and only because it had been in the glove box of his truck when the fire was set.

He studied his poetry shelf. His eyes skipped over works by

Ray Bradbury, N. Scott Momaday, nila northSun, and Dylan Thomas. He found the blue cover he was seeking and pulled it out. Tessa Teshigahara had given this to him when he'd first met her, at a party at the casino. It was a collection of poems by Native American writers, most of them unknowns.

Teshigahara had edited and published the volume and had drawn the cover herself. It featured a simple sketch of a medicine shield. The law officer hadn't had a chance to read it, but he'd glanced through it. And something he'd seen on that glance had stayed with him. He was sure the glance had prompted his memories of the ghost sniper in Afghanistan, and his vision tonight. It might have been affecting his dreams for days without him being aware of it.

Flipping quickly through the volume, which only contained forty poems, he came to page thirteen and a short, thirteen-line poem in four stanzas. *The title!* He'd remembered it. It had reminded him of the war. *Ghosts and Arrows*. The author too. Though he'd forgotten the name until tonight.

Tallulah Whiteheart. Isi's mother.

Ghosts and Arrows

Sky like a bright knife
An altar of buffalo horn
Where warriors dance

Ceremony of life
To pray for arrows
That cleanse the sorrows

A child in gloom
Will wield the moon
To blind the wolf

As ghosts they were
Ghosts they are

Only ghosts
And no more

* * *

GUTIERREZ AQUILA STOOD ALONE ON THE PATIO OF HIS friend's house outside Eagle Pass, Texas. He'd been two days without completing his normal full-body workout. As a stop-gap, he held a grip exerciser in each hand, continually squeezing and relaxing. He was up to a count of five hundred when the door opened behind him, and Eduardo Diaz approached.

The skinny Mexican police lieutenant had grown even thinner in the last few days. And had lost more of his hair. Perhaps it was time to consider replacing this servant, who did not appear to be dealing well with the stress of balancing his work for Aquila with his role as a law officer.

"You sent for me, sir?" Diaz asked.

Aquila did not stop working the grip exercisers. "Yes. I want you to position three of our men at the reservation casino. I want them ready for action, but they are *not* to act until they get specific word from me. Is that understood?"

Diaz nodded. "Certainly, sir."

"There are two people they are to watch for. Concho Ten-Wolves, an American law officer. And Zoe deSaint, one of our own citizens. They should already be familiar with the features and natures of both. Neither is to be touched until I give specific orders. If I give them."

"Understood, sir."

"One more thing." Aquila took a small photo out of his shirt pocket. He held it in his closed hand for a moment, then reluctantly passed it to Diaz. "This woman! Have your men memorize her face. Under no circumstances—even up to their own impending deaths—are they to harm this woman or allow her to come to harm. If she *is* harmed, in whatever way, I will have you and your men skinned alive and fed slowly to my dogs. I trust I'm clear!"

Diaz blanched but nodded. His voice shook. "Certainly, sir." He took the picture and studied it a long moment. He seemed about to say something and thought better of it. Instead, he tucked the photo carefully into his own shirt pocket. "Will that be all, sir?"

"For now." Aquila turned away in dismissal and looked off the patio at the night.

* * *

ZOE DESAINT LEFT HER ROOM IN THE LUCKY EAGLE HOTEL and rode the elevator to the second floor. She wore an unusual outfit for her. Not pants and a T-shirt, but a thick, blue out-of-style dress with tan nylons and orthopedic shoes. A large shawl draped her shoulders and dangled all the way to her waist. Beneath the shawl, at the small of her back, rested a Glock 40. She'd used a temporary coloring spray to add gray highlights to her hair, and a knitted cap sitting atop her head completed the strange ensemble.

It was 10:00 PM. The second floor, which was where management offices and meeting rooms were located, lay quiet, although still brightly lit. As Zoe passed the office of the casino manager, she noted a dimmer light burning inside. Everything was as expected.

It was surprisingly easy to find the names and identify the personal habits of company employees in the United States. They were so eager to give you information and so...regular in their behaviors. So, Zoe knew that Melissa Nolan, chief executive officer of the Lucky Eagle Casino and Hotel, routinely worked until ten while her administrative assistant left hours earlier.

An alcove for a water fountain stood across from the entrance to Nolan's office. Zoe leaned there. She wasn't thirsty but she'd pretend to be if anyone came past. No one did.

At three minutes after ten, Nolan's light clicked off. Another two minutes passed and Melissa Nolan herself stepped out of her office into the hallway. She'd dressed this day in a yellow business skirt and jacket with a starched white shirt beneath. A matching purse hung over her shoulder. She was lovely, showing no sign in her face or hair or clothes of having spent a long day at work.

Nolan startled as she saw Zoe, who had her back turned and was sipping from the water fountain, but the startle quickly faded at what appeared to be an elderly woman simply getting a drink. Nolan locked the office door and started down the hall.

Zoe straightened and drew her Glock. She unrolled the knit cap down to cover her face, revealing it as a ski mask, then stepped up quickly behind Nolan and pressed the tip of the weapon into the yellow jacket.

"Don't scream or run and this will all end easily for us both!" Zoe whispered softly. "I have no wish to harm you."

"My...my wallet's in my purse. You can have it."

"That's not why I'm here. I have a few questions about your operation here. Nothing proprietary. "Let's step into your office, shall we?"

Nolan took a shallow breath that shuddered a little. She turned back to her office. She still held her keys in her hand. As she unlocked the door, Zoe crowded her inside, careful not to be too rough. She didn't want a fight when there didn't have to be one.

"Please stand still!" Zoe ordered.

She locked the door behind them and flipped on the light in the outer office, which was less suspicious than leaving the light off and having someone pass by and hear people inside in the dark.

"What do you want?" Nolan asked, without turning around. "We don't keep any money here."

Zoe heard the nervousness in the woman's voice but admired her control. "I'm not here for money. Or for you. I want some information. I need to know everything you can tell me about Concho Ten-Wolves. And I need to see any official records you have on him. Debts, earnings. Whatever?"

"That won't be possible," Nolan replied.

"It better be. Or I'll stop being nice."

CHAPTER FORTY-FOUR

Concho reread Tallulah Whiteheart's poem a second and third time. An eerie feeling scritched up and down his spine. Too much of it touched on things the woman could not know, and he'd long ago stopped believing in coincidences.

The title, "Ghosts and Arrows," echoed so closely the elements of his clash with the ghost sniper in Afghanistan, which had never been detailed in any official documents. "The child in gloom will wield the moon to blind the wolf." The wolf tied him to the poem directly, although at least wolf was a common word in Native American poetry.

But "wield the moon?" Concho remembered his dream of the moon as he came back down to earth in his backyard, and how the child mummy had blocked his way to it and begged for help. The mummy could easily be represented by the phrase, "child in gloom." But if this poem had any connection to that dream, the mummy's request for help would seem to be a lie, something meant to be used against him. And the repetition of "ghosts" in the last stanza could be interpreted as a threat.

There was more. He considered the four stanzas, each of three lines except for the last. Both four and three were spiritual numbers to many Native American tribes, including the Kickapoo. Three represented the heavens, the earth, and the underworld.

Four wielded even more power, representing not only the cardinal directions but the common pattern by which rituals and prayers were repeated, and sometimes the architectural pattern upon which structures such as lodges were erected. Four was a number used in magic, both light and dark, and Concho could not forget he'd been subjected to magical attacks before on the reservation.

And then the number thirteen. The first thought that occurred to most Americans of European descent when they heard thirteen was its association with bad luck and witches. The number was not commonly endowed with any special significance by Indians. Except in one case, and Concho only knew of it from his research on Aztec mummies. The Aztecs believed there were thirteen heavens, which made the number important to them.

Sliding the book of poems into its place on the shelf, Concho phoned Echabarri, who answered on the third ring.

"Ten-Wolves. What's wrong?"

"Maybe something's right. I've got a suspect for our recent smuggling operation. Which means they're a likely suspect in the murders of those two men we found out by the tree where the sacred deer were born. And they're probably involved with the two men who attacked me on the road, one of which was later murdered in the hospital."

"You're talking about clearing a lot of serious crimes. Who's the guy?"

"Not a guy. I'm talking about Tallulah Whiteheart. And maybe her daughter, Isi."

* * *

Zoe deSaint looked up from Melissa Nolan's computer with irritation. Under threat, Nolan had given up the passwords and Zoe had found and accessed plenty of confidential files on clients of the casino, particularly those who'd accrued debts. She'd found no mention of Ten-Wolves, as Nolan had promised she wouldn't.

Nolan sat across the big desk from Zoe, taped to a chair but ungagged. She couldn't see Zoe's face under the ski mask but correctly interpreted the other woman's body language.

"Told you," she said.

Zoe snorted. "So, this guy doesn't gamble, has never gambled, and doesn't owe the casino or anyone else anything?"

"I've seen him play the quarter slots a few times. He'll lose a few bucks. But he doesn't play cards and I've never seen him make any kind of big wager. If everyone were like him, we'd go broke."

"So, what's his vice?"

"Excuse me?"

"His vice! Everyone's got one. If they don't gamble, they drink, or smoke, or shoot heroin. Or they do bad things to kids."

"That's very cynical."

"Hello. Criminal here who busts other criminals! Why you think I do what I do for a living?"

"I…see your point."

"So, what is Ten-Wolves' vice?"

"He eats a lot."

Zoe barked a short laugh and—despite her predicament—Melissa Nolan smiled.

"You sleeping with him?"

Nolan produced a moue of distaste. "Hardly. He's arrogant enough for ten men. Maybe that's a vice."

"Meaning you want to sleep with him, but he won't oblige." Zoe looked Nolan up and down and shook her head back and forth. "Can't be a problem with your looks. He gay? Maybe that's the issue. A big gay Black Texas Ranger. Someone could have a field day with that if he's trying to hide it."

"You're looking for reasons why someone might blackmail him!"

"Or any kind of secret life. The weaknesses of people in the public eye. You know that yourself."

"Yes, I suppose I do. But I'm pretty sure he's not gay. He has a girlfriend and from the PDA I've seen between them they aren't saving it for marriage."

"Maybe he's got a mistress!"

"I doubt it. I've seen women throw themselves at him. Without success."

"You included?"

"No, not included."

"Don't like the idea of rejection, huh?"

"Since you have me tied to a chair with a gun to my face, I don't see why you need to needle me as well."

Zoe shrugged. "Sorry. I get mean when I'm frustrated."

"Why are you so interested in Ten-Wolves?"

Zoe considered. She shrugged again. "Why not. He disrupted an operation of my employer. Said employer believes it was some kind of double cross, that Ten-Wolves was looking to make a buck out of it. I'm trying to figure out how he found out about it, or who might have put him up to it."

"Ah!"

"Any idea?"

"You must be talking about the smuggling delivery he interrupted on the Rio Grande. Counterfeit money, I hear."

"Yeah, something like that."

"He's lucky that way. Or unlucky."

"What do you mean?"

"I mean, he attracts trouble. He's like…like a traffic obstruction. Criminal traffic. It all somehow has to flow around him. Because of that, some people even consider him a bit of a Jonah."

"People such as yourself?"

"No! Like I said, he's arrogant. And not entirely likable. But I'd stake my position that he's honest. And he wouldn't do anything to hurt this reservation or its people. Or *any* innocents, for that matter."

"I don't believe in angels."

Nolan shrugged. "Believe what you wish. But if you plan on going after him, let me tell you, better people than you have tried."

Zoe turned off Nolan's laptop and shut the lid. She walked around the desk to stand by the casino manager. She pulled a golden scarf from her pocket and tied a knot in the center, then began to twist it around in her hands. Nolan looked suddenly terrified and began to jerk at the tape holding her arms and legs to the chair. Zoe laughed.

"Don't worry. I'm just gagging you. Your secretary will let you loose in the morning. By that time, I'll be long gone."

When Nolan wouldn't open her mouth for the gag, Zoe pinched her nose closed until she had to breath, then pushed the silken knot between her lips and tied off the scarf behind the woman's head.

Zoe stood for a moment, as if considering something. Finally, she added one more comment. "Not sure why I'm telling you this, but I'm not going to hurt Concho Ten-Wolves. It's one thing to take out a bad cop. The law doesn't like it, of course, but it lets them make up a just-so story instead of potentially exposing their own corruption. But, I'm pretty sure now this guy is a good cop. And taking out a good one—particularly one like this who is half a folk hero! Well, that only brings down all kinds of hell that no one with any sense wants."

She patted Melissa Nolan on the shoulder and left.

* * *

AFTER A LONG SILENCE, ROBERTO ECHABARRI FINALLY responded to Concho's comment over the phone. "You think Tallulah Whiteheart is behind the smuggling operation and a bunch of murders spinning off that operation?"

"I do."

"What evidence you have?"

"Not a lot." Concho told the sheriff about his vision and the poem, and what sense he made of them.

"If you're right, we'll have to bring the FBI in. But I doubt Special Agent Della Rice is going to accept your evidence as good enough."

"She won't. That's why I'm gonna have to do what I normally do in these kinds of circumstances."

"Shake the trees," Echabarri said.

"Yep. She's already sent men after me, I think. But once she hears what I've discovered, she'll throw a lot more my way. And something will break."

"Maybe you."

"Maybe. But hey, I've got you around to pick up the pieces."

"Not if the break is too serious."

"I don't break easily."

"How are you going to do it? Shake the trees?"

"Give Isi a call. Share some thoughts with her. Act like I don't know what they mean."

"And she'll report to her mother!"

"That's the idea."

"When you plan to do it?"

Concho yawned. "Tomorrow. Early. Right now, I need a good night's sleep."

"Hope you make it to morning!"

"Me, too."

CHAPTER FORTY-FIVE

Concho awoke. Neither the ambient light nor the sound of the world was correct. Then he remembered. He'd decided that sleeping at his trailer was too risky with so many unknown enemies arrayed against him.

After filing a preliminary report on his findings and suppositions with the Texas Rangers, he'd driven over to the Lucky Eagle Hotel, which generally had a comped room available if it became necessary during one of his investigations. Rolling out of the overly soft hotel bed, he checked his phone for the time—6:04 AM. The usual.

Besides making it harder for his enemies to find him, another advantage of the hotel was hotter water and increased pressure. He took a longer shower than usual, enjoying the needling fingers of the water as they stabbed away at knotted muscles. As he was drying off and sampling a few bites of cheese from the gift basket left for every hotel guest, his phone rang. The ID read Melissa Nolan. Surprised, he swiped to answer.

"Ten-Wolves here."

The voice that responded was Nolan's but rougher than

he'd ever heard, as if she'd gargled with sandpaper. "Can you get to my office?"

"I can. What's up?"

"Just get here!"

"On my way," he said. She'd already hung up.

Dressing quickly and throwing on his gun belt, he rushed to the elevator and in less than four minutes knocked on the locked door to Nolan's office.

"Ten-Wolves?" Nolan called from inside.

"Last I checked."

Nolan opened the door. The light inside was dim, but she looked...rough. Coke bottle sized circles darkened the skin beneath her hazel eyes. Her long blonde hair hung mussed and tangled. The yellow business jacket and matching skirt she wore were wrinkled. He'd never seen her looking less put together.

"What's wrong?"

Nolan said nothing, only waved him inside and locked the door again behind them.

"What's going on?" Concho demanded.

"I was…held prisoner last night. By someone who wanted to know everything she could about *you*!"

"What? Who?"

Nolan shook her head. "I don't know. She wore a ski mask. Her voice wasn't one I recognized. She even hacked into my computer and looked for anything she could find on you. Gambling debts or anything else. She grilled me for half an hour on your vices."

"And what did you tell her?"

The distraught woman began to pace back and forth in front of the Ranger. "Only that you ate a lot and were arrogant."

"Guilty on both counts."

Nolan kept pacing, muttering something beneath her breath. Concho reached out and grasped her shoulders and pulled her to a stop facing him. Her gaze met his for a moment, then dropped, which was not like her at all.

"I'm not the only one who's arrogant," Ten-Wolves said. "Normally, you're worse than I am. But you're obviously scared and it sounds justified. Tell me what happened. From the beginning."

Nolan shuddered. She pulled away from the lawman's hands and walked over to drop into the chair behind her administrative assistant's desk. Her voice rang flat as she explained her late-night visitation. She ended with, "For what it's worth, she said she wasn't planning to hurt you. If you believe it. Said it was too dangerous to hurt a good cop."

Concho nodded. "Sounds like she knows her stuff. How did you get free?"

"My assistant came by early this morning. He…untied me."

"Where is he?"

"I sent him home. Told him to lie down." She snorted. "He was more hysterical than I was."

"I see."

"So, who is this, Ten-Wolves? And what have you brought to my door?"

"Don't know," Concho admitted. "Too many players in this game. But it must have to do with that smuggling operation I told you about."

"I figured that."

Concho studied the woman. "Let me walk you to your room," he finally said. "You take the day off."

Nolan shrugged, then nodded. She rose. "I will. I feel...disgusting."

"Rumpled clothes will do that," he offered dryly.

Nolan glanced at him sharply. She shook her head. However, a faint smile flicked up the corners of her lips before disappearing.

"I'll be half ashamed to be seen with you," the Ranger added. "Is there a back way we can take?"

"Don't push it, Ten-Wolves!" Nolan snapped. But the second smile lingered longer than the first.

GUTIERREZ AQUILA ARRIVED AT THE LUCKY EAGLE CASINO A little after 10:00 AM. The place was already booming, full of murmuring voices, the click-clack of machines working, and the tap and shish of feet moving back and forth.

His three men—four counting Eduardo Diaz—were also here, inconspicuously positioned at slot machines or card tables. Diaz had called him an hour before to tell him that Ten-Wolves was on the scene. Aquila wanted to see this Ranger who'd caused so much trouble, and who had now apparently convinced a trusted operative of his innocence.

Two hours ago, the doctor had gotten a call from Zoe deSaint. She'd claimed Ten-Wolves was innocent of corruption, that his actions in breaking up Jañega's operation had nothing to do with Aquila, that he'd merely been doing his job as a lawman, and to kill a good cop under those circumstances would bring more trouble than it was worth.

Although those statements were patently foolish, he'd pretended to agree with her. He'd told her to back off, and as soon as he got off the phone, he texted the blonde killer, Liana, and ordered her to take appropriate action. Finally, he'd decided to have a look for himself.

There was another reason—he admitted—why he'd come to the Kickapoo Reservation. There was a chance he might see someone else as well, someone of great importance to him. He longed for such a sight.

* * *

AFTER MAKING SURE MELISSA NOLAN GOT SAFELY TO HER hotel room, Concho returned to his own. It was too early to make the call to Isi Whiteheart, so he ordered room service—a breakfast of eggs, sausage, and toast. Although he'd accepted the comped room, he paid for his breakfast and ate it hungrily after it was delivered.

At 9:00 AM, he punched in Isi's phone number from the slip of paper she'd left on his kitchen counter. It rang ten times and went to voice mail. He frowned but left a brief message saying he'd like to speak to her.

Ten minutes later, a text came from the same number. *I'd like to speak to you too. I'll be at the casino around 10:00. We can talk.*

He sent back a "thumbs up."

Right at 10:00, the Ranger headed down to the casino floor. He spotted Isi almost immediately and joined her at the small central bar where she was getting a cup of coffee.

The woman smiled as he approached but held up a finger to beg for quiet until she'd finished taking her first huge sip. The gesture sent a quick spasm of ache through the Ranger. It reminded him so much of Maria and her coffee fanaticism. In fact, several things about Isi Whiteheart reminded him of Maria, but he told himself they were only externals. Inside, the two were nothing alike.

"We need someplace more private to talk," Isi said.

Concho hesitated. Taking her to his room might well send the wrong message, but they did need privacy. It was hard to even hear *yourself* in the casino. He scratched his head.

"I need your help with something," he said. "Something confusing I've just found out. I've got a room here but I'm not sure it's a good idea for us to go there."

Isi grinned. "Afraid I'll jump your bones? Or don't you trust yourself?"

"Neither of those actually. Maybe we could use one of the conference rooms on the second floor."

Isi's grin disappeared as if a switch had been flicked. "Your room is fine. I promise I won't embarrass myself. I threw myself at you once. You can guarantee that won't happen again."

Concho nodded, unsure of what he could say. He gestured

toward the elevators, and they headed for them, Isi clutching her plastic cup of coffee. An eerie chill swept the Ranger suddenly, as if he were being watched by cold eyes. He glanced around but saw nothing out of the ordinary. Shrugging, he walked on.

CHAPTER FORTY-SIX

Zoe deSaint snapped awake in a chair in her room at the Lucky Eagle Hotel. She'd been unable to sleep after returning to her room from Melissa Nolan's office. Her mind chewed over everything she'd learned. Mostly, she tried to imagine every place where her choices in the coming hours could make a difference.

Killing Concho Ten-Wolves would be a bad move for everyone. She'd stayed awake into the morning to call Aquila and explain that to him. It seemed he'd understood. He'd even told her to back off. She wasn't convinced he'd meant it.

She'd twice tried to call Liana as well, and her partner's phone had gone straight to voice mail. She'd left a message telling the other woman to sit tight, that the "operation" was on hold. So far, she'd gotten nothing back. None of this made her comfortable, but tension must have temporarily shut her nervous system down, making her fall asleep in the chair.

Rising, she checked the time. Not long after 10:00 AM. She took a long shower to wash the temporary gray out of her hair, then dressed in her regular heavy trousers, an oversized T-shirt, and a windbreaker to cover the gun tucked in her belt.

Restless, she left the room and headed downstairs, not

worrying she'd run into Melissa Nolan and be recognized. Her disguise had been good. She didn't know what she was about to do. The goal she'd come here for was gone. She needed some new goal to replace it. She wasn't the same wild, drunk woman she'd once been; time to start acting like it.

* * *

"SCREW IT!" LIANA MUTTERED AS SHE LEFT HER MOTEL ROOM in Eagle Pass.

She climbed into her orange Firebird and cranked the engine to life. Tires smoking, she wheeled out of the parking lot and roared off in the direction of the Lucky Eagle Casino.

* * *

"SO, WHAT DO YOU NEED MY HELP WITH?" ISI WHITEHEART asked once they were in Concho's room.

The Ranger took out his phone and swiped to his photos. He enlarged one, held it out for Isi to see. She leaned close, squinting. Her eyes widened.

"One of my mother's poems! I always liked that one. How did you get it?"

"Tessa Teshigahara gave me a book a few months back with this poem in it. I just read it last night, though."

"OK. But what's confusing you about it?"

"See the line that reads 'child in gloom'?"

"Yes. So?"

"I didn't tell you. In fact, no one knows but me and a few others. But along with the counterfeit money I confiscated along the Grande, there was another object. A child mummy made in the Aztec fashion."

Isi stiffened; it was impossible to miss. Concho continued as if he hadn't noticed. "The mummy was bound in a fiber sack, with a turquoise mask over the face. I think this line in your mother's poem is about a child like that."

Isi shoved the phone back into his hands. She shook her head. "Ridiculous!"

The Ranger spoke a little lie. "I haven't told anyone else about the poem or my thinking. I wanted to get your reaction first."

"I have no reaction. It's nonsense."

"Then what's the line about?" he asked. An impulse made him add, "Maybe your younger sister?"

Isi looked trapped. In the times he'd seen her before, she'd been in control of the situation. He understood why. She was smart, terribly smart. But she was also young. She'd surely prepared for her previous meetings with him. She'd run a script she'd practiced in her head.

But whatever script she'd had in mind this time had been depth charged by Concho's mention of the mummy and, particularly, its possible connection to her mother. Now, his left turn into territory concerning her supposedly "ill" younger sister had thrown her completely off.

"You don't talk about my sister!" Isi snapped, her dark eyes flashing.

"Then you talk about her. I don't even know her name. But is that who your mother was referring to with 'child in gloom'?"

"This conversation is over!" Isi almost shouted. She side-stepped around Concho and strode to the door, only a hair's breadth from running. He let her go. He'd accomplished what he'd wanted. Isi would be on the phone with her mother thirty seconds after she was out the door. The trees had been shaken.

The Ranger sighed. He didn't know how involved Isi was in this whole thing, but he felt a little like a heel for breaking her down this way. She'd shown him a weakness and he'd exploited it in the name of the law.

He caught his reflection in the mirror over the sink and made a face at himself, then shook his head. Isi might well be a murderer, or an accessory to murder. The dead deserved justice, whether guilty or innocent.

* * *

WEARING A BEARD, A WIG, AND A JANITOR'S UNIFORM, A disguised Doctor Gutierrez Aquila loitered down the hallway from Concho Ten-Wolves' room in the Lucky Eagle Hotel. He'd followed the man and Isi Whiteheart here and had seen them enter the room together in apparent friendliness.

His emotions worked at him, biting and gnawing. Part of him wanted to race down the hallway, kick in the door to the Texas Ranger's room, and confront him. Part of him wanted to scream and shriek in anguish.

He did neither. He waited and watched. Until suddenly the door to the room burst open and Isi Whiteheart rushed out, wiping at her face with a hand as if fighting tears. He took an involuntary step forward, but the woman was fumbling with her phone, then flung it to her ear and spoke to someone he couldn't hear.

Aquila froze as she turned toward him. She paid him no mind, only stopped at the elevators a dozen steps away and punched the down button angrily. The elevator opened and she stepped inside.

She'd paid him no mind. But why should she? She couldn't see through his janitorial disguise to the professor she'd known at Universidad Nacional Autónoma de México. She couldn't see the man who'd fallen in love with her and who she had claimed to love as well.

"Claimed!" He nearly vomited the word.

His glance traveled down the corridor to the closed door of Ten-Wolves' room. A rage suffused him. An image came to mind, of him walking to that door and knocking, calling out that it was the janitorial service, and when the man inside opened up, of emptying ten shots from a pistol into his belly.

But that would be too easy, too…unsatisfying. He needed a better plan, a more personal one.

CHAPTER FORTY-SEVEN

Concho finally made a call he'd been hesitant to make. He explained his thoughts on the situation to agent Della Rice and was met with the expected skepticism. Rice could offer nothing more constructive, however, and reported no progress on the two bodies they'd found with Concho's stolen arrows in them.

"You still have that helicopter at your disposal?" Concho asked at conversation's end.

"Yeah, why?"

"Maybe keep it ready. I've got a feeling it might be needed."

"I don't schedule my life and work based on your feelings, Ten-Wolves."

"But knowing you, it'll be ready anyway."

Rice scoffed and hung up.

Next, Concho called Roberto to report baiting the hook for Tallulah Whiteheart.

"Better be extra careful now," Echabarri replied. "The Whitehearts aren't known for patience or finesse in dealing with trouble."

"Right. That's why I'm going home. Don't want to be here among a lot of civilians if they send someone after me."

"You can hang out at the police station."

"I'll consider it. I need to check with John Gray-Dove anyway. He's supposed to have my truck repaired soon."

"All right. Just be careful."

"Doing my best."

Concho hung up. He took a quick bathroom break before heading downstairs to check out. As he crossed the lobby to the reception counter, a man came toward him with an intent look on his face. Pausing, Concho dropped his left hand to the butt of a Colt .45.

The man looked to be in his early forties, with short, dark hair graying at the sideburns. He was tall, a little over six feet, slender but of muscular build. A handsome fellow of Hispanic heritage, with the face and demeanor of an aristocrat. He paused a few steps away; his coal-black eyes glinting with an ill-concealed anger.

"You are Ten-Wolves," the man said. "A…Texas Ranger!"

"I am."

"You are scum!"

Concho felt the urge to arch an eyebrow, but it wasn't a talent he possessed. "Usually, people need to get to know me before they call me names," he replied. "I don't believe we've ever met."

"You have debased a beautiful young woman. For that, you are scum."

It took Ten-Wolves a few seconds to realize who the man must be talking about. "If you mean Isi Whiteheart, I promise you I've not debased her in any way. But I am curious as to why you think it's your business?"

The man spat on the floor at Concho's feet; a droplet struck his boot and glistened. He bit his lower lip to keep from punching the fellow's lights out.

"If you have *any* honor, you will meet me in fifteen minutes out back of this hotel," the man said.

The surprise of the statement helped Concho calm down. "It's been a while since I've been challenged to a duel," he said dryly. "I'm a little rusty. What weapons are we supposed to use?"

"You have a knife at your belt." The man jerked his chin toward the bone handle of the Bowie sheathed at Concho's right side behind his holstered Colt. "We will use bladed weapons."

"You have a name I can put on your tombstone?"

A small confident sneer curved the fellow's lips. "Only if it becomes apparent a tombstone is needed. Fifteen minutes!" He turned and walked off.

* * *

Zoe was sitting aimlessly at the central casino bar drinking coffee when she overheard a snippet of conversation between two female staff members picking up drinks for their customers.

"You see Ten-Wolves this morning?" one woman asked the other.

"I did. Now *that's* a man."

"Too bad he's spoken for."

The second woman laughed. "I'd like to speak for him."

The servers got their drinks and moved off, leaving Zoe thinking. So, Ten-Wolves was here. At the casino. Maybe it was time to talk to the trophy himself. She finished her coffee and left a tip for the bartender as she headed off in search of the man she'd once intended to kill.

* * *

As the last of the fifteen minutes passed, Ten-Wolves stepped out the back door of the Lucky Eagle Hotel into a construction lot. Three trailers sat parked there. One was the construction maintenance office. The head of that office was

Finn Hansson, but he was usually in the building doing something and was seldom at his desk.

Another trailer served mostly for storage while the third was a little nicer, with red trim around the door and windows. Concho didn't really know what purpose it served, though he'd been involved in a drug bust there once.

A recently constructed plank fence surrounded the area to keep kids and onlookers away, though there were places where people could slip through. A few piles of dirt and gravel lay scattered around on what was mostly barren ground.

In front of a tall pile of red clay, Concho's challenger stood stretching. He turned as the Ranger stepped into the impromptu arena and drew a wicked looking Bowie knife from his belt, the weapon made famous by Jim Bowie, of Alamo fame.

Concho drew his own knife, a pretty standard Bowie except for the bone handle. The heavy cutting blade was ten inches long, thinning at the end and with a slight upward curve of the tip. A cross-guard of steel between the blade and the hilt provided protection for the user's hand. His opponent's knife looked an inch or so longer, but the lawman probably still had reach on him with his long arms.

Concho's gaze roamed the site. No sign of anyone here as backup for his opponent, although they could be hiding behind one of the trailers. The Ranger had considered calling Echabarri as his own backup but the simmering anger inside him pushed him recklessly forward. Still, he made one more attempt to resolve this without a fight.

"You best reconsider. I've done nothing to Isi Whiteheart so you're gonna get hurt for no reason."

"I have had much practice with the blade," the man replied. "It is you who will be hurt."

The fellow swished his knife in the air a few times, as if he were flourishing a sword, and the Ranger had no difficulty imagining him striking a fencing pose. He even wore a bullfighter's tight gray pants and a long-sleeved white silk shirt open at the chest.

"He thinks he's in a movie," Concho muttered to himself. Out loud, he called, "What's your connection to Isi anyway?"

The man repeated something from earlier. "Only at the point of dying." He started forward.

The Ranger didn't like the grip he had on the knife with his right hand. The splint on his broken little finger made grasping the hilt difficult. He switched the weapon to his left hand, then crouched a little as his opponent closed.

Though he was bigger and younger than his opponent, Ten-Wolves did not make the mistake of underestimating the man. The fellow was tall and lean, but strongly built and clearly in peak condition. And if he were trained, as he'd claimed, he'd be a dangerously formidable foe.

At four paces away, the man transitioned his stride into a lunge, with his knife held low and spiking for the belly. The Ranger whipped his own blade across. The two knives struck each other, casting away steel sparks as they rang together.

Instantly, the man spun off his left heel, swinging around with the long blade slashing. Concho leaped back. The edge of the other Bowie whiffed past his chest but caught nothing. The Ranger held his own attack, waiting as he judged the other man's skill, hoping to find a weakness and an opening.

The man stretched to his full height and stalked to his right, forcing Concho to turn in a circle to ward him off. Again came the lunge, dazzling quick. The Ranger blocked once more. The blades clanged.

The day was cool, but the sun stood high. Sweat began to bead on Concho's face and run down his chest beneath his shirt. His irritation began to grow; he fought to control it but wasn't completely successful.

The stranger stepped back. "Do you know, this blade is modeled on the original knife James Bowie carried."

"That make it cut better?" Concho snarled in return.

The man smiled. "I own the original actually."

"Doubt it."

"No, no, it is true. At your Alamo, when James Bowie was found in his bed by Mexican soldiers at battle's end, he did not even put up a fight. He was shot like a dog. And his famous knife was taken by one of the soldiers and brought to Mexico. I acquired it only a few years ago. And I had this model made. And today I will return it to Texas. In a way. It is a perfect weapon for disemboweling Tejano scum."

"If you think insulting Jim Bowie or Texas is going to piss me off enough to make a mistake, then you don't know me very well."

"I don't need to know you to kill you," the man snapped. Again, he lunged.

CHAPTER FORTY-EIGHT

Zoe looked for Ten-Wolves on the casino floor and in every one of the hotel restaurants. She couldn't find him, but a small bribe to the concierge got his room number and an indication he hadn't checked out. She knocked on his door, with no answer. She called his room. No answer. She went outside to the parking lot. No sign.

An impulse sent her around the building. She came to a plank fence closing off the rear of the hotel. A couple of loose boards showed her where others had made a way through before. She pulled one back and peeked through.

A gasp almost escaped her. Concho Ten-Wolves and Doctor Gutierrez Aquila were fighting each other with knives. She couldn't tell who was winning.

* * *

As his opponent lunged and stabbed, Concho shifted to his right and hooked his blade into the other. The cross guards locked. The Ranger twisted his wrist, pulling the other man's arm out of position and drawing him closer; he struck with his right hand, using the heel rather than the fist to protect his damaged finger.

The blow caught the man under the chin but was not a solid hit. The fellow staggered backward but the knives came unhooked and the trick didn't disarm the foe as the lawman hoped.

The man backpedaled, shaking his head to clear it. His left hand slipped behind his hip and came out with a second knife, much shorter and slenderer than the first, with a straight blade. A throwing knife.

Concho still wore his holstered Colts. He'd hooked the restraining straps to keep them from falling out in the fight. He considered drawing a gun and putting a stop to this battle. In the next instant, he shoved the thought aside. He wanted this now, to finish it with cold steel.

With his face flushed in anger from having been struck, the man darted closer, swiping with both knives. Concho leaped backward. The man pursued. Concho blocked one knife as it sliced in and twisted aside to avoid the second.

As the shorter blade swept impotently past his side, Concho hooked at the man with his Bowie. The other fighter blocked, and again the cross guards of the two knives locked. The Ranger lunged, using the weight of his body. His opponent flung backward; this time the knives didn't come free and the Bowie ripped out of the man's grip.

Concho charged, snapping a kick with his right boot. The blow struck the man's leg above the knee. The leg buckled. The man flung his second blade as he fell. The Ranger batted the flashing steel aside and threw himself forward.

As the man tried to rise, the big lawman switched his Bowie from left hand to right and locked the fingers of his left around his enemy's throat. With brute strength, he dragged the man upright. His right hand swept in with the Bowie, hacking down beneath the chin. He stopped. Just as the razored edge of the blade dimpled the man's neck, he stopped. The kiss of steel brought a tiny bright line of red but did no serious damage.

"Could have taken your head," Concho snarled. "Still could. Add it to my collection. So, at the point of death, tell me who you are and what's your connection to Isi Whiteheart?"

The man's eyes flashed with defiance. He would have spit in the Ranger's face if the grip on his windpipe hadn't nearly closed it off.

"I can tell you who he is, Ten-Wolves," a woman's voice called from behind the Ranger.

Concho spun, dragging Aquila with him by the throat to put the man between himself and the voice. He saw a tall woman with short, dark hair standing by a loose board in the fence. She had the build of a weightlifter and held a semi-automatic pistol with both hands. But the gun was pointed at the ground.

"His name's Aquila," the woman continued. "Gutierrez Aquila."

The Ranger released Aquila's throat and twisted him around so he, too, faced the woman. But he kept a hand on the back of the man's neck and kept the blade of his Bowie pressed to the pulsing beat of the right carotid.

"Zoe deSaint!" Aquila called. "Kill this Ranger and I'll triple your pay."

Zoe shook her head. "Can't do that Doctor Aquila. It's the wrong thing. For all of us." She looked past Aquila to meet Concho's gaze. "He's a Mexican citizen. Very prominent. Considering that he may have wanted to kill you but failed, I doubt you'll be able to hold him on much of anything once his government gets involved."

"You want me to let him go?" Ten-Wolves asked.

"It'd be best for everyone."

"No!" Aquila shouted. "Men! Kill both these fools!"

The freezing hand of realization slid down Concho's back. Aquila hadn't been completely honorable. He'd brought help. The Ranger twisted around again as three men burst around the corner of one of the trailers with the blued steel of guns in their hands. From the roof of another trailer came the boom of a shot. Concho neither saw nor heard where it went.

Shoving Aquila away from him and toward his three followers, Ten-Wolves' hands flashed for his Colts. His thumbs unsnapped the restraining straps, his fingers gripped the handles, and the pistols leaped into his fists. Aquila had thrown himself down, out of the line of fire.

All three men cut their weapons loose on Concho. All carried pistols, some kind of semi-automatic. One had an Uzi knockoff. Bullets slashed the dirt around the Ranger; they sliced the air like angry hornets.

Concho stood amid the hail of fire, his guns rising. He double-actioned the triggers. Aquila's man on the left went spinning around, his weapon flying. The man on the right staggered and dropped to one knee as blood sprayed from his thigh.

Ten-Wolves kept firing, the butts of the .45s slamming back into his palms as the empty brass casings ejected into the cool air. The foe in the center of the three took two bullets and stopped as if he'd run into a wall. He crumpled.

The man on one knee screamed defiance and swung his weapon up again. Concho shot him in the forehead, cutting through a lock of dark hair, which dropped to earth. The man fell and his gun clattered on rocky soil.

Only seconds had passed. The three gunmen were down but it wasn't over. There'd been the shot from one of the trailer roofs. From a rifle. Concho's gaze rose; he scanned the roofs. A shadow in black stood atop the trailer with the red-trimmed door, behind an air conditioning unit. He held a long rifle in his hands. Like a sniper. He drew a bead on the Ranger.

Two shots snapped from behind Concho. He flinched but nothing struck him. The man with the rifle, though, he suddenly stretched up on his toes, then plummeted off the roof, his weapon falling with a *thunk* to the shingles.

Concho twisted around. He saw where the shot had come from that saved him. The woman named Zoe deSaint. She knelt. Blood spattered her white T-shirt and ran from a wound in her lower left side. But she held her pistol in both hands and it was pointed toward the roof where the sniper had hidden.

The Ranger's eyes must have looked confused; deSaint smiled wryly into them. Then something else swept through her own eyes. "Look out!" she shouted.

Concho felt it. Maybe intuition. Maybe the brush of a breeze from movement behind him. He swung around yet again, right hand rising instinctively with the Colt extended. Gutierrez Aquila was lunging toward him, only two steps away, the recovered Bowie in his fist.

Concho fired. The gun kicked back into his palm. The echo of the shot deadened the air as Aquila stumbled. Concho sidestepped. Aquilla fell on his face but pressed his hands against the ground and rolled over. His eyes glared, then softened as they looked on death. The knife lifted a few inches before dropping down onto his chest. Aquila closed his eyes.

CHAPTER FORTY-NINE

CONCHO HOLSTERED HIS PISTOLS. HIS RIGHT HAND STUNG; HE shook it back and forth. He'd never noticed pain from his broken finger while in the middle of the firefight, but it hurt now.

But the pain was nothing to the sensation of being alive. He could easily have been dead. He drew in a deep breath of cool air. Even laced with the scent of spent gunpowder, it was glorious.

Zoe deSaint had lain down on her side nearly against the fence. She'd dropped her gun but was still alive, though the Ranger could hear the grind of pain working in her as she breathed. He strode toward her and went to one knee to examine her wound. She'd been shot in the side but the sniper rifle bullet, while fast-moving, was not a huge chunk of lead. He thought she'd live, and likely fully recover.

"Thanks," Concho said. "The man had a bead on me."

"Thanks back. They'd have killed me as soon as they finished you."

"Reckon so."

"Aquila dead? Or just wounded?"

"Fatal wound, I'm afraid."

Zoe nodded.

Concho pulled his phone out. "They've got a good medic on staff here. I'll call him."

Zoe nodded again.

The Ranger swiped up the number for Sam Reyes, the nurse practitioner who managed the Lucky Eagle infirmary. As he started to press call, a new voice and the click of a gun's hammer being cocked froze him.

"Don't do that!" the voice said.

Zoe was looking past the Ranger, surprise etched on her face. Without making any sudden moves, Concho turned his head to look as well. Though her hair was shorter and darker now, he recognized the woman who stood behind him with the muzzle of a Glock pointed at him. Tall, slender, and striking. He'd seen her once before, on the stairs in the casino. He'd been going up while she was going down and they'd both taken second looks.

"Didn't you used to be blonde?" Concho asked dryly.

"Liana!" Zoe said. "Don't."

The woman named Liana ignored Zoe for the moment. She chuckled at the law officer's comment. "Blondes may have more fun, but brunettes get the drop."

"Liana!" Zoe said again.

"Better for you to be quiet, Zoeita," Liana said softly. "I'm doing your job here. And you might want to know, Aquila offered me extra to take you out, too."

"Aquila is dead," Zoe snapped. "We haven't been paid yet and we're not going to be. No need to shoot the Ranger."

"What if want to?"

"Do I get a vote?" Ten-Wolves asked.

Liana ignored him. She puffed a breath. "Aquila really dead?" she asked Zoe.

"Truly dead."

Liana shifted her gaze fully to Concho. "If I lower my weapon, you're not going to do something mean like try to shoot me, are you?"

"Wouldn't dream of it."

The woman nodded. She let the barrel of her pistol sink toward the ground, then uncocked the hammer and holstered it behind her back. She glanced at Zoe.

"Can you walk? We need to get the Texas out of here."

"And go where?"

Liana shrugged. "Mexico, I guess. I can drop you off at the bar you were working at before this all started."

Zoe shook her head. "I'm not going."

"What have you got here?" Liana demanded.

"Don't know. Something better." She glanced at the Ranger. "You going to arrest me?"

Concho shrugged. "For what? Saving my life? I'm not aware of any crimes you two have committed, though apparently you both contemplated some."

"Contemplating some right now," Liana said, giving Concho a slow once-over.

Ten-Wolves felt a flush taking hold but pushed it away with, "Don't make me read you your rights?"

Liana laughed. "Such a charmer." She glanced again at Zoe. "I'm gone. You ever get back in country...Well, you'll know how to find me."

"Right," Zoe said.

Liana gave a brief nod to them both, then slipped back through the hole in the fence and was gone.

Shaking his head in surprise at his out-of-character words to Liana, Concho resumed his phone call and told Sam Reyes where and why his help was needed. Next, he called Roberto and told him to bring deputies with him to the crime scene.

As he swiped off the call, Zoe spoke. "Since he's dead, I guess I can tell you. Aquila was behind the smuggling operation you busted. At least from the Mexican side."

"I was beginning to figure. That why he sent you and your friend to kill me?"

"He sent us to investigate. And, yeah, kill you. He expected you were crooked, that you were in on it."

"Just in the right place at the right time. At least from my standpoint."

"I learned that in the last couple days investigating you. But why were you and he fighting? I mean, he wanted you dead, but I didn't think it was personal enough for a knife."

"He misjudged something he saw. About a young woman I was speaking with."

"The one you're 'already in love' with?"

"No. A woman named Isi Whiteheart. Seems *he* might have been in love with her. Though I've got no idea how it came about."

Zoe frowned. "Young, you say? How young?"

"Twenty-three, twenty-four."

"Then I know who she is. Who she has to be."

"And that is?"

"Rumor went around certain circles in Mexico a couple years ago. I only heard it because I make a habit of checking on the people I work for. While Aquila was teaching at Universidad de México he supposedly had an affair with a student. A girl from the United States. When the school found out, he wasn't fired from his job but left through some 'mutual agreement.' I bet it's the same woman."

"Makes sense," Concho said. "And could be a prelude to blackmail."

Zoe nodded. "Especially since it's known that Aquila wanted to move to the States and teach here. If that rumor came out, he'd never get hired."

"Gives us motive," Concho said. He pulled his phone out again. Sam Reyes burst out of the hotel and froze as he saw the dead bodies. His eyes shifted back and forth. Concho waved and the young Kickapoo medic rushed over.

Ten-Wolves pointed at Zoe.

Reyes nodded and dropped to his knees beside deSaint, quickly opening the small briefcase he carried. Concho rose to his feet and stepped away. He called Della Rice, who answered promptly.

“I’ve got better evidence now,” he told the FBI agent. “Bring that helicopter and meet me in the parking lot of the Lucky Eagle.”

“Where we going?”

“The Whiteheart farm.”

“Gonna be gunplay?”

“Maybe.”

CHAPTER FIFTY

Concho left Zoe deSaint in the care of Samuel Reyes and several Kickapoo police deputies, who were told *not* to arrest her. She said she'd be here when he returned if he changed his mind. He believed her. Every instinct told him he could trust her.

He met Della Rice in her helicopter in an open field at the edge of the casino's parking lot. Echabarri accompanied him to make it official; it was best for everyone if even the FBI were invited to any investigation on reservation lands. Agents Will Bolin and Bihn Bui arrived with Rice, armed and armored. Bui gave Concho a bulletproof vest with FBI printed on it. It was even his size. He donned it. Echabarri already wore his own.

"Just picked up something on the Rez grapevine this morning that might be relevant," Echabarri said as the chopper got airborne and roared west toward the Whiteheart Ranch.

"What's that?" Rice asked.

"Rumor says the Whitehearts have been constructing a landing strip. And it's possible they have a plane. We know Isi Whiteheart has taken flying lessons locally."

"Good for smuggling," Concho said.

"My thoughts," Roberto agreed.

"Or for fleeing arrest," Rice added.

"That, too," Ten-Wolves said. "I wonder why they didn't use that method to bring in the shipment I busted up, though?"

"The strip is not supposed to be completed," Roberto said. "Maybe they needed the money from *that* operation to finish it."

"We need to get up high and spot the strip," Concho said. "Make it our priority."

"Why?" Rice asked. "If it's not completed?"

"Guess you never saw *Return of the Jedi*?"

"What? Are you talking *Star Wars*?"

"'I'm afraid the deflector shield will be quite operational when your friends arrive,'" Concho quoted in Emperor Palpatine's voice. Then, "No recognition? No?"

"I have no idea what that nonsense means."

"The Ranger is saying the airstrip is probably a lot more finished than we were led to believe," Bihn Bui explained.

Della shook her head. "All right, Bui. You're designated as Ten-Wolves' translator from here on."

Concho and Bihn laughed. No one else joined them.

* * *

THE BIG, BARBED WIRE FENCE SURROUNDING THE WHITEHEART Ranch might have stopped any land vehicle short of an armored half-track, but it couldn't do squat about a helicopter. The FBI chopper soared over, rotors throbbing against the clouding sky.

They spotted the landing strip easily. Half a mile behind the ranch house itself, beyond a grove of hardwood trees, stretched a packed-down dirt runway. It stood out as a tan and sandy line through the Texas scrub. A large, warehouse-style building stood to one side with a pearl-colored Honda Accord parked outside. There was even a tower, though clearly incomplete.

"That car!" Concho shouted. "That's the one seen at Earl Blake's office when the mummy was stolen. That building is where the plane will be. And I'll bet Tallulah Whiteheart is in there with it."

The wide door of the building stood open, and even as the lawman spoke, a small plane nosed out from inside. It was under power, with the propeller spinning.

"They're running!" Echabarri shouted. "Someone must have called to tell them we were coming."

The small plane swept onto the runway and began to pick up speed.

"Don't let it take off!" Della Rice snapped to the chopper pilot.

"How you expect me to stop it?"

"Get in front of it! Block its way into the air!"

The pilot looked shocked but shrugged and obeyed his boss. He worked the chopper controls, sending the aircraft diving straight toward the speeding plane. The pilot of the plane saw them. Its speed faltered for an instant, then increased.

"They wanna play chicken!" Rice shouted. "We can't let 'em win."

The chopper pilot was game. He continued to dive straight toward the small airplane, then swung directly into its path and hovered. The rotors kicked up streams of dirt and sent them whirling away.

Concho's hands were gripped tight on his seat when the plane's pilot finally blinked and pulled up on the throttle. The little craft wheeled to one side. The engine stalled. The propellor faltered and cranked to a stop.

"Land!" Rice ordered.

The helicopter jolted as it hit the ground. Concho slid open the door on his side and bailed out. Will Bolin did the same on the other side. The door of the plane flung back, and a man leaped free. His hands held a rifle.

Concho already had his left-hand Colt drawn. He lifted it to shoot but Bolin fired first with the bolt-action .30-06 hunting rifle he carried. The bullet struck the other man's rifle and ricocheted away, tearing the weapon from the gunman's hands and wringing a shout of pain from his throat.

Bui came third out of the chopper and took a stance directly in front of the nose of the airplane, his Sig Sauer 9-millimeter drawn and pointed at the pilot through the plexiglass windshield. That pilot was Isi Whiteheart. She raised her hands.

Della Rice also exited the helicopter, her service weapon drawn. She, Concho, and Bolin approached the plane. Bolin grabbed the rifleman—who'd been wounded from the ricochet—by the shoulders and shoved him against the aircraft, pulling his arms behind him for cuffs.

"Nice shot!" the Ranger complimented Bolin.

The young agent grinned. "Might have been a little luck involved."

Concho chuckled. The windows along the plane's side showed no other armed figures inside. Ten-Wolves peered through the door. Besides Isi, there was only one passenger—Tallulah Whiteheart.

"Mrs. Whiteheart. Would you and your daughter step out of the plane."

"I see no reason to comply," Tallulah said. "You have no right to come on our land and interrupt our private affairs."

Della Rice leaned her own head in the plane. She wasn't as polite as Concho. "When you've got the FBI, the Texas Rangers, and the Kickapoo police telling you to stop, you stop! You don't send someone out with a rifle to shoot at us."

"He did not know who you were. Perhaps you were bandits!"

"Not with FBI written all over our helicopter."

"Momma," Isi said, as she unlocked her seat belt and slid free of the pilot's chair, "we should go along. We have to."

Tallulah sighed like an empress told that she must feed her servants. She, too, unsnapped her seatbelt and rose. Concho and Della stepped back as the two women exited.

Isi still wore her outfit from earlier, jeans, a white shirt, and a buckskin fringed vest. Her hair was pulled into a ponytail. Tallulah Whiteheart wore a heavy brocade dress of silver and had her dark and still lustrous hair piled atop her head in some elaborate coiffure. She glared at them all but seemed to reserve her greatest disdain for Roberto Echabarri. She jerked her chin toward him.

"I see the white man's lapdog is with you."

Roberto blushed but said nothing.

Della Rice laughed. "Only one white man here. And he's not in charge. I am. So, you better find another line of attack."

Tallulah shrugged. "It is all the same."

Before Della could respond in kind and have the next few minutes descend into name calling, Concho interrupted. "Where's the child mummy?"

Tallulah flinched slightly but responded with, "I don't know what you're talking about."

"I'll have a look," Bui said.

"You will not!" Tallulah snapped. "I do not give you permission to search my property."

"He doesn't need permission," Della Rice said. "That perk disappeared the minute your guy pulled a gun on us. This is a crime scene now."

Tallulah started to protest more but Isi tugged on her arm and she fell silent.

Concho stopped Bui, though. "I'll do it!"

The Vietnamese agent shrugged. The Ranger stepped past him into the plane, having to bend almost double to avoid hitting his head on the roof. It took him only seconds. A large metallic case caught his attention. He knelt, unsnapped the latches, and opened it. Inside, nestled in silk lining, lay the mummy with its turquoise mask and obsidian eyes.

"I think I know who you are now," the big officer murmured. "I'll make sure you can rest soon." Cradling the case gently, he stepped back out of the plane and gave Della Rice a nod.

Rice grinned triumphantly. "Now we've got you for theft," she said to Tallulah. "You stole this from the coroner's office. And Tased the doctor while you were at it."

"One cannot steal that which belongs to you," Tallulah retorted.

Concho looked at Isi. The young woman seemed resigned to a bad outcome for her day. He asked her, "You're the one stole it, aren't you?"

Isi nodded. "I didn't want to hurt anyone, but we had to have her back."

"Her?"

"Do not give them this satisfaction," Tallulah snapped at her daughter.

But Isi was beyond resisting the crush of events now. "My sister," she said.

Tallulah threw her hands in the air and turned away with disgust.

"I thought so," Concho said. "When did she die?"

Della Rice stared at the Ranger with confusion, but she'd worked with him enough to let him have his head.

"A year ago," Isi answered. "In Mexico. Just before I finished at the university, she came…to visit me. For a…spa there that promised to help her. It didn't work. She went downhill very quickly. She died but…" her glance swept toward her mother and away again, "but Momma couldn't let her go."

Concho turned toward Tallulah. "You're Nahua, aren't you? Aztec! At least partly."

Tallulah drew herself to her full height, which was not inconsiderable. "I *am* full-blood. A descendant of queens while *your* ancestors were nothing but slaves."

Concho ignored the insult. As for Tallulah's full-bloodedness, he doubted it. But it didn't matter. The woman considered herself an Aztec queen of the past. She'd wanted her lost child treated as the Aztecs treated their loved and honored dead. But she'd not been able to let go of her anger and… Meskwaa would have said the woman's anger disrupted the child's passage into the afterlife. Concho didn't know what to think.

Ten-Wolves looked back at Isi. "Did Gutierrez Aquila perform the mummification?"

Isi looked startled. "How did you…What do you know of Aquila?"

Concho had used his phone and the internet to look up information on Aquila while on the way to the Whitehearts'.

"He was a medical doctor, a professor at the University of Mexico while you were there. He had some unorthodox ideas about how to treat wasting diseases, which is what I imagine your sister suffered from."

Isi nodded.

"And," Concho continued, "you had an affair with him."

Isi gasped. Tallulah rounded on the Ranger. "She was seduced by the beast," the woman shouted. "Used by him."

"Momma!" protested Isi.

"The man degraded my oldest daughter with his...attentions. And his foolishness *killed* my youngest daughter."

"And since you knew he wanted to move to the States and teach here, you decided to blackmail him," Concho said.

"He had overstayed his welcome in his homeland," Tallulah replied. "He thought Americans ripe to be plucked by his silly theories. Perhaps they would have been. I let him think I might help. But I would never have allowed him to establish his filthy practices here. I only sought some small measure of justice!" She smiled unpleasantly. "He, of course, believed he could work his way back into my good graces and thus win Isi for his own. I would have died first."

Concho nodded. "Who killed David Flores in the hospital?" he asked. "Someone hired him to kill me, and when he failed you were afraid he'd talk so you murdered him with a poisoned dart."

"I did it!" Isi said. "Both things. Hired him and killed him!"

Tallulah turned on her daughter. "What foolishness!" she shouted. She looked back at the Ranger, and for the first time something like an appeal appeared in her eyes. "Do not believe this silly girl. I did both those things." She drew herself up again. "And I do not regret them."

CHAPTER FIFTY-ONE

Concho stood talking to Della Rice while the FBI forensics team Rice had called in went over the plane inch by inch. They found little besides the mummy and suitcases full of clothes and items suggesting a long trip. A large amount of Mexican currency suggested the destination.

"So, which one of them you think did it?" Rice asked. "Killed Flores?"

"My money's on the mother. Isi's trying to protect her. Regardless, Tallulah gave the orders."

"Not Sam Whiteheart?"

"Not this time."

Rice nodded. "What if we never find out the whole story?"

The lawman shrugged. "The courts decide."

Rice hmmed a response, then went off to talk to one of her agents. Concho walked over to Isi Whiteheart, who was seated on the ground next to Rice's helicopter. A second helicopter, which had carried the forensics team, sat about fifty yards away.

Half a dozen armed agents stood between the choppers and nearly thirty members of the Whiteheart family and staff, including Sam Whiteheart. It had seemed for a while as if there'd be a fight to take Tallulah and Isi out of here, but Tallulah had calmed the situation down. Now, both sides merely watched.

Concho squatted beside Isi. When she finally looked up, she asked, "Come to gloat?"

The Ranger shook his head. "I thought you'd wanna know, Aquila is dead. He came to the hotel. Looking for you, I think."

Isi sucked in a breath, held it for a moment before releasing. Her shoulders slumped further. "I don't care. You kill him?"

"Afraid I did. He challenged me to a duel, of all things."

"A duel? Over what?"

"Over you."

The young woman shook her head back and forth. "He...he didn't understand how to love anyone but himself."

"Maybe so. He certainly seemed obsessed with you."

"I should be glad he's dead, but…"

Concho nodded. "Just thought you should know." He rose.

"Ten-Wolves!"

"Yes?"

"My mother. She… My sister's death hurt her badly. She'd been praying. She tried everything." A humorless smile flitted across her lips. "Even magic. Maybe you can help her? If you would?"

"I'll see what I can do. I doubt it'll be much."

"And my sister?"

The Ranger sighed. "Awful as it is to say, her body is evidence right now. But I'll make sure she's returned to your father. She deserves a proper internment. She'll get it."

"Thanks."

Concho wanted to tell the young woman to speak the truth when the case came to trial, to not waste her life trying to protect her mother. It wouldn't have done any good. He walked away.

* * *

AFTER A LONG AFTERNOON OF BUREAUCRACY AND FILING reports to various law enforcement agencies—including his own—Ten-Wolves finally headed home. He stopped by John Gray-Dove's shop on the way and found his truck ready. It felt good to be back in a familiar vehicle after driving the sheriff office's SUV.

Scudding clouds had moved into the area, bringing a drop in temperature and a fitful rain. But as if the end of the violent day were a signal, the fitful became the frightful. Thunder-boomers and squalls began to hammer Maverick County and the Rez. The Ranger drove home with his truck shaking in the wind and his wipers swishing out a quick rhythm. Thunder growled angrily and lightning stabbed purple through the evening gloom.

He waited in his driveway for the rain to let up before dashing into his trailer. The lights were off, the air inside cold and lonely. He kicked on the heater for one of the rare times this winter and hung up his gun belt. His filthy clothes got dumped into the washing machine.

After changing into a ratty pair of pajama bottoms and a T-shirt worn soft with use, he checked the fridge for something to eat. No leftovers. He had eggs but he'd been eating a lot of eggs recently.

He checked his cupboard. The two cans of tuna didn't excite him. He should have picked up something at the Lucky Eagle but had just wanted to get home. Hoping for a miracle, he glanced in the freezer. On top of the meat pile lay a package of two rib-eye steaks he'd once intended to grill for himself and Maria Morales.

Thoughts of Maria deepened an already descending melancholy. He sighed. He wasn't used to going a day without speaking to her. It had been several now and some part of him feared he wouldn't speak to her again. He couldn't stand that.

He took out the steaks. They were about the only thing in

the freezer he could thaw quickly in the oven. Eating them would only up his self-pity quotient, but sometimes when you wallow, you want to wallow all the way.

He placed the steaks on a baking tray and stuck them in the oven. The rain had slacked again, and he heard the sound of a vehicle pulling into his driveway. "What now!" he growled. "Someone else wanna shoot me? Or is it more work? Everybody needs something from Concho Ten-Wolves!"

Aware that he was feeling sorry for himself, he stalked to his doorway. Night had fallen. He flipped on the outside light and threw the door open. Someone stepped out of the car. A shadowy figure moved toward him through scattered raindrops.

Despite his comment about someone coming to shoot him, he didn't really believe anyone who wanted to kill him would simply pull into his driveway and walk up to him. He pushed open the screen and waited.

Maria Morales came out of the darkness. She strode up the three steps of his stairs and inserted herself into his arms. He folded her into his chest. She'd been crying; he could see. But he said nothing. He held her.

Sometime later, in the kitchen, Maria flipped on the oven light and peeked in to see what was cooking.

"*Two* steaks?" she asked, arching an eyebrow.

Concho grinned, and felt it go all the way to his toes.

"I knew you were coming," he teased, "so I *baked* you a steak."

A LOOK AT BOOK SEVEN

WHITE LINE RAZOR

Experience the pulse-pounding return of Texas Ranger Concho Ten-Wolves in this captivating contemporary western! A.W. Hart delivers another thrilling tale, packed with action, suspense, and a mesmerizing blend of Native American heritage.

When Concho Ten-Wolves stumbles upon two suspicious vehicles concealed beneath a rugged country bridge, he senses trouble brewing—a potential drug deal shrouded in secrecy. As he cautiously delves deeper, the air erupts with gunfire, and he discovers a young Native American woman, bound and silenced in the trunk of one of the cars. Plagued by amnesia, she pleads for assistance, her motives obscured by uncertainty.

Is she an innocent victim ensnared in a web of deceit, or does she harbor a darker secret? With a separate case already demanding his attention, Ten-Wolves initially considers leaving the mystery to the local authorities. However, when a relentless attempt is made on her life and she beseeches him for help, their shared heritage resonating between them, the Ranger's resolve solidifies.

Determined to unravel the enigma, Concho Ten-Wolves embarks on a perilous journey, ready to confront any obstacle standing in his way.

AVAILABLE NOW

ABOUT THE AUTHOR

Charles Gramlich lives amid the piney woods of southern Louisiana and is the author of the Talera fantasy series, the science fiction novel, *Under the Ember Star*, and the thriller, *Cold in the Light*.

His work has appeared in magazines such as *Star*Line*, *Beat to a Pulp*, *Night to Dawn*, *Pedestal Magazine*, and many others. Several of his stories have been collected in anthologies, such as: *Bitter Steel* (fantasy), *Midnight in Rosary* (vampires/werewolves), and *In the Language of Scorpions* (horror).

Charles also writes westerns under the name Tyler Boone. Although he writes in many different genres, all of his fiction work is known for its intense action and strong visuals.

Made in United States
Troutdale, OR
01/19/2024